TWICE SHY

By Sophia Holloway

Kingscastle
The Season
Isabelle
The Chaperone
Celia
To Catch a Husband
An Independent Woman
Twice Shy

TWICE SHY

SOPHIA HOLLOWAY

Allison & Busby Limited
11 Wardour Mews
London W1F 8AN
allisonandbusby.com

First published in Great Britain by Allison & Busby in 2026.

A CIP catalogue record for this book is available from the British Library.

First Edition

ISBN 978-0-7490-3359-0

By choosing this product, you help take care of the world's forests. Learn more: www.fsc.org.

FSC
www.fsc.org
MIX
Paper | Supporting responsible forestry
FSC® C018072

Printed and bound in Great Britain by Clays Ltd. Elcograf S.p.A

EU GPSR Authorised Representative
LOGOS EUROPE, 9 rue Nicolas Poussin, 17000, LA ROCHELLE, France
E-mail: Contact@logoseurope.eu

For K M L B

CHAPTER ONE

Elizabeth Ashling took up the pearl drops from their blue velvet bed to fix in her ears, while her maid slid the final pins into her hair. She reflected upon how different she felt from the first time she had sat before this same mirror, only three years previously, and suppressed a sigh. She had been anticipating her first ball, and been so excited that her maid had shaken her head and claimed it was all but impossible to dress her hair properly for all her fidgeting. Tonight Ditcham was beseeching her mistress to abandon the long face that she said would have suited a wake rather than a come-out, and did so with all the authority of one who had been her mother's tirewoman and had known her from infancy.

'Well, it is not my come-out, thank goodness. My cousin will be the focus of attention, but I promise I shall not give anyone the opportunity to say that I am not delighted to be present.'

'It is high time you were out in society again, Miss

Elizabeth, and enjoying yourself at your age. As for being admired, well, there is no reason you should not find yourself the belle of the ball, so lovely as you look, and the image of your poor dear mama.'

'I sincerely hope you are wrong. It would put both Cousin Amelia and my aunt's noses very much out of joint. Besides, Amelia is an exceedingly pretty girl, and I am sure my aunt has very reasonable expectations of her making a most advantageous match before the Season is over. Amelia, at least, will not disappoint her.' There was a bitter stress upon 'at least'.

'It was never your fault, not one bit of it, as I said then and will say now, for all that you frown at me.' The maid clasped the single string of pearls about her mistress's neck. 'Cruel it was, and unfair, and—'

'Thank you, Ditcham, that will be all. I shall do very well.' Elizabeth softened the dismissal with a smile, and a hand on her maid's arm as she rose. 'You mustn't wait up for me.'

Ditcham sniffed, and declared she would be ready to attend her mistress at whatever hour of the morning she retired. She then twitched the folds of the spangled gauze scarf that draped over Elizabeth's elbows, and gave a nod indicative of approbation at the final effect.

Lady Chalford viewed her niece with eyes equally as critical. Her approval was tempered by the fact that she had no wish that her niece should detract from her daughter's launch into Society. She had chaperoned Elizabeth with what could even be described as pleasure, those three years past, when Amelia was still firmly in the schoolroom, and there was every chance of Elizabeth making a reasonable match for which she could take no small degree of credit. After all, it had been she who had taken the girl into her own home when she was a quiet thirteen-year-old, immured in the schoolroom at Dowlands. She had given her the benefit of worldly wisdom and how to go on, without which, in the absence of a mama, she would have been singularly unprepared to take her place in grown-up society. That it had ended as it did, with the embarrassment, the pitying looks, made her doubly determined that Amelia would be a hit.

Not that this was unlikely, she told herself. She smiled indulgently upon her elder daughter, as she watched her self-consciously adjust the pearl and diamond-chip bracelet, a gift for this special occasion, about her wrist. Miss Amelia Ashling had, at just gone seventeen, a figure womanly enough to appeal to the most demanding of gentlemen, without being buxom, and which owed nothing to padding or wax enhancements. Her face was heart shaped, her complexion, despite some fears during the previous year, was flawless, and her features attractive. She beamed at her mama and cousin, and squeezed that damsel's hand quite tightly in her excitement. Lady Chalford looked at the pair together, her daughter golden-haired, her niece a contrasting brunette. Amelia had a thrilled glow about her that the more experienced Elizabeth lacked. Elizabeth, thought her aunt, looked elegant, cool and composed, though it might make Amelia seem gauche, and her ladyship had a lingering doubt that she should have permitted Elizabeth to wear the plain three-quarter dress of bluebell-coloured silk over a straw satin underdress. It was certainly appropriate to a young woman not in her first Season, but it did not make Amelia's faintest shell pink appear to advantage when they stood together, and tonight she wanted her daughter to outshine every other girl present. It was not a foolish aspiration, given her looks.

Lady Chalford had the honesty to admit that although she herself had been accounted a remarkably good-looking girl in her day, her daughter's beauty owed much to her sire. Lord Chalford, though now rather more solid in build than twenty years previously, was frequently described as 'distinguished-looking', and had been remarkably handsome. All three Ashling brothers had been thus blessed, and it had been no surprise when the second son, Edward, with little beyond good lineage and good looks, had married well. Cecilia Dowty might have had her pick of suitors. Lady Chalford cast a glance at her niece's profile; how Elizabeth looked like her mama. Dear Cecilia had brought, with her hand, the Dowlands estate and ten thousand pounds a year. Her gentle, calm good sense, added to the obvious affection in which Edward held her, had proved a very steadying influence upon one whose youthful excesses had caused some concern. He had proved a model husband, but when Cecilia and their son had been carried off within a week of each other by diphtheria when Elizabeth was ten, he had become reclusive, and turned increasingly to intoxicating liquor. His friends and family had shaken their heads and done what they could, but to no avail. He had shunned everybody, including his daughter, and drunk himself slowly but inexorably into the grave. It had been the Christian thing to do, taking the poor girl under her wing, and Edward Ashling's morose inebriation was something that was discreetly forgotten. At least Elizabeth's chances of matrimony had not been harmed by it. What damage, other than to himself, might the poor man do? Lady Chalford permitted herself a sigh. Little had they known.

His sudden death, when Elizabeth was on the very verge of a respectable alliance, had been 'most inopportune' in Lady Chalford's view, since it ruined any plans for a lavish wedding, which would have reflected upon her good taste. Worse was, however, to follow. It became apparent that he had been persuaded into some highly risky investments, which had failed and left his daughter with an encumbered estate and no capital. At this point Lady Chalford had resorted to her vinaigrette and feared the worst.

Elizabeth's grief was tempered by the fact that her father's abandonment of her after her mother died had made her feel orphaned long before he actually died. She had wept often enough in those lonely years, and had no tears left. Cast into full mourning, she had expected her anticipated engagement to be longer, and her wedding a quieter affair, but not that the Honourable Henry Freshford would pay a visit of condolence, murmur about 'changed circumstances' and thereafter ignore her completely. It had all been the whisper of the week in Society, and Lady Chalford had been forced to accept some most unpalatable insincere commiserations from ladies who had been expecting to make just as insincere felicitations.

Elizabeth had withdrawn briefly to Sussex with a heart, if not broken, then at least severely bruised, and in the knowledge that everyone was aware she had been jilted. Henry had not been courting her for her wealth, she knew, for his family were not poor. He had seemed genuinely taken with her, and, after a period of natural caution, she had moved swiftly from surprised delight to infatuation. He was everything a girl could wish for: handsome, thoughtful, just a trifle dashing. Then everything had changed. Whatever he had felt for her was so shallow that he abandoned her when she was no longer 'a good match'. He had proved beyond doubt what she had already feared, that men spoke of love and affection, but they could not be trusted. One loved, laid oneself open, but to them it was no more than words. First Papa had rejected her, then Henry. Disillusioned and dejected, Elizabeth had had nothing to do but contemplate the disaster that had befallen her, and the perfidious nature of the male of the species. Her aunt, insistent that she should not be left alone, had brought her to reside once more at Marden Hall, whilst her uncle and Wimborne, the family man of business, struggled to rescue what they could from the financial disaster that was her legacy. By the following summer, it looked very much as if the creditors would compound no more, and even the house and home farm would have to be sold. What they had not accounted for was a rescue from an unexpected source.

The Honourable Gerald Ashling, the youngest of the brothers, had gone into the army, and beyond letters home and a period of furlough to recuperate following a wound at Salamanca, he had been on the periphery of the family for well over a decade. He had joined Wellington's 'family', the group of staff officers about the Great Man, following Napoleon's escape from Elba. Before his departure he gave Wimborne very precise instructions about what to do with the accumulation of pay, of which he had spent but little. In the course of the war in the Peninsula, he had come into contact with Mr Nathan Rothschild, whose efforts had ensured the army was paid. He pressed Wimborne to keep the closest of eyes upon what Mr Rothschild did and to do the same, however risky it might appear. Thus, when everyone was selling out of Funds upon rumour of an Allied defeat in Belgium, Wimborne, desperately unhappy, and with the bankers telling him he was mad, followed the Rothschild example and bought stock.

Waterloo thus made Gerald Ashling considerably wealthier, but he did not live to enjoy the fruits of his acumen. Gravely wounded upon the field of battle, he lingered some three weeks before expiring, and left all his worldly goods to his niece, Elizabeth Cecilia Ashling, to be held in trust until her twenty-fifth birthday or her marriage, by his eldest brother, William, and Josiah Wimborne.

In the space of little over a year, Elizabeth had been hopeful debutante, penniless relative, and then, if not an heiress, at least the possessor of a very respectable competence. She had begged her aunt not to make her go to London for her second Season, and in view of the impossibility of her achieving any marriage, that lady had acquiesced and permitted her to remain in Sussex. With the recovery of her fortune there was pressure brought to bear upon her to return to London for the 1816 Season,

Lady Chalford being keen to have her niece off her hands before Amelia's come-out, but Elizabeth, still haunted by the idea that she would be an object of pity and hushed, behind-the-hand conversations, withstood every entreaty and even command. She had neither the intention nor wish to marry, she said, and would rather learn more about the management of her estate from Frimley, the Marden land agent, so that upon coming of age, she could live in peace and quiet at Dowlands, with some suitable female companion.

This Season, however, Amelia was to make her bow to Polite Society, and Lady Chalford was determined that Elizabeth should not remain behind.

'Think, my dear, how odd it would appear. It would be said that your uncle and I were behaving very shabbily towards you.'

'But if it was made clear, Aunt . . .'

'In what manner? Would you take out an advertisement in the pages of the *Morning Post*? Believe me, Elizabeth, what you ask is not possible. I understand, truthfully I do, your reluctance, however little I may like your future plans, but you are still underage and in your uncle's care, and so this Season you will be with us in Mount Street.'

Elizabeth had, perforce, to submit, and if she did not look tonight like a young woman delighted to re-enter society, she had, her aunt noted approvingly, the good breeding not to exhibit any missish behaviour. The clock struck the hour, Lord Chalford emerged from the library just in time to wish the ladies of his household a pleasant evening and crack a mild jest, before the front door was opened and a breath of cool evening air reached them as they descended the steps to the waiting carriage.

Amelia was silent during the short journey, but fidgeted. Lady Chalford had been careful in her selection of parties through which she might ease her daughter into Polite Society. She was confident Amelia would not be overawed, but the ball at Devonshire House was going to be the first 'squeeze' of the Season, and she might be forgiven her agitation. Elizabeth sat composedly, and watched her cousin with sympathy.

Elizabeth withdrew into herself, and though she smiled and curtseyed prettily as they were presented to their hostess, she felt remarkably hollow and alone. However, she revived a few minutes later as she heard the announcement of the Earl and Countess of Godmanchester. Lady Godmanchester had been, three years ago, Miss Turville, and Elizabeth's closest friend among the debutantes. She had made a very good match, and whilst circumstances, including her ladyship's presenting her lord with a son and heir shortly after their first anniversary, had precluded their meeting, they had remained frequent correspondents. She entered the brightly lit room on her husband's arm, looking much as Elizabeth remembered her, and when she caught her friend's eye she greeted Elizabeth affectionately.

'How nice to see you at last, Elizabeth. Do tell me we can enjoy a comfortable chat later on. Oh, but do not let it be too late, for Godmanchester will not let me tire myself, and will drag me home unconscionably early.' Her voice dropped to a whisper. 'I have discovered I am increasing again, which annoyingly means a curtailed Season for me, and he is most careful of my health.' She turned and smiled at her husband, and Elizabeth realised with a start that the swift glance they exchanged spoke volumes. He did look inordinately proud and solicitous.

'I shall be sure to do so, Helen. You will not be dancing, I take it?'

Lady Godmanchester pulled a face. 'Alas no, upon strict instruction. Though I do see it is sensible. It is bound to be a cause of speculation among the tabbies. I shall need your company very much, stuck as I will be among the mamas and dowagers.'

With which she passed on, and Elizabeth schooled her features into polite interest once more.

It was something over an hour later when she found her friend seated upon a sofa, fanning herself gently.

'You are not feeling faint, are you?' Elizabeth looked suddenly worried. She had no experience of ladies in expectation of a happy event.

'Just a trifle hot. It is nothing. Lucius Radstock has just gone to find me some lemonade, but you can be sure he will return with Godmanchester. I said nothing, but he is frighteningly acute, and they are close friends. Even if it were only the heat he would fetch him to me, but, oh, trust him to guess at something more.' She blushed, and her eyes misted slightly. 'Though it might be he has guessed from Godmanchester's demeanour. Bless him, he is so pleased.' She sighed and took Elizabeth's hand. 'I only wish I could see you as happy as I am, my dear friend.'

'I think you found the best of men, Helen. I doubt I

could be as fortunate, and if not, then I am happier single.'

'Do not say so, please. To think of you hiding yourself away in Sussex . . .'

'Hiding? No such thing! Were I but older it would be easy. I admit that at present the thought of having to have a companion and oh, all the constraints, is irksome, but far more irksome it would be to be wed to some man or other without real love. And that is rare. You are very fortunate.'

'I am. He is such a dear. Overprotective, of course, at the moment, but . . .'

'Well, even I would not deny a man the right to feel so in such circumstances.'

'Even you?'

'Ah.' A dimple peeped in Elizabeth's cheek. 'I would prefer to deny men everything, but . . .'

'Your lemonade, my lady.'

Elizabeth flushed and half turned, looking over her shoulder. Sir Lucius Radstock presented the glass to Lady Godmanchester, and she wondered if he had overheard her. If he had done so he gave no sign, and Elizabeth heaved a sigh of relief.

'I took it upon myself to tell Godmanchester that you were a trifle indisposed,' the grey eyes held far too much understanding, 'and he will be here . . . Ah, now.'

'My love?' Godmanchester's handsome face wore a frown of concern.

'My lord, really. It is nothing, except that the warmth of the room became a little oppressive. I beg you will not look so, nor whisk me away on the instant, for it would be as well to announce everything in the newspaper, and I shall have no peace from the busybody mamas with their sovereign remedies and recommendations from now until I have to retire from Society.'

'Not immediately then, but soon.' He smiled, but the worry remained in the hazel eyes.

'Oh.' Lady Godmanchester put her hand to her lips. 'How imprudent of me. Sir Lucius, I beg of you . . .'

Sir Lucius bowed. 'Not imprudent, my lady, since I had already surmised, and you may be sure I shall not reveal anything, especially to any, er, "busybody mamas". My felicitations, to you both.' He acknowledged his friend with the briefest of touches upon the arm. 'And now I find myself somewhat *de trop* and will go in search of something rather stronger than lemonade. Ladies.'

With a bow and a smile he turned, and Elizabeth watched his tall form weave its way between the guests until lost from view.

'Good fellow, Lucius,' remarked Godmanchester, a little gruffly. 'Now, my love. If you are perfectly sure you are not unwell I will, most reluctantly, leave you, but be advised I shall return within the half hour and bear you off home.' He lifted his wife's hand to his lips and kissed it.

'My lord, what will people say?' She coloured.

'That I adore my wife, which is perfectly true. Half an hour, my dear, no longer.' He smiled at her, spoke a few words to Elizabeth, and withdrew.

'You see how fortunate I am, Elizabeth?' Lady Godmanchester blinked away a tear. 'When he offered for me I could not claim to have had more than a slight *tendre* for him, a predisposition towards him, perhaps. But then,

I did not know him, the private "him", you understand. But oh, before the end even of the honeymoon, my feelings for him were as strong as his for me. Forgive me. I am emotional. You must put it down to my delicate situation. There, I am quite composed again.'

'What need for apology?' Elizabeth patted her hand. 'Indeed, it is I who should apologise, for I have not congratulated you, which was remiss, though I hope you knew it, even unspoken.'

'Of course I did. You know, perhaps one reason I felt unwell was lack of food. I am really not able to take more than a dry, sweet biscuit in the morning, and my appetite today was wayward, but I did see that there were spiced apple tartlets. Shall we go and see if there are any remaining, and then I will return here quietly to await my lord.'

Lady Godmanchester took her friend's arm and they made their way to where various delicacies had been set out, the fair head of the countess contrasting with Elizabeth's own dark locks.

Lady Godmanchester laid her head against her husband's broad shoulder in the darkness of the carriage, letting her fingers entwine with his, and sighed.

'I am sorry if I seemed dictatorial, my dear.' He spoke gently, and breathed in the fragrance of the perfume in her hair.

'No, no. I was ready to leave, I promise you, but I was so glad to be with Elizabeth again. I asked her to visit me tomorrow afternoon. I told her I wished she might be as happy as I am, though I doubt that is possible.'

'Say that again.'

'I am so happy, blissfully happy, Giles.' She sighed again, and he turned slightly to kiss her.

'My love.'

She murmured something unintelligible, and her hand touched his cheek. What she had meant was not just that nobody could be as happy as they were, though it was true, but that she thought that Elizabeth was refusing to admit the possibility of such happiness. Thinking about it tonight was too difficult, so she let herself drift, secure in her own deep contentment, until the carriage drew up at her own door.

CHAPTER TWO

The Honourable Amelia Ashling made no attempt to conceal her delight at the success of her first ball, and positively bounced into her cousin's room next morning, her hair still in curling papers, and eager to discuss the previous evening in minute detail. Youthful excitement, rather than any puffed-up idea of her own worth, was the cause of these transports, and, beyond requesting that her cousin did not make her spill her morning chocolate on the coverlet, Elizabeth did nothing to restrain her. After all, a girl's first ball ought to be memorable. Hers had been, and she had foreseen nothing but pleasure for the rest of the Season. It had been a delusion, but it would be cruel to ruin Amelia's innocent delight. Having lived in her aunt's house since she was thirteen, Elizabeth had been more of an older sister to her cousins Amelia, nearly four years her junior, and the even younger Anne. She held her sweet-natured but biddable cousin in deep affection, and so Elizabeth sat in bed and listened patiently to the litany of introductions, interjecting only the occasional murmured agreement.

'Did you not think Isabella Crowthorne looked a positive fright in that dress cluttered about with knots of pink ribbon? Mama says that simplicity is best, and although I would have liked those paste buttons we saw in the haberdasher's, I know she was right not to let me purchase them for my gown last night. Mama says . . .'

It was apparent that Amelia had developed no firm thoughts of her own, and was currently an echo of her mother. Elizabeth secretly hoped that, as she unfurled her petals, she would gain the confidence to hold her own opinions, not least because it would be unfortunate if she accepted the offer of a man simply because her mama told her it was what she should do.

'. . . And Mama says that Lady Cowper actually sought her out to say she was delighted to have been the one to provide the vouchers for Almack's, having observed us last week, and she said to Mama that she thought I would "break hearts".' Amelia giggled. 'Me! Was there ever anything so funny? Why, when you think of how little attention James's friends paid me at Christmas . . .'

Elizabeth smiled. It was hardly likely that Amelia's brother's Oxford friends, barely two years older than Amelia herself, would think of his sister, still officially in the schoolroom, in a romantic light. This was especially true since James treated his nearest sibling with a studied casual air that belied their underlying deep affection. However, it would not be prudent to tell Amelia this. She was a generally sweet-tempered girl, not prone to scowls and sulks, and willing, thus far, to be guided entirely by her mama.

Elizabeth wondered whether she was so biddable because she simply sailed through life expecting everything to go well, or because it was easier not to upset her parent. Amelia had proved an able pupil at music and her watercolours, of which her mama made much, but was not given to deep thought. She would, thought Elizabeth, be the perfect wife for a man of moderate intellect who would delight in a helpmeet who would defer to him with any problem beyond the running of the house, and never challenge his authority. If Elizabeth thought that lily-livered, she did at least accept that it would make for a peaceful and contented existence. For herself, she was inclined to think she would be driven to distraction, especially since men had a vastly inflated idea of their own importance. She was grateful that she had escaped the confines that marriage would have put upon her, and had resolved to revel in the freedom of her single state rather than bemoan spinsterhood.

'I am sure Lady Cowper was paying your mama a compliment as much as you, Cousin, and as long as you do not actually set out to "break hearts", for that is not appealing in a girl, you will be very popular.'

'You sound like old Aunt Risborough.' Amelia grinned, and her eyes twinkled. 'But you are barely four years my senior, so I do not know why you should want to be like her. You will be wearing quizzy hats and moth-eaten sables like she does, next.'

'Oh no!' Elizabeth laughed. 'Not the sad sables! They really are atrocious, are they not? And how can they be so moth-eaten when they reek of camphor?'

'Perhaps it is Aunt Risborough who smells of camphor.'

Both young ladies collapsed in giggles for a moment, then Amelia reverted to the ball.

'By the time I went to bed, my feet positively ached from dancing.'

'That must have been that man who trod on your foot.'

'Oh, how did you know? There was one!'

'Indeed, and you should have warned me, for he trod on mine later. I would have cried off and had him fetch me a glass of champagne instead, had I known. I only danced because my aunt positively pushed the man at me. I am sure he had no control over his lower limbs at all. He danced like a frog.'

'He was quite amusing and very polite, except that he did not even seem to notice when he crushed my toes. I was glad that Mama had given me strict orders not to dance more than once with any gentleman, for he did request a second.'

'I doubt any woman would care to dance twice with him.'

'True. Nor would I have wished to stand up with Sir Lucius Radstock. He dances well, but he is very dry. He spoke to us while you were with Lady Brightlingsea. Mama seemed to find him amusing but I think he was mocking me a little, although I cannot be sure.' She frowned, then her brows lifted. 'But I would not have minded dancing again with Lord Bensthorpe, or Mr Selborne.' She blushed. 'He said that his evening was quite ruined when I refused him a quadrille.'

'Yes,' responded Elizabeth drily, 'I did notice him withdraw to the card room shortly afterwards.'

'Wretch!' Amelia pouted, but mirth bubbled up again.

Elizabeth smiled, and set her chocolate cup to one side. 'Now, you must leave me to get up. I am going riding in the park this morning.'

'Oh, with whom?'

'Just a groom. You see, I am going for the riding, not the company. Mind you, if that hack my Uncle Chalford hired turns out to be anything more than a slug, I shall be surprised.' She coloured. 'I am sorry, that was ungracious. It is very good of him to find me a horse, but his idea of a mount suitable for a lady is very . . . staid.'

'Mama never really liked horses, and I prefer to be in a carriage, so I suppose . . .'

'No, no. There is no fault, excepting mine. I only wish I could have brought Pallas up with us for the Season, but there.' She sighed. 'No point bemoaning the fact now, though, so off with you. Oh, and I fear I shall not see you after luncheon, for I believe you are to visit Lady Ellesmere this afternoon, and I am engaged to visit Lady Godmanchester.'

With which she shooed Miss Amelia from the bed and rang for Ditcham.

Elizabeth could not but dwell upon the evening herself, as Ditcham twisted her hair into a knot on the top of her head. Amelia might regard it as a triumphant dream, but for Elizabeth it had dissolved into a nightmare. At first she had thought herself at ease and under control, and indeed, until shortly after the Godmanchesters had left, she had been enjoying herself, in a mild way. Then it had happened, an encounter that shattered her equilibrium. She had accepted that she was bound to meet her erstwhile suitor, Henry

Freshford, at some point. He was the Viscount Syston now, and she knew that he had married, but she was praying she might not have to greet them in the house where they had met, and in such similar circumstances. It would be almost too much to bear. Elizabeth was unconsciously focusing upon the ignominy of three years ago, wondering if it would be brought into people's minds again, and she would be the object of pitying looks and snide remarks. Whilst she was in fact spared Henry, she suffered almost as great a misfortune in that she had come face to face with Aurelia Northcott, who had made a brilliant match, and who had seen herself as Elizabeth's rival at her come-out. Perhaps it had been that they had looked too alike, both brunettes, both with good complexions and regular features. If Miss Northcott had the more perfect mouth, there were many to swear Miss Ashling had the finer, and more naturally arching brows, and if Miss Northcott had the sweeter singing voice, Miss Ashling was the better dancer. The main difference between them had been ambition; Aurelia Northcott had set out to make as stunning a match as her modest fortune would permit, and woe betide any whom she saw as standing in her way. Elizabeth did not aspire to more than the vague wish that some eligible and reasonably handsome man would appear out of nowhere and sweep her off her nimble little feet, but Miss Northcott saw every man who so much as cast Elizabeth an admiring glance as a recusant who ought to be worshipping her elegant self. That Henry Freshford had looked favourably on her for a short time only, and had then transferred his adoration, most perfidiously, to Elizabeth Ashling, was a personal affront. It rankled until the moment when it was rendered unimportant by her own conquest of a marquis, who had been a widower some years and was not considered likely to remarry. He might be forty, and prone to ponderous witticisms, but Lord Rendlesham was perfectly willing and able to keep Aurelia Northcott in the style she deemed her right, would place her on as high a pedestal as she demanded, and give her a title to which she assumed every other debutante must aspire. Not content merely with her own success, she had revelled in Miss Ashling's sudden ignominious withdrawal from the 'lists', vanquished and unwed.

The Marchioness of Rendlesham had chosen to appear fashionably late at the Duchess of Devonshire's ball, having already made an appearance at Lady Merton's rather overshadowed rout earlier in the evening. It had given her the chance to enjoy that lady's chagrin at having picked the worst of dates for her party.

Marriage had given the former Miss Northcott the supreme air of assurance. Indeed, those who were not enamoured of her suggest she had secretly regretted that there had been no marriageable dukes available when she had accepted Rendlesham. She certainly swept in, bedecked in diamonds and with a supercilious look upon her face, and, as bad luck would have it, came up face to face with Elizabeth. For a fleeting moment there had been no recognition, then the sapphire-blue eyes hardened, and the smile had become fixed. There had been a stiff acknowledgement, an exchange of formal insincerities, and then her ladyship had moved on, but not before Elizabeth had heard her comment to a dyspeptic-looking lady in lilac.

'One wonders why on earth dear Lady Chalford, with that sweet daughter of hers to launch, would care to advertise past failures.'

Elizabeth had stood very still, though the room seemed to spin about her for a moment. Her kid-gloved hands clenched involuntarily, and she took a deep breath. The colour had drained from her face, but then returned in a rush. It took all her self control not to turn and run from the room, but she had regained her composure, and if her manner seemed a trifle brittle thereafter, she successfully concealed her inner turmoil. She had danced, mechanically rather than with any pleasure, including the quadrille with the hapless man who had trodden on her toes, and which had added a final dismal note to the evening. Her aunt and cousin, caught up in who had said what and danced with whom, barely seemed to notice with how much relief Elizabeth had climbed into their carriage at an advanced hour.

The trouble, she thought, and sighed, was that last night was just the beginning. Weeks and weeks of this stretched before her, of wishing that she could be invisible. If only Aunt Chalford had let her remain in Sussex. There was no point to her coming to London, none at all. For all that her aunt retained the faint hope that she would find a husband at this late stage, Lady Chalford was deluding herself. Elizabeth had resolved not to let herself be exposed to the humiliation and hurt again. At least she thought that she could avoid it, but if Lady Rendlesham and her friends chose to rake up the past, that was what she faced, even without falling into the trap of believing the shallow lies that men offered as 'love'. She shut her eyes.

'Have you the headache still, Miss Elizabeth? Would you not be better laid upon your bed rather than out in the park in that nasty cold wind? I could burn pastilles if you so wished.'

'No, Ditcham, it is not a headache, I promise, and the chance to let the wind blow away my foolish thoughts would be welcome. I am visiting Lady Godmanchester this afternoon, so would you lay out the fawn twilled silk and my green spencer.'

'As you wish, miss. And I ought to mention there's a nasty mark on one of your satin slippers that you wore last night, and I am not sure as it will come out, for the fabric is damaged.'

'Oh dear, how vexatious. I had thought it was only my toes that were bruised. I think gentlemen should produce certificates of competence before requesting to dance with one. There was a man last night who is a danger to every toe in London.' Elizabeth smiled at her maid, who shook her head, but thought that whatever had blue-devilled her mistress would pass quickly enough.

It so happened that Lady Chalford had not been blind to her niece's failure to enjoy the evening, and whilst her daughter's palpable success weighed most with her, she did spend some minutes wondering what might have occurred to put Elizabeth out so much. She had not entertained the false hope that Elizabeth would spend an evening of unalloyed pleasure, but when she had seen her early on during the ball, she had seemed in tolerable spirits, and several gentlemen had sought introductions as partners. Admittedly, one was Colonel Bettison, who had been a friend of Elizabeth's late uncle Gerald, and another was Lord Farncombe's hapless heir, a weak-chinned youth inclined to poetry. The Honourable Gregory Escott had eschewed the normal mistakes of youth; he did not give his mama sleepless nights over heavy drinking or the muslin company, nor was his father forced to advance him his quarter's allowance to cover his debts, beyond those to his tailor, which was expected. Instead, he had determined that he was a poet in the Byronic mode, and turned the simplest phrase into a grandiloquent outpouring littered with excessive, and sometimes random, emphases. He awaited admiration of his poetic talent, but in fact the rest of the Polite World simply tolerated his folly and waited for him to grow up. He was a pleasant enough youth, and everywhere received, and Lady Chalford had introduced him without any thought but that he might be anything more than a reasonable partner for the cotillion. Neither of these gentlemen had been seen by Elizabeth as a threat, the one being too old, and the other too juvenile.

Lady Chalford was wise enough to know that her niece now regarded men with the utmost suspicion, but retained the hope that somehow, somewhere, there might be a gentleman who would see past her unapproachable, if not antagonistic, manner, and find a way to make himself acceptable to her. Elizabeth might talk of living the single life at Dowlands, but her aunt was under no illusions that, once the novelty wore off, such an existence would prove lonely and miserable. Single ladies were difficult to invite to any function, and, with age, generally became eccentric. She herself had had such an aunt, and it was not the future she wanted for her much-loved niece.

She was sure that none of the gentlemen could have given Elizabeth cause to be upset. However, at some point in the evening something had happened, something untoward. The gentle cynicism in Elizabeth's eyes had been replaced by a ghastly emptiness by the time she had seen her at supper. She had danced thereafter like an automaton, she who could dance with such vivacity and joy in every step. Elizabeth herself would certainly not reveal the cause and Lady Chalford saw no reason to ask Amelia if she had heard or seen anything. Not only had the dear girl been caught up in her own excitement, but Amelia was largely ignorant of what had happened three years past, and how it had twisted her cousin's view of the world. She had been but a fourteen-year-old and firmly in the schoolroom when 'The Disaster' had occurred, and had been kept from all but the sketchiest details by her mama, for fear that it might make her unnecessarily nervous and cautious at her own come-out.

Lady Chalford was not unfeeling, and it distressed her to think her niece had been made unhappy, but she was at a loss to know what to do about it. She sighed, instantly dismissed the idea that she might mention it to her husband, and having come to the conclusion that there was nothing to be done but hope that it was a passing case of agitated nerves, set it on one side to think of more pleasant things. The most pressing of these were the decisions upon which of the invitations that had arrived in the course of the morning should take precedence in the following weeks, and whether attending the military review in Hyde Park was likely to give Amelia an unfortunate predisposition towards young men in regimentals. They did look so dashing, but none she had ever encountered had a feather to fly with, and they were universally high on the matchmaking mamas' list of dangers. It was with thoughts of scarlet cloth and gold tassels, rather than Elizabeth's disquiet, that she rang for her dresser.

CHAPTER THREE

Elizabeth's every worst fear about the horse that her uncle had selected for her was fulfilled. It regarded her with patent suspicion, as someone likely to want it to go at a pace it had little inclination to attain. It had four legs, yes, but calling it a horse was, in her opinion, an error. What her uncle, who was well aware that she was a considerable horsewoman, was thinking when he selected it, she could not imagine. Perhaps, as Amelia had said, he had reverted to thinking about what he would select for his daughter, if she had to ride in London.

It had been Elizabeth's intention to go for a ride rather than be 'seen'. Riding around Hyde Park was undoubtedly something that many people did as a social exercise, taking the opportunity to meet and exchange gossip rather than simply take the fresh air upon horseback. From choice, Elizabeth would have preferred the freedom to gallop, but this would have attracted the most severe censure, since it was forbidden, even assuming she had been able to force her mount to such an expenditure of energy. As it was, even a sedate canter proved more than it was happy to maintain for more than a hundred yards or so. Elizabeth was faced with the alternatives of kicking the beast in an unseemly effort to get it to keep to even a moderate pace, or maundering along at a desultory trot. The only advantage that she could see was that nobody would wish to be seen riding beside her, assuming they could get a real horse to match the pace.

On the other hand, it prevented her passing the highly polished barouche of Lady Rendlesham without exchanging courtesies, just as she emerged from Hyde Park at the conclusion of her inadequate ride. Lady Rendlesham was not a rider, but it did not take an expert to tell that Elizabeth was mounted upon a hired beast of dubious worth. It was therefore too good an opportunity to be wasted. Lady Rendlesham commanded her coachman to halt, waved her gloved hand and nodded, smiling, at Elizabeth.

'Dear Miss Ashling, riding out in the fresh air so early, I see. No doubt it is good for the complexion, or is it indigestion? I never can remember, never having been worried by either. Lady Cumnor – oh, have you been introduced . . . yes . . . Well, Lady Cumnor and I were saying how well you look upon a suitably mettlesome steed. You were accounted quite the horsewoman, as I recall.'

Lady Cumnor blinked, having said nothing of the sort, but made a vague gesture of agreement. The smile on Lady Rendlesham's face grew, for it was an insult couched in the most unexceptional terms, but one which Elizabeth was bound to feel. The retort that sprang to her lips, had, perforce, to be bitten back, for she had not the added experience of the married lady of fashion to reply in kind, and knew she would be openly offensive, which was unthinkable in front of Lady Cumnor. She was therefore reduced to bland inanities. Complaining about the horse would do nothing but give pleasure to her torturer. Elizabeth wondered why on earth Aurelia should seek to continue to denigrate one whom she must have considered 'defeated' three years since, and decided it was simply a natural malevolence.

With a condescending nod of her elegantly bonneted head, indicating dismissal, Lady Rendlesham had her carriage move on.

Elizabeth gritted her teeth, and smiled as falsely as the ladies in the barouche. Even when upon horseback, it seemed, London was determined to ruin any chance of not only pleasure, but even contentment. How could one feel liberated upon a creature as uninspiring as the one she had been given to ride?

It was therefore an out-of-temper Miss Ashling who returned to Mount Street, a little dusty and most displeased with life.

Her mood was not improved by finding that, in her absence, Mr Escott had called, been cast into apparent despair by her absence and had left a bouquet of garish red roses with a message, which turned out to be in rhyme. This offering, at which she took one appalled glance and then flung upon the table in disgust, was pounced upon by Amelia. It sent her into whoops of laughter, which were only curtailed by her mama's arrival upon the scene to deliver an admonition on unladylike 'yelling'.

'I am sorry, Mama, but this . . . Oh, it is just too funny! Mr Escott has written a poem to Elizabeth.'

'Then it is hardly your place to be reading it, surely, Amelia,' remonstrated Lady Chalford gently.

'Oh no, Aunt,' interposed Elizabeth, still fuming. 'At least if it gives Amelia some merriment it has done something, other than fill me with the strong desire to stamp these roses into your new carpet.'

'Oh dear! Is it that bad?'

'Worse, if possible. Go on, Amelia, read it out, if you can bear to do so.'

Amelia tried to school her features into a semblance of disinterest, cleared her throat, and promptly choked over the first line. It took her three attempts before she managed to recite the short stanza.

'Fairest of fair, yet beauteous dark,
Alas, your absence in the Park
Leaves me disconsolate and low.
For without speech you cannot know
The heights to which your vision bright,
Carried me speechless, yesternight,
And these poor flowers, no words possessing,
I leave, my stolen heart confessing.'

Tears were streaming down Amelia's cheeks from laughter.

'I think,' enunciated Elizabeth slowly, 'that I feel ill.'

'He is very young, and working under strong emotions,' remarked Lady Chalford soothingly.

'Then he should spend his time in curbing them, rather than in producing such nonsense.' Elizabeth was clearly not mollified.

'Are you not being a trifle harsh, my dear?'

'Harsh? No, for "nonsense" seems a generous term.'

'But you will not be uncivil to him, will you, when next you meet?' Lady Chalford gave a small, nervous smile. 'You must not be seen as cruel and unfair.'

'Nobody would think me cruel if they had to read that,' Elizabeth fumed, pointing at the note, 'but since, thankfully, they will be spared it, I suppose I shall have to appear unmoved.' She sighed. 'He only had one dance with me. What perversity of fate made him select me, of all people, as his latest goddess?'

'He did not actually call you a "goddess",' noted Amelia judiciously.

'No, but he will, I have no doubt. That, do not forget, was merely written upon finding me not at home. Oh goodness, what if he writes pages of it?'

'Or there is a literary soirée, and he reads them,' declared Amelia, collapsing once more into helpless laughter.

Her mama glared at her and sent her immediately to her room to compose herself, and sit for an hour with the book of homilies that her Aunt Risborough had sent her. Levity, she said repressively, was not to be encouraged in excess. With Amelia gone, Lady Chalford set about soothing her niece's ruffled feathers, with limited success.

'You might be making too much of this, my dear. It is most provoking, I am sure, but is in no way your fault, as anyone would accept. Young men in the grip of the poetic urge may select their muse upon the flimsiest of premises, but thankfully their interest tends to wax and wane quickly, and they transfer their fleeting adoration elsewhere. It is just bad luck, like catching the mumps.'

At which point, with the analogy of Mr Escott as a disease, even Elizabeth began to laugh.

The subject was carefully avoided at luncheon, and afterwards Elizabeth set off to visit her friend, declining the offer of the landaulet, and stepping the short distance to Brook Street accompanied by a footman. She found Lady Godmanchester reclining upon a sofa, but looking in good health.

'I am not near as invalidish as I must appear, Elizabeth, but I have been recommended to put my feet up as often as possible. I do find myself in need of rest if I am to go out in the evening, and later, as one becomes larger, it does help prevent one's ankles from swelling.'

'You seem very unperturbed by the prospect.'

'Well, one is less concerned, the second time, I think. The loss of one's figure is sad, but once the sickness passed, and the baby quickened, I have to admit I was very content whilst carrying George, and Godmanchester is a perfect dear about it all, putting up with the odd humours that afflict ladies when increasing without complaint.' Her eyes misted. 'He even said he thought me beautiful when I was positively huge, and waddled rather than walked, and once I was safely delivered, came down to London, and bought me the most beautiful sapphire bracelet, "for being brave". As if one had a choice!'

'Marriage suits you, Helen.'

'My husband suits me,' she corrected. 'I am very well aware that many women are not nearly as fortunate as I am. I dread to think what marriage must be like where there is no mutual love, or even deep affection. Can you imagine being married to Lord Newlyn, who never does anything but find fault, or a man with an erratic temper?' She shuddered. 'No. I am blessed with the best of husbands, so how could marriage not suit me?'

She was entirely sincere, and Elizabeth could not, though it went against her every experience, find a fault in what she said, nor indeed would have had the heart to disabuse her, had she been able to do so. The memory of her parents' devotion was clouded by the ensuing misery of loss, and that was the only relationship that she had seen as truly complete.

The major problem that Elizabeth foresaw was that her dearest friend, and only true confidante, would not be able to comprehend her actions. How could a woman so happy in the bonds of wedlock see that she recoiled from them in distrust and even fear? It created a chasm between them, which Elizabeth regretted. However, she was perfectly willing to share the baleful news of her couplet-writing admirer.

'I did not encourage him, I swear, Helen. Indeed, one might more readily have complained that I was too aloof and distant.'

'By which, you know, you probably placed yourself upon the pedestal to which he raises his eyes,' Lady Godmanchester remarked sagely.

'Tell me how I might leap down from it immediately and I will be eternally grateful! It is horrible! What if his verses become known?'

'I hardly think they will. Printing and binding is quite expensive, I believe.' Lady Godmanchester's eyes danced, as her friend's widened in horror.

'Published? No, please, tell me that is in jest!'

'Oh, Elizabeth, of course. Unless he has a patron, of course.' She giggled.

'You are being cruel, Helen. Very cruel.' Elizabeth pouted theatrically. 'If you only knew . . .'

'Go on then, tell me what he wrote.'

'I threw it away.'

'Shame. Can you not remember any of it?'

'Remember? It still haunts me. It began with something like "Fairest of fair, yet beauteous dark, Alas, your absence in the Park, Leaves me despondent, sorry, disconsolate, and low."'

'Dark and, er, park, what fortuitous rhyming.'

'I am sure,' declared Elizabeth repressively, 'that giggling is bad for the unborn child. Too much bouncing up and down might jangle its nerves.'

'Really?' Lady Godmanchester laid a hand on her barely rounded stomach. 'And I thought it might make Baby a happy little soul.' She smiled. 'Seriously, having a poet dragging about after you, sighing, and singing your praises, is an encumbrance, but scarcely your own fault.'

'But it makes one ridiculous, and . . . Oh Helen, the Awful Aurelia is as spiteful as ever. We met last night, very stiffly civil of course, but she made such a comment to another lady as she turned away as must have been intended for my ears also, wondering why my aunt, launching Amelia into Society, would be prepared to "advertise past failures". And those were her exact words.'

Helen Godmanchester's normally open, pleasant expression clouded, and she frowned. 'Oh no, you poor thing. She is the most hateful woman, but I assure you she has not been keeping her sharp tongue just for your return. She has a reputation for it, and often against those who are entirely without fault, not engaged in any female cattiness. I think she just assumes everyone is her rival, and being married does not mean, to her, not wanting to flirt outrageously and be admired by the gentlemen. She still expects adulation. I was sorry for her for a while.'

'Sorry? For Aurelia?'

'Yes. I mean after George was born, I truly realised how fulfilling life could be, and yet she has not shown any signs of wanting a child. Perhaps, I thought, if she was longing for a baby, and so far there have been none forthcoming . . . But I heard her say to Lady Carterton that she was actually relieved, since "breeding mars the figure". What sort of woman is that?'

Elizabeth did not reply. She saw her friend's point, but was herself unconscious of any maternal impulse.

Helen gave her a lopsided smile. 'Ah, I see it in your eyes. You think me addled. But if you found the right man, Elizabeth . . .'

'I would be amazed. Oh, do not look so tragic. I shall promise to be as fond a godmother as any could wish, if you have a little girl. I was of course immensely cast down last time that you "only" had a son.' She grinned, and patted her friend's hand. 'Come. I did not visit you to make you low spirited. Indeed, I had hoped you would cheer me, after an evening of misery and a frustrating morning. I have not even begun to tell you about the hack my uncle selected for me.'

Elizabeth proceeded to distract Lady Godmanchester with a description of the horse, and her efforts to make it move. She even managed to make herself smile, but knew that her acceptance of the beast was transient. She would be filled with disgust the very next time she saw it.

The sound of male voices and a baritone laugh made Lady Godmanchester look towards the door, and a few moments later her lord, and Sir Lucius Radstock, entered. Sir Lucius was still smiling at whatever sally his friend had made, and Elizabeth was quite surprised. She had thought his features formed for sobriety at their first encounter. Both ladies made to rise, but Lord Godmanchester shook his head.

'No, no, please do not get up, ladies. We intrude, I know, but I wished to find out whether my lady felt better than when I departed this morning.' His eyes were on his wife.

'Much better, sir, I assure you, and before you ask, I took a little boiled chicken and fruit at luncheon. Such indisposition as I suffer is transitory and not, I must stress, a reason for you to worry.'

'"Concern" sounds better, I think. Lucius will vouch I have not been biting my nails to the quick, or tearing my hair.' He smiled, and turned to his friend, who nodded.

'And Sir Lucius, I have not as yet presented you to my

dearest friend, Miss Ashling. Last night I was singularly remiss, but shall remedy it now.'

The introduction was made, with less formality than if it had been made in a public place, and Lady Godmanchester invited the gentlemen to remain and take tea, though with a twinkle in her eyes.

'Er, thank you, my love, but we were going to adjourn to the study. We have been racking our brains for a name for Lucius's new filly, and something Greek might prove suitable.'

'What is her breeding, Sir Lucius?' Her ladyship's interest was polite.

'Out of Debutante, by Run To A Standstill.'

'Then "Wallflower" would be appropriate. There are many debutantes who stand an awful lot.' There was a very slight edge to Elizabeth's voice, but Sir Lucius was not sufficiently acquainted with her to note it.

'Very clever, Miss Ashling, though I am sure it has not been a role you have played.' His compliment was a little ponderous, he would have acknowledged, but her response took him by surprise.

'There are even less acceptable reasons to be returning for another Season, are there not?' She did not hide her bitterness, thinking that he must have recalled how she had been jilted.

Both gentlemen looked blankly at her, and then at each other.

'No insult was intended, ma'am.' It was Sir Lucius's turn to sound prickly.

'And I am sure none was taken,' interjected Lady

Godmanchester calmly, giving her friend a glance and tentative smile.

'No, Sir Lucius, none taken.' Elizabeth obeyed the unspoken plea, though her voice lacked conviction.

'Well, despite having the problem of naming the filly solved, I think we will leave you ladies to tea.' Lord Godmanchester decided withdrawing was the safest course. Once in the privacy of the study, Sir Lucius asked the obvious question.

'Why did Miss Ashling rip up at me like that?'

'I have absolutely no idea, my friend, none at all. The gentle sex are a mystery, even to the married.'

Elizabeth, meanwhile, was contrite. 'Oh Helen, I am sorry. That was unforgivable. I can only apologise profusely. It is like touching a raw wound, even now, and I flinch.'

'Does it still hurt your heart, or your dignity?' Lady Godmanchester was perspicacious.

'Oh, my dignity now. I do not pine for what might have been with Henry Freshford.'

'But you have not met him yet?'

'No, and that will be awkward, embarrassing perhaps, but I will not weep at it. It is the fear that memories will be revived.'

'Well, Lucius Radstock knows nothing, and nor does my lord. I would vouch no gentleman will recall what happened, and it might be that the ladies have as short memories. It was the talk of but a few days.'

Elizabeth did not mention the second meeting with Lady Rendlesham.

* * *

Upon her return to Mount Street, she found her aunt laid upon her bed to rally her strength for the evening's entertainments. Meanwhile, her cousin, who felt no need to spend any part of the day in idleness, was at the pianoforte, working upon a sonatina that she hoped to have at a sufficient standard for public performance. Her fair brows were puckered, and the tip of her tongue protruded in concentration. She did not at first notice Elizabeth's arrival.

'It sounds well enough, Amelia, but if you have to pull such faces, I doubt it will stand you in good stead with your admirers.'

'Oh!' Amelia jumped. 'I am sorry, Elizabeth. I was trying so hard to get past these mordants. My fingers are tying themselves in knots, and I think the notes are starting to dance before my eyes.'

'That is clearly a sign, Cousin, that you should abandon the exercise for the day and come and tell me about the visit to Lady Ellesmere. I shall ring for tea, and then you can begin.'

Lady Ellesmere was Amelia's godmother, and a lady of whom Amelia had spent her early years in awe. She was always attired in the latest fashion, regardless of her figure, which was considerably larger than when she and Lady Chalford had been girlhood friends. Money was no object to her, since she was blessed with a wealthy and indulgent husband, who regarded her production of eight additions to the family tree, five of them sons, as a sound reason for her fuller figure, and never showed the slightest regret that the sylph-like maiden he had married had become 'voluptuous', nor queried her choice of raiment. Other than in a refusal to dress her age, Lady Ellesmere was a sensible and pragmatic lady who viewed Amelia's come-out in almost the same way as she might one of her own daughters, the eldest of whom was already settled in an establishment of her own, whilst the second would not make an appearance upon Society until the following spring.

'Godmama was in very good spirits, and also very generous. She gave me a prodigiously pretty shawl of Norwich silk, and said she herself wished to take me out on Thursday afternoon and purchase me an Angoulême bonnet, which she says will look ravishing.' Amelia giggled. 'I am not sure that Mama regards my going shopping with Godmama as a good thing, but it might be the hat we saw the other day, which was monstrously expensive, so she agreed. Do you think I should refuse any other purchases she might choose to make, or should I accept nicely, and then let Mama decide whether or not I should wear them?'

'The latter, since Lady Ellesmere might otherwise take offence. And to be fair, I do not think her taste is at fault, other than she cannot see that so many garments are designed to flatter the youthful figure, which she now lacks. She certainly did not deck Maria in unsuitable clothes when she came out, as I remember. Everything was very modest and suitable, though very expensively made. I think you will have a lovely outing, and return laden with packages. You will remember to make something very elaborate for Lady Ellesmere's birthday, won't you? You do the most delightful embroidery.'

'Mama has already said exactly that.' Amelia paused, and then changed the subject. 'Oh, and she asked me to remind you that it is the Durnfords' this evening. I am not sure why she stressed it to me, but I am assuming it has some importance to you.' She was clearly hoping that Elizabeth would reveal what that was, but her cousin merely thanked her.

When she went upstairs however, Elizabeth was looking very solemn. Lady Durnford was Syston's sister. She must meet Henry and act as if nothing had ever happened between them. She sighed. She had dreaded it, but her aunt was right to make her face it early on. It was also far better to meet him fully prepared, rather than be thrown into confusion by a chance encounter. It did not, however, make it easier to contemplate.

CHAPTER FOUR

Elizabeth had not been able to rid herself of the questions revolving in her mind, even as she made her preparations for the evening. How different would he find her after three years passing? How would she compare with the woman he had chosen in her stead? Would he pretend they had never meant anything to each other? Had he told his wife all about her? She did not even know the lady's maiden name. Perhaps she knew her. Aunt Chalford had kept all details from her when fresh, and she had never thought to find out later. She felt a little sick, and Ditcham worried at her pallor. She blamed it upon the particular shade of her gown, which brought a repetition of the complaint that it was too sombre a dress for such an occasion, and that her aunt would be displeased.

'No more, Ditcham, please. The gown is perfectly suitable.'

It was, in fact, a lilac silk with ecru lace about the neck and sleeves, and Elizabeth had worn it as she emerged from mourning. On a lady of more advanced years it would have been considered charming; on a girl of not yet twenty-one it was almost a statement that she considered herself outside of the coterie of marriageable young women, which would be regarded as extremely odd.

In an effort to placate her maid, Elizabeth selected a necklet of diamonds that had belonged to her mother, with diamond drop earrings and a diamond star that shone from among her dark locks, but it was clear that Ditcham was unhappy dressing her in such a manner.

Lady Chalford was as horrified, and more vocal. 'What can you be thinking of, Elizabeth? Were it not so late I would have you go up and change immediately.'

'If you are unhappy, Aunt, I can tender my apologies and remain here.'

'Oh no. I see what you are about, trying to make me leave you behind so that you might avoid meeting Syston. Well, you shall not do so, even if you are dressed like some timid widow, creeping out into Society. Really, Elizabeth, I had expected better of you. People will say you have given up on catching a husband.'

'Given up? No, ma'am. Rather I have no interest in "catching" a husband as if he were a rabbit in a snare. I deceive nobody, and no gentleman will think I am setting my cap at them.'

'I despair of you, truly I do. What your poor dear mama would say . . .'

'Is irrelevant, surely, Aunt.' Elizabeth's chin went up. 'I am convinced she would not want to see me an object of pity. Since I advertise the fact that I do not seek a husband, none can pity me when I do not find one.'

Lady Chalford shook her head and was only distracted from saying more by her daughter's appearance. Amelia looked a picture, as her mama had known she would when she selected the palest aquamarine-blue silk trimmings for the gown to show off her fair hair, with its hint of gold. There was a sparkle to her eyes that matched Elizabeth's diamonds, and Lady Chalford knew that at least her daughter would win hearts.

Lady Durnford's party was well-attended, and it was some time after eleven o'clock when Elizabeth almost literally bumped into the Viscount Syston, who was on his way to procure his wife a glass of ratafia. Despite having mentally prepared herself, Elizabeth forgot everything, and just said 'Oh', in a small voice. Henry made an indeterminate sound in his throat, bowed politely and coloured, as if the act had driven the blood into his cheeks.

'Miss Ashling, your servant. I hope I find you, er, well?'

So that was how he wanted it to be, forgotten, set aside as an aberration. He was distant, barely more than formal, this man who had professed himself charmed beyond words by her merely smiling upon him, giving him her first waltz, the man who had pressed fervent kisses upon her fingers, whispered words of love and had told her his plans for his future, their future, with shining eyes.

'I enjoy my customary good health, sir.' He would find she could be as distant.

'Yes, well, good, excellent. I regret I must not linger, for I am upon an errand of mercy.'

He made it sound as if it involved rescuing someone from

disaster, she thought, and wondered, all of sudden, why he had seemed so much her own knight in shining armour. The fair, slightly wavy, hair seemed less lustrous, the blue eyes more faded, and of dash there was no sign whatsoever. Was that the effect of marriage, or just that she was no longer a girl in her first Season?

'I will not delay you, if your task is so urgent.'

'Urgent? Ah, not exactly that. My wife, I do not think you have met my wife,' and he said it ponderously as if she might not otherwise understand, 'is in need of refreshment. Such a hot evening.'

'Then you must complete your errand without delay. Good evening to you, my lord.' Elizabeth inclined her head, and turned away, her thoughts jumbled.

She was filled with anger that he should think it necessary to hold her at a distance, as if she might throw herself upon his chest and make a scene after all this time, and disappointment that he showed no emotion other than embarrassment. He might have been friendly, as an old acquaintance not met for some time, but no, he preferred to treat her as merely someone who would receive a nod or bow in passing.

She was also confused by the fact that seeing him cost her not one pang. She had thought that it would, for the sake of the girl she had been. He was the love of her innocence, of her hope that a husband's love would be stronger than her father's, before she found out what the real world meant. Yet there was nothing but negative emotions in her heart. She was curious, however, to see Henry's wife, and manoeuvred herself so that she could see him leave the room with refreshments, and thereafter follow at a discreet distance. She watched him weave his way to an embrasure, where a middle-aged lady with a steely expression and a young woman with a long face at variance with her *retroussé* nose and reddish-brown hair were sat. The latter looked up at his approach and spoke briefly, extending her hand to receive the glass, but she did not smile at him. As evidence it was circumstantial, but Elizabeth did not think the Systons enjoyed the relationship that her friends the Godmanchesters enjoyed.

Still in contemplation, she turned, heading to where Amelia was in conversation with Lord Nuneaton, a gentleman with many years' experience upon the Town. Her colour was a trifle heightened, and Elizabeth thought perhaps he was being a little extravagant in his compliments. She did not notice Mr Escott approach from her right until he was before her and bowing.

'Miss Ashling, I am transported.'

Elizabeth bit back the response that she wished he might be transported to the Antipodes.

'You are, sir?' Her voice was not encouraging. 'I can conceive of no reason why that should be so.'

'But you are here, in the Midst of the Multitude, and suddenly the mundane has become Gilded by your Brilliance.' He put a clenched hand to his mouth as if bottling up further flowery comment, but then let it fall, and continued. 'I called yesterday, but you were engaged upon Equine Exercise. The Image of you in my Mind, upon your Noble Beast, brought some Diminution to my Disappointment.'

It was odd, she thought, the way she could hear the stressed capital letters in his speech, and wondered if he thought in alliterative phrases even when ordering his dinner. The idea of the Slug being a 'noble beast' brought an unwilling smile to her lips. He saw it as encouragement.

'Ah, Her Lips convey that my humble Words please. I am in alt.'

'I would far prefer it if you refrained from talking about me in the third person, Mr Escott, as if I were not actually present.'

'You are ever present in my Thoughts.'

Try as she might, she was unable to prevent the look of disdain crossing her features. 'I do not consider that fitting, sir.'

'My Goddess!' he breathed, reverently.

'It needed only that!' She groaned, and closed her eyes. Her fists clenched in frustration, stretching the fine kid leather taut. She had agreed that she should not berate him or be cruel at their next meeting, but this was insupportable. 'Mr Escott, this must cease. You are making yourself look foolish. I beseech you . . .'

'Ah, she beseeches, but really she Commands!' Mr Escott pressed his hand over his heart. 'If I cease it is Bowing to an Injunction from the Divinity Herself, and yet I disobey, my Muse. The very fire in your eyes Inspires, the way you look down upon me from your Olympian height crushes me to dust as a Man, but remoulds me in a Poet's form.'

'It does what?' She sounded appalled.

'It remoulds me, so that the ink flows upon the Page as Bright Blood does in my Veins.'

'Sir, you place far too much importance upon a . . . a fleeting image in your head. I am no goddess, I assure you, merely a woman. You need only be firm with yourself.'

'Merely a Woman?' The idea seemed alien to him. 'How could I Dare to use such an Epithet?'

'Just repeat it to yourself,' she replied, rather caustically, 'several times a day.' She was losing all patience. 'I am sure you will realise your error very soon, Mr Escott. I am entirely, er, unworthy of the elevation that you have bestowed upon me.'

'Alas! She Frowns!'

For an awful moment Elizabeth feared he was about to lay his hand to his forehead in another theatrical gesture, but he refrained, and seemed instead to withdraw into some inner contemplation.

'Mr Escott?'

'She frowns, and from that blessèd Brow, unbid . . . Ah yes, I feel the Verse upon me.' He smiled beatifically at her, turned and was gone, no doubt in search of pen, ink and paper.

Sir Lucius Radstock was bored. This was nothing new. Every Season he wondered why he came to London at all, and then accepted that it was a very convenient way to meet up with friends for a few weeks, and to keep a finger upon the pulse of Society. To refuse the invitations that were delivered to his door would be rude in the extreme, since if he did not wish to socialise, why be in Town at all. Therefore he accepted a fair number of them, and made an effort. This effort only went so far, and though he was unfailingly courteous, he did have a reputation for a dry humour, which could be most off-putting to any damsel foolish enough to try and ensnare him with dimples and limpid looks.

He was in most things a moderate man; he wore his clothes well, but his tailor was never permitted to try anything that might be thought of as daring, or setting a fashion; his neckcloths were snowy white but not showy; he was convivial in his club but neither drank nor gambled to such a degree as might lead to notoriety. In fact, he almost risked being a dull fellow. However, he was wealthy, good-looking and single, which put him high on the list for any hostess wishful of holding a successful evening, especially since he could flirt decorously with any lady he was seated next to at dinner, be she the hostess's irascible mama-in-law or tongue-tied daughter who needed bringing out of her shell. Among the gentlemen, he was noted for his knowledge of all things equine. If you wanted advice on a riding horse, whether a well set up bit of blood and bone to hunt in the shires, or a good-looking hack for town, Lucius Radstock was the man to whom you should turn.

His only real extravagance was his horses, be they to ride or drive, and his treasured brood mares. Having had some success upon the Turf with several fillies, he now spared no expense sending them to the finest and most expensive stallions standing, and had indeed bought more, so that he was establishing a small stud of his own at his place in Berkshire. He would never rival his friend Lord Egremont, but was respected in the bloodstock circle. His closest and oldest friend, Lord Godmanchester, whom he had known since Eton, was not as besotted with all things quadrupedal, but interested enough not to be bored by the latest news of a promising colt, or a threatened laminitis, and was quite prepared to give his friend a hint if he went on too long about such things.

They were standing a little to one side of where Lady Godmanchester was in conversation with a worried-looking lady about the outbreak of measles at Harrow, and Sir Lucius was regaling Godmanchester with the latest news from his head groom, which had greeted him upon his return to his town house.

'I only wish I could have been there, having missed Debutante dropping hers. Madrigal is a lovely mare, and this is her second foal by Soothsayer. Truth Song, her first, looks to have potential. Grafton offered me a good price for her, but I fancy bringing her on myself for the Oaks, year after next.'

'And what will you call this one, Lucius, the colt?'

'What a clunch!'

'Not very flattering name, I must say.' Godmanchester grinned, and followed Radstock's gaze, as he watched Mr Escott. 'Ah, Farncombe's Folly might be better.'

'Farncombe is as sane a fellow as you or I. The poet nonsense must come from the distaff. Maria Farncombe is one of those ethereal, wan females always going on about her "poor nerves" and sighing.'

'There speaks the horse breeder, my friend, looking at bloodlines.'

Sir Lucius laughed softly. 'I almost pity Lady Chalford's niece.' He paused. 'Has there been some sudden death in the family? Miss Ashling is not in black gloves, nor are Lady Chalford or her daughter sombrely clad, but Miss Ashling seems in some distant mourning.'

'Perhaps some relative of her mother's? My wife did not mention it, though, and we saw her this very afternoon in colours.'

'And black gloves would be sufficient for some great-aunt or other. How odd.'

'You could ask her, Lucius, for she is coming this way.'

Sir Lucius watched the lilac-clad figure coming towards Lady Godmanchester, her head held high in what looked suspiciously like defiance at the world.

'Oh, by the by,' he murmured, taking in the lady's firmly closed mouth and furrowed brow, 'I rather think I am going to call the colt Premonition.'

'Good evening, Miss Ashling.' Lord Godmanchester bowed, smiling slightly. 'I see you were waylaid by Mr Escott.'

'Waylaid, my lord?' She acknowledged both gentlemen politely, as Sir Lucius, a fraction behind his friend, made his bow. 'I would as soon have been waylaid by highwaymen.'

'But then you would have lost your diamonds,' noted Sir Lucius logically.

'But retained my self-respect, sir. There ought to be a law against' – she paused, and made a frustrated noise – 'live poets.'

'An interesting idea,' murmured Sir Lucius, smiling, 'but are you suggesting all poetry should cease to be written, or that poets should have to, er, pour out their inner ramblings in secret meetings, in fear of the Law banging upon their doors and arresting them?'

Elizabeth opened her mouth to speak, and he thought she might suggest some bloodthirsty penalty, but suddenly the hard look disappeared, and she gave a twisted smile. 'You ought not to tempt me, sir. Perhaps, poetry could be kept confined in locked boxes until after the poet's demise, with an instruction to the executor to read it and destroy anything . . . gushing.'

'The practical Miss Ashling.' Lord Godmanchester smiled. 'And I thought young ladies would be flattered to be the object of a poet's golden phrases.'

'There speaks one who has not had to suffer them, my lord. Only a ninny would be flattered by the pretentious effusions such as Mr Escott brings forth, and I am not so young a lady as to be deceived by words, which mean nothing.' Her smile disappeared with the last phrase, and her look became almost challenging.

'Do you thus condemn poets for not just what they say, but for the fact that they say, rather than act, ma'am?' Sir Lucius raised a questioning eyebrow.

For a moment she frowned, considering. Sir Lucius was struck by the thought that she was indeed far from a ninny, but a woman who really did think. He wondered if she were some blue-stocking with a rabid interest in botany, or Etruscan art. It might account for her unusual manner.

'I think that might be the case. They also dwell far too much upon "love", as if it provided the only reason to exist.'

'You hold love in so lowly an estimation?' Lord Godmanchester sounded puzzled. He had thrown a swift glance at his lady, who had looked up as if aware of his gaze by some telepathy, and smiled with her heart in her eyes.

'I hold what poets term "love" so, my lord, though I will admit that in a few most happy instances, there is a real meaning to it. Genuine love is a too solid and magnificent a thing for mere metre and alliteration.' She smiled. 'There. Am I forgiven, sir?'

'Indeed, ma'am.' He laughed, and coloured slightly at having betrayed his feelings.

Lady Godmanchester had brought her conversation to an end, and rose to slip her arm through her lord's. 'Now what can you have said to put my husband to the blush, Elizabeth? You were not flirting wickedly, I hope?' Her eyes danced.

'Flirting? Me?' Elizabeth looked almost shocked.

'Do not look horrified. I meant only in the most discreet and social manner. I myself have flirted, quite wildly, this evening.' She looked up at her spouse. 'Are you not jealous, my lord?'

'Since I observed you "flirting", as you term it, with Sir Francis Sellers, who is old enough to be your grandfather, my love, no, not at all. Mind you, you made his evening. He went away with quite a spring in his step for a man who uses a stick.'

'He did, did he not?' She squeezed his arm slightly. 'You keep watch over me, sir?'

'Of course, since you are the most beautiful woman present.'

'Now who is flirting, my lord?' She laughed, and it was her turn to blush. 'And with your wife, too!' She turned to her friend. 'Elizabeth, did Mr Escott regale you with sublime couplets?'

'Do not bring up the subject of poets with Miss Ashling, Lady Godmanchester,' Sir Lucius recommended, with a wry smile. 'She has quite gruesome ideas on how they should be treated.'

'Not "gruesome". Merely severe.'

'Oh dear. If I must hear those, I had best be fortified first. Shall we go and seek out the enticing strawberry terrine I have heard is being offered?'

Sir Lucius offered Miss Ashling his arm, and noted the briefest of hesitations before she took it.

Most ladies would have taken pleasure in being seen upon Sir Lucius Radstock's arm. Elizabeth was wary rather than pleased. He was certainly not going to flirt with her, but had shown an inclination to engage in verbal fencing, and that risked probing far too deep, though there was a trace of excitement to it. Helen had described him as too percipient by half, and Elizabeth thought her friend slightly in awe of him for that reason. Elizabeth would certainly not be in awe of a man, but she thought it would be safer to remain at a distance. Her conversation with him was therefore brought into the domain of the socially mundane.

After a few minutes he did not respond to her comment, but paused and then asked, abruptly, 'Why do you choose to revert to inanities, when we had a more interesting topic of conversation before, Miss Ashling? You have genuine views upon matters, and I found your animadversions upon the poetic muse far more entertaining.'

'I had not realised, Sir Lucius, that you expected to be entertained, and the subject is one I would far rather forget, especially when I hear the word "muse".' She sounded displeased.

'My apologies, ma'am. I thought perhaps you had thought better of voicing opinions that might be considered out of the ordinary. It would be a pity if you did, since they were most refreshing.'

'Let me assure you, sir, that I have no fear of being so considered. I spoke my mind, which was intemperate, but I did not make my thoughts known in order to provide "refreshment".' There was a tartness to her tone.

'I am wondering why you seem so determined to treat everything I say as offensive, Miss Ashling?' Her attitude provoked him, and he could not quite comprehend it. It made him unusually terse, and as edgy as she was.

Before she could reply, Lady Godmanchester espied the strawberry terrine, and they were once more drawn into a four-way conversation. If Lord Godmanchester noticed a sudden frostiness between his best friend and Miss Ashling, he did not mention it later. Nor did he comment upon Sir Lucius withdrawing upon the pretext of wishing to speak urgently to a gentleman with whom Godmanchester knew he had spoken only half an hour previously, and muttering under his breath, 'Women . . . incomprehensible. Impossible!'

CHAPTER FIVE

'I thought how Lord Nuneaton singled Amelia out last night a very promising sign, did not you, Elizabeth?' Lady Chalford clearly wanted agreement.

They were seated, eating a light luncheon and contemplating a visit to Lady Chalford's preferred milliner. Her ladyship had decided that the bonnet that had seemed just right with Amelia's new pelisse made her look too old. She had noted that Lord Nuneaton was remarkably taken with Amelia's fresh youthfulness, and wished to show it to advantage, although Amelia was keen to appear older and more sophisticated than her seventeen years. Amelia said nothing, kept her gaze lowered and concentrated upon peeling an apple, though her cheeks reddened.

Elizabeth had retreated into the background once her friend had retired for the evening, and had had opportunity to watch her cousin. Amelia was inexperienced and was unprepared for certain situations. It seemed to her that she found Lord Nuneaton's manner oppressive, and had wilted under his gaze. His broad compliments had not been to her taste, but she did not know how to curtail them whilst remaining respectful of his years and position. Elizabeth had fumed on her cousin's behalf. Had he behaved so with her, she would have put him in his place, regardless of who he was, but poor Amelia had simply become flustered. She had been far more her normal self when she had been entertained by Mr Southram, and Lord Carbrooke, who had both made her laugh with their mock outrage at each other in their rivalry to bring her a glass of champagne. It was an easy bantering that remained light and innocent, and since neither young gentleman was above twenty-five, and reminded her of her brother, she did not see that beneath the badinage, both were very taken with her. Elizabeth avoided answering her aunt, and asked a question of her own.

'So, who won the right to fetch you your champagne in the end, Amelia?'

Amelia laughed and her blush was not embarrassed, but of pleasure. 'The honour went to Lord Carbrooke, though I was sure to promise that if Mr Southram is at Almack's on Tuesday, I will keep the first quadrille for him. He seemed so downcast.'

Lady Chalford did not pursue this conversation and threw her niece a look of mild reproach. Even she saw that the superior rank of Lord Nuneaton would not count for much when put against younger and more dashing gentlemen. When Amelia excused herself to go and dress for the afternoon's expedition, she frowned at Elizabeth.

'I do not think that was well done of you, Elizabeth.

Lord Nuneaton's bestowing of his interest upon Amelia does her no harm in the eyes of the world. I do not say I am convinced it is more than interest, but if he were to offer for her . . . She would lack for nothing.'

'Except a man to whom she might be deeply attached. I saw her last night, Aunt. I think he frightened her a little. He is perhaps too much a man of the world, as well as being nearly old enough to be her father. She looked acutely uncomfortable.'

'She will soon learn how to receive more fulsome compliments. I do not pretend that they are quite what I would like her to hear, but one cannot expect a gentleman who has not looked, I swear, at a young woman in a decade, to instantly remember how best to approach them. Amelia is very fortunate.'

Elizabeth held her tongue. She thought he had looked the sort of man who looked at 'young women' very frequently, but of a very different class from that contemplated by Lady Chalford.

Madame Minette abandoned several lesser customers to her minions at the entrance of Lady Chalford and her charges to her exclusive premises in Conduit Street. Lady Chalford herself was an old and regular customer, and, for a more mature lady, showed off many styles to great advantage. She was what Madame Minette thought of as a natural hat wearer. That this Season she was bringing out the delightful Miss Amelia, whose open features and golden hair could be framed well by almost anything on display, and would draw admiring glances and more custom, guaranteed personal attention. Elizabeth, content to watch and listen, watched her cousin try on a variety of chip straws and villager hats with satin bows, grosgrain ribbons or bunches of cherries. Amelia was not a decisive girl, and her mother could see her capturing the noble lord's heart if not his name, in several of them. Throughout the swapping, debating and a very little subtle haggling over the price if three hats were purchased, Elizabeth thought herself a mere bystander, until Madame whispered to an underling and sent her into the rear workroom. She returned with a low-crowned beaver in a dove grey, quite masculine in style, but with a stiff, deep red plume up the left side.

'As I recall, Mademoiselle Ashling is the equestrienne, *non*? I thought perhaps . . .'

She nodded to the underling, who presented the hat to Elizabeth and took up a mirror. Madame herself adjusted the tilt to the veriest hint of a dashing angle and stood back to admire.

'There. I knew it. Mademoiselle is *ravissante*.'

It was true, thought Elizabeth, that the hat was very becoming. But her habit was a dark blue.

'It looks very nice, but the colour, is it not a little . . . depressing?' Lady Chalford was thinking of a grey habit to match.

'Ah, but with the red as a highlight, a high collar and cuffs perhaps, milady— A little *militaire*, and with silver buttons.'

Lady Chalford's eyes narrowed as she considered this image.

'But my habit is still perfectly serviceable,' remonstrated Elizabeth, trying not to let herself be carried away with the image in her head, combined with that in the mirror.

'You look to advantage upon a horse, my dear, and the habit is three Seasons old,' Lady Chalford remarked pragmatically.

Elizabeth thought that even in the wonderful hat and a new habit she could not look to advantage upon the Slug, but could not mention this to her aunt. It was so tempting.

Madame saw the wavering and sensed the victory. 'Upon another, mademoiselle, it would be wasted. I think perhaps I imagined you when I designed it, *hein*?'

Elizabeth was not deceived, and yet . . .

'We will take it,' announced Lady Chalford, raising a gloved hand to still any comment from her niece, 'and we will see about a new habit, Elizabeth. There.'

Lady Chalford had made her decision, although technically the money would come from Elizabeth's allowance. The footman accompanying them left the shop balancing three hatboxes, and hoping the ladies would not purchase anything else.

'We will arrange for the tailor to come tomorrow. No point in waiting, since the Season is advancing.'

'Aunt, are you sure? The cost of the hat is not so substantial, but with a new habit . . .'

'My dear, it would be a foolish thing to buy a hat and have nothing to wear with it, and you do look lovely on horseback.'

'I do not ride for appearances' sake.'

'No, Elizabeth, but your appearance is important.'

'I . . .' She shook her head, giving in. 'As you wish.' It would not gain her suitors, which was her aunt's aim. At the same time the idea of a new habit, combined with that hat, was secretly rather exciting.

Once returned to Mount Street, Lady Chalford retired to restore her strength for the evening's entertainment by resting for an hour or so upon her chaise longue with a book of sermons, and her eyes shut. The young ladies were not so inclined, but fortified themselves with tea and little biscuits, and Elizabeth set about discovering her cousin's true thoughts upon the person of Lord Nuneaton. This proved more difficult than she imagined, but not for the reasons that she had expected.

Amelia had taken the easiest course and thrown all thoughts of her most illustrious admirer into a dark recess of her brain. She was therefore able to concentrate upon the far nicer prospect of the other debutantes with whom she was establishing giggling friendships, contemplating presentation at Court, and, by no means least, the rivalry of her younger potential suitors, although as yet she saw them simply as fun and friendly.

'Mr Southram is so droll. He said he would have to call Lord Carbrooke out if he persisted in coming first with me, but hoped, as a friend and a good shot, Lord Carbrooke would have the grace to choose neither swords nor pistols, but something a little less damaging, such as walking canes.' She giggled. 'He then realised that this might seem as though he were not prepared to face great peril on my behalf, and spent several minutes describing how nasty being prodded with a walking cane might be. He nearly had me in whoops.'

'And what was Lord Carbrooke's response to this?'

'Oh, he was determined not to be outdone, and looked terribly serious, and began enumerating the advantages and disadvantages of different woods. And his eyes twinkled so. I declare it was the best twenty minutes I have spent all month, and Julia Wingate said that several of the less generous young ladies present were very put out at me having two gentlemen "paying court", as she put it, all that time.'

Miss Wingate was Amelia's bosom companion among the debutantes. Having had two older sisters make their come-out before her, she was a little more confident than Amelia, and a keen watcher of all that went on about her. Since one of her married sisters, the other being near her confinement, was also enjoying the Season, she also heard rather more of the *on dits* than the sheltered Amelia. Elizabeth judged that in years to come she would become a formidable fount of gossip, but she was without malice.

'And what about Lord Nuneaton?'

'I do not for one moment imagine anyone would be jealous of me having to spend time listening to him.' Amelia sounded sulky. 'Why, he is quite old, perhaps nearly as old as Papa, and says things that put one to the blush. I am not sure Mama would have approved of half of them, and you can be sure I did not repeat any of them to her. I would think I must have been the object of pity had any of the other girls seen me.' She paused, frowning. 'I do hope Mama does not expect me to dance with him. He looked as if he would be a very clumsy dancer.' Then she brightened. 'But then Papa has not danced since the New Year's party at home, and it was unusual for him to do so. I think he had taken a little too much rum punch.' A giggle escaped her. 'But not as much as Harry Festing.'

'Mmm, that is not an episode I particularly wish to recall.' Elizabeth tried to look severe.

'He did not mean to fall asleep on your bed, I am sure.'

'No doubt. He simply wandered upstairs and opened the door that approximated to where he would find his bedchamber at home, and collapsed happily upon my bed. The fact that he had also applied far too much hair oil in achieving the look that he thought fashionable, and that it ruined my lace-edged pillow, was the final straw.'

'Even James could not shake him awake.'

'Given the chance, I would have shaken him harder, but I was banished from my own bedchamber.'

'He was very contrite next morning.' Amelia grinned.

'He was very hungover.'

'And you do not normally eat such a full breakfast, Cousin. He did look decidedly unwell at the sight of your plate.'

'He did, did he not.' Elizabeth's eyes glittered.

Both young ladies then collapsed laughing, and Elizabeth only regained her composure when Amelia returned to the subject of the previous evening.

'So, do tell me, Elizabeth, what Mr Escott said to you that put you in such a temper. I overheard Lord Templecombe say you looked so fierce that he did not dare approach you.'

'Then some good at least came of the encounter. Lord

Templecombe is such a bore, and thinks himself highly amusing.'

'But Mr Escott?'

'Oh Amelia, he really did call me "goddess", to my face.'

'He didn't!'

'He did, I promise you. And he speaks with the most weird emphases in his speech, as if trying out each phrase for use in a stanza. Fortunately, at the point where I might have had to "accidentally" throw a glass of wine over him, he suddenly had inspiration for a poem and walked away, without so much as a bow or word of valediction.'

'How rude of him.'

'I was just glad he went. He had me all on edge, and then—'

'Then what?' Amelia's curiosity made her interrupt again.

'Oh, it is nothing. I went in search of Helen Godmanchester. Lord Godmanchester spoke to me, and he had Sir Lucius Radstock by him. They had clearly seen everything, and thought it funny. Sir Lucius' – Elizabeth nearly ground her teeth – 'was particularly entertained. Perhaps I should have sold tickets.'

'He is rather intimidating.'

'No such thing, Amelia. You must not be afraid of men who simply like to act clever.'

'I am not sure that it is an act.'

'Hmm.' Whilst she would not admit such a thing, Elizabeth knew that Amelia was right. There was no danger of Sir Lucius being slow to get one's hidden meaning. If only he did not seem to mock with those grey eyes of his, and that slight smile. She felt at a disadvantage with him, and Elizabeth was most unwilling to be in that position with any gentleman.

'Elizabeth?'

'I am sorry?'

'I asked if Lady Godmanchester would be remaining in London for the whole Season, in view of her condition. Mama said she is increasing.'

'I do not know, Amelia. It is hardly my place to enquire. I suppose it will depend upon what advice she is given by her doctor, and upon Lord Godmanchester.'

'Ah yes, of course. They will know best.' Amelia nodded sagely. Elizabeth blinked at her cousin's blithe and total acceptance of male superiority, and opened her mouth to speak, but thought the better of it. It was incomprehensible to her, and yet she knew her aunt believed the same and was perfectly happy in that belief. To disabuse Amelia might be to make her life less comfortable.

'I expect Lady Godmanchester will be glad to get back to the country, and her little boy. It is so much nicer and less fraught.' Amelia sighed.

'I thought you could not wait for your come-out? Are you disillusioned already, Amelia?'

'No, not disillusioned. It is terribly good fun, but . . . I think it will be very tiring after a while, and London is getting hot and stuffy.'

'It is nice if you walk in the mornings. The afternoon promenade is far more fatiguing.'

'But getting up early is difficult. I nearly fell asleep again this morning, and last night we were not even at a ball, so I had not been dancing all evening.'

'Yet you did not seek your bed when we arrived home this afternoon.'

'Oh no. I do not feel the least tired now. It is just in the mornings that I feel the perfect sluggard.'

'You ought to meet my horse, though on second thoughts he never ceases to feel the sluggard. If it were but a morning malaise I could ride properly in the afternoons.'

'I prefer to be driven, then one may converse without worry.'

'Worry?'

'Horses are unpredictable. The coachman is far more capable of keeping them under control from his box than I am sitting upon one.' She looked at Elizabeth's incomprehension. 'I know you think me a sad, weak creature not to enjoy riding, but there you are.'

'I am sorry, Cousin. I accept it is merely a difference of opinion, but I cannot understand it. Yet you must not think that I condemn you as weak because of it. Now . . .'

At this moment the butler entered with a missive, delivered, he said, by Mr Escott.

'He did not ask to see me, did he, Ribston?' Elizabeth eyed the butler with concern.

'No, miss. He merely requested that it be brought to you. No response is, I believe, required.'

Elizabeth took the note with rising apprehension, and broke the wafer. She groaned.

'Bad news, Elizabeth?'

'In a sense, yes. Here is the result of last night's inspiration. Good grief, there are six stanzas of it.'

'Ooh, how exciting.'

'Not at all. He has added a note at the end.' She paused. 'He says that this kept him up until "Aurora's advent", but that he thinks it is one of his best and wishes me to see it before he, oh no, reads it at a "poetic gathering" tomorrow night at Lady Cowper's. We have invitations for that. I can feel my sick headache coming on already, Amelia. You are warned. He . . .' She paused, and then, to Amelia's surprise, began to read the poem aloud.

It was greeted by stunned silence. Elizabeth continued to read silently to the end of the missive, her cheeks gradually becoming suffused with colour, and she did not make any further comment. With unusual tact, Amelia did not pry, thinking the verses simply too awful. They were, but were not Elizabeth's primary concern, and she left her cousin almost immediately, her brow furrowed.

In the privacy of her room, Elizabeth unfolded the letter again. The verses were bad, and that annoyed and embarrassed her, but what was worse was Mr Escott's conclusion.

The difference that your Pulchritudinous Presence has made, even in so Swift a time, to my works, inclines me strongly to the belief that you were Sent by the Omnipotent to Inspire Me in all my Doings. You Must know already, how I revere You, most excellent Maiden. I am Convinced that You will not only be the Ideal Helpmeet, but the Lydia to my Horace, and a Fount of Felicity. Be Assured that it shall not be long before I Reveal All, Offer All, and Anticipate your Acceptance with Joy.

Elizabeth sat upon her bed heavily. It was, of course, quite ridiculous. No man could fall in love with a woman upon the basis of two public encounters, and indeed Mr Escott did not mention 'love' at all. He had simply decided she enabled him to write better poetry – though on the evidence of the stanzas before her she doubted this – and therefore assumed she would be pleased to marry him to advance his 'career'. Were it not so appalling it would be laughable. Her first thought was to cry off from any evening parties that she thought he might attend, but common sense told her that to do so would be impossible, and that it might even encourage him, thinking her overwhelmed by the honour he did her. That she despised him, and that until the next month she was underage and could only enter into an engagement with her uncle's permission, had clearly not occurred to him. His self-belief was total. Well, he was in for a shock. Elizabeth looked grim. He would find his plans overset, and that his 'goddess' was the sort who was quite capable of launching thunderbolts.

CHAPTER SIX

Lady Chalford, when told of the forthcoming outburst of poetry, and Elizabeth's consequent reluctance to be present, responded in a way that Elizabeth found most unsympathetic.

'Not attend Emily Cowper's soirée, when she has been so kind this Season? Nonsense.'

'This is a very particular thing, Aunt. I shall be a laughing-stock. I am sorry, for Lady Cowper has been kind to you, as her friend, and to Amelia, but . . .'

'You are part of this family, Elizabeth, and you will act as such.' Lady Chalford waved away Elizabeth's remonstrance. 'You may not like it, indeed I know you cannot, but I assure you that not being present when Mr Escott delivers his verses will only ensure that they are repeated to you until you are heartily sick of them.'

'I am after one perusal, Aunt.'

'You would be the more so if everyone you met for the next week quoted them at you, but if you hear them first hand, then that will not happen.' She paused. 'At least,' she amended, 'not nearly as much.'

Elizabeth groaned.

'Perhaps,' offered Amelia, 'he will have gone over his lines again and, er, improved upon them.' She did not sound hopeful of this.

'Or made them even worse.'

'It might not be clear that he means you, Elizabeth.' Lady Chalford joined her daughter.

'Oh, it will, ma'am, since he alludes to me by name.'

'Oh dear.'

'And compares me to Queen Elizabeth.'

'He does? Was not she the one who had lots of people burnt at the stake? Hardly felicitous.' Lady Chalford's history was sketchy.

'No, that was her sister. Queen Elizabeth was the one whose sailors defeated the Spanish Armada. She is also famed for not having married, so why, other than the name, he picked upon her—'

Her ladyship interrupted. She did not applaud her niece's erudition, but rather warned her against sounding too bookish. 'It is better to err on the side of ignorance, my dear, especially in something such as history, which everyone knows is about the past, which is best left to itself, being full of violence, immorality and peasants in misery.'

This comprehensive dismissal of the subject left Elizabeth so much at a loss that Lady Chalford was able to introduce an entirely new topic of conversation and refuse, steadfastly, to return to Elizabeth's forthcoming lauding in verse.

* * *

It was with a sense of impending doom that Elizabeth prepared for Lady Cowper's soirée, which she would otherwise have had a reasonable expectation of enjoying. Whilst she did not sing at such functions herself, and considered herself a mediocre pianist, she did enjoy the sound of both the piano and the human voice, excepting when that voice was Mr Escott's reading his poetry. She resolved to sit out of his line of sight, lest he address the verses directly at her, and strive to remain impassive.

Lady Godmanchester was present, but her lord was not in attendance.

'He has strong views upon "caterwauling by amateurs",' she whispered to Elizabeth, and giggled. 'He has sought refuge with Lucius Radstock for dinner and a quiet evening of piquet. Poor dear.'

'Well, at least they will not be present to hear me thoroughly embarrassed by the Awful Escott.'

'Oh, he isn't reading, is he?'

'Yes. And he sent me a copy of the verses that I might be the first to see them. I only wish I could be the last. They are truly terrible.'

'If they are then they will be shown up by others. I know Miss Campsey is singing, for her sister told me so, and she has a delightful voice, and Sir Oswald Tiverton writes the most diverting ballads, treating things like losing a button in the grand histrionic manner. Last time I heard him my eyes watered.'

'They may do so at Mr Escott's offering, but it will be from pain at hearing poetry mangled. At least he is not opening the proceedings.'

A harp was being placed in the centre of the space set aside for the performances. Elizabeth folded her hands in her lap and tried, valiantly, to concentrate merely upon the music. After a while she did relax a little, and when Mr Escott had not appeared by the time that refreshments were being served, she had even begun to hope that he might have lost his voice, or suffered an attack of nerves and bolted. This was not, however, the case, and as everyone settled for the next performances, Amelia dug her cousin in the ribs.

'He has come, Elizabeth, after all, and goodness me, what has he done with his neckcloth?'

Mr Escott was formally attired as befitted an evening party, but was advertising his bohemian credentials with an arrangement of muslin that he considered 'original'.

'It is perfectly ridiculous. It is lopsided, limp and looks likely to collapse at any moment. I would swear it is not fully starched. Well, if he looks a figure of fun, perhaps people will not actually listen to what he says.'

However, after a very melodic Italian aria, Mr Escott was ushered to the front. He had in his hand a scroll of vellum, from which, after clearing his throat three times, he began to read in his heavily accentuated manner.

'My Queen thou art, as Gloriana named,
As Faerie Queen to this poor Spenser stand.
Let my poor lips address thy soft white hand
And offer thee my poet's heart inflamed.
Elizabeth, such syllables alone . . .'

'If he has an inflammation of the heart, he ought to consult a physician,' whispered Elizabeth to Amelia from behind her fan, as that damsel fought to control a fit of the giggles.

'You should be flattered, Cousin.'

'No, he should be flattened. There are sixty lines of this pretentious drivel to sit through, and I have already seen Hyacinthe Consett smirking at me. I shall never live it down, never.'

'He looks like a town crier, holding his poem like that.'

'What a pity he is not in a town somewhere far away, like Truro.'

There was a stifled snigger, which turned into a gasp of pain as a young lady received a rap across the knuckles from her mama's fan, and then Elizabeth noticed Lady Rendlesham. She was smiling, not at Mr Escott, but at her, and it was the smile of one enjoying her acute discomfort. Elizabeth fought the rising blush, and her hands gripped each other tightly as if for mutual support. Lady Godmanchester, seeing this, placed her own hand lightly upon her friend's arm. 'It will soon be over and forgotten, you know.'

'Yes, by all except those who wish to recall it for their own ends. Oh, Helen, this is ghastly.'

It seemed interminable, but eventually he drew to a close.

'*. . . And at your feet, for nimble dancing formed*
I lay my vocal tribute thus, and part.'

There was silence, and then Lady Cowper applauded, encouraging her guests to a polite but not over-enthusiastic response. Mr Escott beamed, and bowed as if he had just performed *Hamlet*.

'I think,' muttered Elizabeth, 'I would rather have a tooth drawn than listen to him again.'

'You know, I am not at all sure he will get further invitations to perform his verse in public, Elizabeth. Lady Cowper is a connection of his mother's, and must have thought it a generous act, but . . .' Lady Godmanchester gasped. 'Oh dear, he is coming this way.'

Mr Escott was indeed threading his way towards them, and made his bow with an exaggerated flourish. 'As I said, O Muse, I lay my offering at your feet.'

'Where I may tread upon it. How convenient.' Elizabeth's lip curled.

'Fair Cruelty, you do not mean it. Your Words are Barbs, but I see your Intent, which is to spur me to better and greater things. You are right. A Poet must always be seeking Perfection and not rest upon His Laurels. I think I strained a metaphor in the fifth stanza.'

Amelia dropped her fan, and bent to pick it up, thus concealing the biting of her lip.

'Do your . . . efforts take you many hours, Mr Escott?' Lady Chalford feared that even one as confident of his self-worth as Mr Escott might realise he was being laughed at by her daughter and insulted by her niece.

'Dear ma'am, I am Inspired by the Moment, but perforce Refashion and Sculpt the lines until they sit Felicitously upon the Page. When I am Unhappy at the Result I may lose my Appetite for a Whole Day. It is most Distressing.'

'I wonder at it that you are not thinner, Mr Escott,' Elizabeth murmured, but he remained lost in his own thoughts, and only when addressed once more by Lady

Chalford did he emerge from the contemplation of his own sacrifice to Poetry, and withdrew as a mezzo-soprano began to sing.

Elizabeth did not sleep well, tossing and turning between dreams in which mocking laughter followed her through a series of wildly improbable scenes. When she did waken fully she felt jaded, and greeted her maid rather blearily. Ditcham was, however, forcefully cheery, and adjured her mistress to make the best of what was a bright morning.

'Though the breeze is easterly, and that is always a chill one, Miss Elizabeth, so do not forget your tippet. You can take Miss Amelia for a walk in the park. It will do you both the power of good.'

'You make her sound like a lapdog, Ditcham,' murmured Elizabeth, yawning. 'However, fresh air may well clear my head, and walking early may avoid encounters with persons liable to spout poetry at one.'

Ditcham found this remark somewhat cryptic, but nodded in agreement nonetheless. Elizabeth rose and dressed, and knocked upon Amelia's door to see if she was prepared to face the day. Untroubled by nightmarish dreams, Amelia was feeling quite energetic, and perfectly happy to accompany her cousin to see the spring flowers coming into their full glory. They breakfasted together, and then set forth to Hyde Park, tippet-wrapped. It was impossible for Amelia not to comment upon the previous evening, but she tried to do so in a way that might make Elizabeth feel better.

'Lady Godmanchester is, I am convinced, quite right

about Mr Escott. Nobody is going to ask him to read his verses at their evenings, and I am sure most people regard him as a silly boy.'

Elizabeth smiled at this, coming from Amelia at seventeen, when Mr Escott must be all of four and twenty. 'Are Lord Carbrooke or Mr Southram "silly boys" too?'

'Well, they are youthful,' admitted Amelia, 'but they are not silly. I mean they can say silly things to entertain one, but they are not prone to stupid fancies like Mr Escott.' A faint colour came into her cheeks. 'I spoke with Lord Carbrooke's mama last night, very briefly. She commented upon my gown, and seemed very nice.'

Which implied, thought Elizabeth, that her son had mentioned Miss Ashling several times, and his cautious mama was finding out as quickly as possible what sort of a girl she was. She said nothing. It was then that a large bay horse cantering towards them was slowed by its rider. Sir Lucius Radstock touched his hat and nodded to the ladies.

'Taking the morning air, I see. How are the Misses Ashling?'

'Quite well, I thank you, Sir Lucius.' Elizabeth was conscious that there was a smile lurking in his eyes, and was suspicious.

'And did you enjoy yesterday evening?' He spoke casually.

'Well, I most certainly did not, sir, and if you as much as mention poetry I shall most likely pull you from your horse and murder you with my hatpin,' Elizabeth snapped at him.

'Oh.' He looked quite taken aback for a moment, but

then his lips twitched reprehensibly. 'That would be a very gruesome demise and probably the first such case to come before the criminal courts. I, er, take it that young Escott was present.'

'Present and presented, Sir Lucius. Sixty lines.' She sounded exasperated.

'And all about my cousin, sir. He likened her to Gloriana,' offered Amelia.

'Good Lord, how glad I am that Godmanchester and I did not attend. I quite understand your threat of violence upon my person in that case, Miss Ashling. I can only apologise and say that I merely assumed it would be an evening of insipid music and dull conversation.'

'So you gave it the go-by, Sir Lucius.'

'I did, and without a single qualm, ma'am. I can think of few worse ways to spend an evening.'

'Worse, sir, is having execrable verse spouted while everyone in the room knows one to be its object, and being the recipient of sly smiles and silent mockery.'

'You must needs develop a thick skin, Miss Ashling, and ignore them.'

'Easy to say and hard to do, Sir Lucius. If only I were a man.'

He blinked. 'Forgive me, but I think you make a better woman than you would a man, ma'am.'

'Yes, but if I were a man I would not be a "muse" and if any fellow got my back up, as Mr Escott has done, I could' – she paused and considered the options – 'punch him on the nose.'

'You are in a most bellicose humour this morning, Miss

Ashling. I am fortunate, therefore, that I am mounted upon a decent horse and can retreat at speed.'

'Very lily-livered of you, sir.' Elizabeth could not keep the tremor of a laugh from her voice.

'Ah, but discretion is the better part of valour. I shall avoid death by hatpin, and wish you a good day. Ladies.' Sir Lucius touched his crop to his hat once more and trotted away.

'I find Sir Lucius rather disconcerting, Elizabeth. One has to concentrate so hard to keep up with him.' Amelia sighed, but then the sigh became a groan. Walking, or rather swaggering, towards them was Lord Nuneaton, his smile predatory. There was no way in which they might turn about without being extremely rude, and perforce had to accept his greeting with a good grace.

Lord Nuneaton made his bow to them both, but it was almost immediately clear that he regarded Elizabeth as of no more consequence than a dutiful abigail in attendance, and his attentions were entirely focused upon the very uncomfortable Amelia. Elizabeth listened and observed with revulsion, and could well understand why poor Amelia had stiffened at his approach. His smile was positively reptilian, and Elizabeth was conscious of feeling that his inappropriate compliments and leering expressions emanated not from a lack of experience in recent years, but rather a pleasure in discommoding a young woman set at a disadvantage by her innocence and youthful respect for her seniors. Elizabeth, by contrast, was several years older, more worldly-wise, and not at all afraid of putting their unwanted companion in his place.

'I am glad to see that you have wrapped up warmly, Miss Ashling. I would hate to think of a pernicious breeze harming your "neck".' Nuneaton's comment might have been seen as considerate, had he not invested the word with significance, his focus not been upon her bosom and his eyes twinkling wickedly as though he were imagining her disrobed entirely. He awaited Amelia's blush with relish.

'Whereas you have no such need, my lord, obviously possessing such a thick skin.' Elizabeth's riposte was swift and acerbic, and took the lascivious peer by surprise.

'I beg your pardon.' Nuneaton had forgotten Elizabeth's presence.

'Why, you must either possess very thick skin or be lacking in wits not to see that your "attentions" are not to my cousin's taste, sir. Indeed, they would not be to the taste of any elegantly brought-up young woman. One can only suppose that you have essayed them too long upon women of an entirely different calibre.'

'And what would you know of them, ma'am?'

'Thankfully very little, but pretending they do not exist does not mean being ignorant of their existence.'

'And I think' – his lordship's eyes narrowed, and his voice lost any pretence of cordiality – 'that you would be wise not to meddle where you have no right.' He looked her up and down, taking in the drab pelisse and the stern expression that made Elizabeth look older than her years. Not having taken an interest in her at parties, he assumed she was some indigent relative. 'I doubt very much that Lady Chalford would share your attitude.'

'Then you do not know my aunt, sir. There are limits,

and you overstep them. We wish you good day, my lord. Come, Cousin.' With which Elizabeth took Amelia by the elbow, and strode purposefully away, head held imperiously high. Lord Nuneaton's chagrin was thus invisible to her.

'Oh dear,' whispered Amelia. 'What if he complains to Mama? Will you not be in trouble?'

'No, Amelia.'

'But you have heard how she is pleased that he pays me attention.'

'Yes, but she has not been privy to his manner.' Elizabeth halted, and turned to her younger cousin. 'Dear Amelia, your mama would have been horrified to hear what Lord Nuneaton said to you. It is beyond all that is seemly, and you can be assured that he would not have dared speak so in her hearing. You need not be concerned about what he may say, since I have every intention of broaching the subject with my aunt as soon as we return home.'

'He is the most repellent man' – Amelia shuddered – 'and I do not know how you dared to confront him.'

'It was not daring, Amelia, for he can do me no harm.'

As soon as she had divested herself of her outside attire, Elizabeth sought out her aunt, who was making a list of those to invite to a dinner the following week.

'May I speak with you, Aunt?'

'Of course, my dear, as long as it isn't about that "you know what" last night.'

'It is not. Amelia and I encountered Lord Nuneaton in the park.'

'Oh, did you?' Lady Chalford sounded cautiously pleased.

'It was not a pleasant encounter. His behaviour, his language, his looks . . . he put Amelia to the blush intentionally, and the poor child did not know how to counter him. When he lost all sense of propriety, I myself made our disapprobation clear.'

'Oh dear. You got up in your high ropes no doubt and said something cutting.' She sighed. 'I do wish you were not so . . . belligerent, Elizabeth. You will get a reputation as sharp-tongued and waspish if you do not take care.'

'You are the second person to call me belligerent, or rather he termed me "bellicose".'

'Lord Nuneaton?'

'No, Sir Lucius Radstock.'

'Do not tell me you bit his head off too.' Lady Chalford put a hand to her cheek.

'If I did, he took it in good part, ma'am, but Sir Lucius is not the problem. Nuneaton is beyond the pale, truly.' Elizabeth, reluctantly, repeated his comments to Amelia, and her aunt frowned.

'Well, how disappointing. He is always perfectly reasonable with me. Are you sure . . .'

'You, dear Aunt, are not an innocent of seventeen. I watched him. He wanted to put her to the blush, took pleasure in her embarrassment. It was . . . disgusting.' Elizabeth shuddered.

'What a pity, and just as I was beginning to have hopes. Oh well, there are, as they say, more fish in the sea.'

'Hopefully not more sharks, ma'am.'

CHAPTER SEVEN

Elizabeth did not encounter Mr Escott for the better part of a week, although whether through good fortune or some indisposition on his part she did not know. However, she returned from an afternoon with Amelia at the Royal Academy exhibition to find Lady Farncombe paying a morning call upon her aunt. Lady Farncombe had been regaling Lady Chalford with a litany of her ills, which all fell just short of preventing her attending all the most interesting social functions. Lady Chalford greeted her daughter and niece as if they were a relief force.

'Amelia dearest, and Elizabeth too. What did you think to the exhibition? Lady Farncombe has been telling me that her son Gregory has been three times already, because there he thinks that one of the paintings will inspire him.'

'Oh, which one, ma'am?' Amelia enquired innocently.

'He has not decided that yet. He says that the arts must inspire each other. When Gregory was still in leading strings he was painted by Hoppner, who said he was a joy to paint. I like to think that it is one of the reasons my Gregory now paints such pictures with words. It is that mystical connection.' Lady Farncombe beamed at Amelia, who looked to her mama, unsure how to respond.

'Yes, well, I am sure we all appreciate the arts,' Lady Chalford declared bracingly, and cast Elizabeth a very swift but warning glance.

'Poor Gregory has put himself into solitude this week, because he said he needed to prepare himself. I am not entirely sure what he is preparing himself for, but I assume it is some great epic piece. Only this morning he emerged, and declared that he would come with me to Lady Chesham's ball, so it must be going well.' Lady Farncombe sighed with maternal relief and pride.

Elizabeth said not a word, but her heart sank. She had a horrible feeling that she knew exactly why Mr Escott was 'preparing himself'. It was not something she could reveal even to Amelia.

She dressed for the ball with a distracted air that had Ditcham accuse her of wool-gathering, being uncharacteristically indecisive over her choice of gown and jewels. Her plan was actually quite simple. She would not dance at Lady Chesham's ball, upon the pretext of a strained foot. This would enable her to keep out of the way, and if Mr Escott was determined to press his suit upon her, he might do so away from the dance floor and public gaze. She would let him say his piece, or as much as made his intentions clear, and then she would crush him, once and for all. She had no compunction about doing so, since he had not considered her or her feelings for one second, and was self-obsessed. Nor had she any fear of failure, though she admitted his carapace of self-delusion was thick. By the time she had derided his verse and his character, she thought he might be guaranteed to loathe her, and this torment would be at an end. In this determined, if not warlike, frame of mind, she prepared for the evening.

Lady Chesham's ball was clearly going to go down as a veritable squeeze, and be accounted a great success, though the evening was warm, and the ladies' fans were practical rather than merely decorative. Helen Godmanchester had qualms about attending at all, but feared that crying off entirely would have her husband determined to whisk her back to Northamptonshire immediately, when she would, at the very least, dearly like to remain in London for a few more weeks. She thought it prudent to advise him that she wished to make little more than an appearance, and perhaps speak to a few friends, and would then slip home, freeing him, she said with a smile, to go to his club without any feeling of guilt. He had to acknowledge that since she had announced her condition, he had been in close attendance, like a watchful guard dog. She found it touching rather than constricting, but regretted that he was giving up his own pleasures.

They arrived just after the Chalford party, and so she had no difficulty in finding her friend.

'You will not mind if I drag you from the dancing for just a few minutes, Elizabeth? The night is too sultry, and I have told Godmanchester that I will retire very early. This heat saps my energy.'

'Indeed it must. It is so oppressive I might hope for a thunderstorm, though it will inevitably mean a sleepless night.'

'You dislike them so much?'

'I do not enjoy them particularly, but Amelia is terrified by them, and will most certainly be in my bedchamber and seeking refuge beneath my counterpane with the first distant rumble.' She shook her head in mock sorrow. 'Amelia would make a poor gun dog. I think she would be gun-shy.'

They laughed and went to sit in an alcove where an open window gave a whisper of fresher air. Elizabeth exhibited a slight limp as she did so.

'Oh Elizabeth, what have you done?'

'Shh, Helen, nothing of import. If asked about, it is merely a slight strain. In fact, it is nothing at all, but I wish to keep out of the way this evening, and the dance floor would be dangerously public.'

She explained the situation to her friend, who entered into her sympathies far more than Elizabeth had expected.

'Foolish boy. He is living in some bubble of his own invention, and you are quite right, he would have no compunction about making a declaration somewhere totally inappropriate.'

'Any declaration would be inappropriate.'

'Yes, but you know what I mean. How vexatious! And you would, I am sure, have enjoyed dancing. Why is it that young men remain so juvenile for so long? I declare Mr Escott has no more awareness of others than my darling George, but he, sweet lamb, has the excuse of being not yet three.'

'I think,' said Elizabeth, with a look of mock seriousness, 'I would prefer an offer from George.'

Helen Godmanchester giggled, and whispered, 'Yes, but he would be offering you the chance to build him a tower of blocks.'

'Even more reason to accept, then.'

The two ladies enjoyed a very light-hearted conversation before Lady Godmanchester was discovered by a lady with whom she had been at school, and Elizabeth moved away, rather more at ease than when she had arrived. This even extended to her walking less stiffly. Sir Lucius Radstock, talking to Lady Cowper, caught sight of her, and his eyes narrowed for a second.

Mr Escott arrived quite late, having been assailed by the opening lines of a sonnet whilst engaged in tying his neckcloth, and then being rendered incapable of mere physical activity until the first iambic pentameters had evolved to his satisfaction. He was polite but vague to his hostess, but since that was his normal manner, she was in no way offended.

In seeking out Miss Ashling he was more than usually focused, though she thought she might have led him a merry dance through the salons had she so wished. Instead, she stood her ground and waited. He approached with a fervent crease to his pale brow, and one lock of sandy gold hair 'fallen', after much coaxing, in just the correct manner to look tidy yet disturbed by poetic agitation. He made her a brief bow, already speaking as he did so.

'You received my Offering, and you await me in

Anticipation. Behold your Slave, who yet demands your Attention.'

Elizabeth schooled her features into calm disdain, though she already felt the urge to slap him. 'I have never been in favour of slavery, Mr Escott, and I am not one to accede to "demands". However, if you have private matters to discuss with me, it would be preferable that we speak in less public surroundings. I believe Lady Chesham has left doors open onto the rear terrace, with it being so warm.'

'Then let me lead you, as Orpheus did Eurydice from the Depths, to the terrace forthwith.'

'That analogy, Mr Escott, is neither complimentary to Lady Chesham's ball, nor likely to inspire me with confidence, since Eurydice did not escape Hades.'

He offered her his arm, and she took it, though she tensed, seeing Lady Rendlesham gazing at them with a far from pleasant smile upon her lips. As they passed her she nodded, graciously, and murmured, 'Mr Escott, Miss Ashling. What a delightful couple you make, a contrast of light and dark. I do declare even I might be tempted to write lines upon such a vision.' She gave a tittering laugh and turned away. Elizabeth had no doubt that anything that occurred to Aurelia Rendlesham would be waspish.

The terrace was cooler, and the lanterns hung about it did not bathe it in so much light that a couple might not find somewhere in at least slight shadow. Elizabeth hoped most sincerely that none had seen her departure and assumed it a tryst of her choosing. Thankfully, it was also not so late as to have attracted any other couples. She steered her escort to the alcove to the right of the doorway, thinking most would look to the terrace end for an assignation.

'Mr Escott, your letter, and the information contained—'

'You understand. It is Pointless for me to repress my Feelings. A Poet *is* Feelings, and above All things I am a Poet. You must See how much I need your Inspiring Presence at my Side to fuel my Verses. I Need you as a Fish needs water.'

Elizabeth had a mental image of him flapping about like a landed fish. 'Sir, your interest in me is, I assure you, transitory, and nothing could be less likely to bring either of us happiness than . . . Mr Escott, get up, sir!'

He had gone down on one knee, and was looking up at her in a manner reminiscent of the Honourable James Ashling's favourite spaniel. 'My Muse, my Goddess, you will not fail me.'

'You are living in a bubble of your own devising.' Elizabeth unconsciously echoed her friend's words. 'There is absolutely no reason why I should be even tempted to accept an offer from you, assuming that is what you are about to waste your breath upon, and . . .'

He looked, for a moment, stunned, then confused, and then simply disbelieving. She could not be trying to refuse him. That was an impossibility. He grabbed her hand.

'Miss Ashling . . . Elizabeth . . . You cannot mean . . .' He attempted to press kisses upon her wrist as she drew her hand back, sharply.

'I made you free of neither my name nor my hand, sir, and—'

'The lady would be mightily relieved if you stopped behaving with as little decorum as a village swain at a revel-rout.' Neither Elizabeth nor the lovelorn youth had noticed Sir Lucius Radstock leaning nonchalantly against the doorframe. 'However, that would seem to be too much to be hoped for, so I take leave to tell you that I shall remove you forcibly into the rose bed below, if you do not instantly take yourself off. I will also have no compunction in informing your father that you need taking in hand.' The voice was bored, and not a little supercilious.

Mr Escott, very red in the face, and suddenly feeling far less the man of the town and more green stripling, stammered something incoherent, and scrambled to his feet. He cast Sir Lucius a look of loathing, and one of despair at Elizabeth, indicative of his belief that, had he not been interrupted, she would have been won over by his protestations of undying devotion. With a hasty bow, he withdrew, scowling. Elizabeth pursed her lips, an action that Sir Lucius interpreted as natural irritation.

'He was becoming a nuisance, ma'am?'

'Yes, but I was quite capable of dealing with him. If you think you have in some way rescued me, sir, then you labour under a singular misapprehension.' Her tone was civil, but only just.

'Forgive me. You did not seem to be encouraging him. Indeed, I was under the impression that you did not appear to be enjoying the young man's attentions one jot. I think you were perhaps unwise to have permitted him to bring you somewhere private, however damping your intentions.' He raised an eyebrow.

'No, of course I was not "enjoying" his attentions, but I was quite capable of sending him to the right about when he became too tedious. As well put up with him as any other . . .' She halted, aware that she was about to sound churlish and unforgivably rude.

'. . . Pretentious young cub?' He smiled, seemingly unabashed, but the eyes looked very hard at her. She nodded. No, he thought, that was not what she was going to say, though she chose to accept his offer of escape.

'Young men can be very irksome, sir.'

'How fortunate, then, that I am no longer a "young man", and thus am able to solicit your hand for the next dance without fearing that I might irk you. And please do not tell me that you are unable to dance through sustaining an injury, for I have watched you hobble on one side and then the other, Miss Ashling, and feel obliged to tell you that that hare will not run.'

She had had no intention of accepting any offer from him, whether of refreshment or to dance, but this disarmed her. She coloured slightly, conscious that to decline in the face of his seeing through her ruse would appear petulant. Then she laid her hand upon his arm, not daring to glance into his face as he led her back into the ballroom, and into the set that was forming.

Elizabeth had almost forgotten how much she enjoyed dancing with a gentleman who was adept at the exercise. What a pity it was that one had to be engaged to dance by the man, selected by him, picked as carelessly as a buttonhole flower, regardless of his own abilities. Had she not been intensely annoyed with Sir Lucius she would have exulted in the fact that, for the first time this Season, she had a partner who made it all seem natural. The momentary distaste had crossed her features so fleetingly that only Sir Lucius noticed, and she otherwise played the part of delighted and delightful partner perfectly well, making such small talk as the movements of the dance made convenient.

At the conclusion, Sir Lucius led her from the floor, aware that several jealous matrons eyed her 'success' with disfavour, and wondered why, instead of enjoying her triumph, Miss Ashling seemed put out by it. She certainly stiffened, and her thanks were patently insincere, her look a dismissal as obvious as the one he had given her unwanted poet. He bowed, as coolly civil, and withdrew in good order. He was confused, and more than a little piqued, since he had ended what he saw as an embarrassing interlude for her. With his thoughts thus still upon her, he went to join his friend Collingbourne, who was trying to catch his eye.

'Stealing a march, are you? For shame, Lucius. What need you of a wife with a neat little fortune? I have been fobbed off with the excuse that the lady's shoes were most unfortunately pinching, and that she had resolved not to dance this evening. Yet there she was, and with you, sly dog.'

'Perhaps she has seen you dance, my dear Collingbourne.' Sir Lucius grinned at his friend, and then looked to where Miss Ashling was in comfortable conversation with the Dowager Lady Keynsham.

'I'll admit I'm no caper merchant, but dash it, Lucius, I am not likely to tread on the delightful Miss Ashling's toes.'

'Ah, are you one of those who would pay her court?' Sir Lucius concealed his chagrin well, and, to all intents and purposes, was smiling in a benign and almost avuncular fashion on his erstwhile partner.

'Dashed good-looking girl in a sort of reserved way, and worth a good few thousand, so they say.'

'They?' He cast a sidelong glance at the Viscount.

'Foxton, for one, and Bensthorpe's aunt heard it from Lady Chalford herself, and I ask you, would she be wrong?'

'Not wrong, but perhaps keen to have her niece established and out of the way while she launches that fair chit of hers onto the Marriage Mart.' The cynicism in the voice was marked.

'You think it is a hum, then?' Lord Collingbourne looked disappointed.

'Not necessarily. Do not let me put you off, my dear fellow.' Sir Lucius wondered what made him encourage his friend in what would almost certainly be a fruitless effort, and decided that the thought of Miss Ashling beset by unwanted suitors had a certain uncharitable appeal to it. The London Season was an endless round of young women doing all in their power to attract a suitable *parti*, and one who showed every sign of wanting to keep the whole crowd of them at arm's length had novelty value. He had spoken out of chagrin, to be sure, but her cavalier treatment of him when he had come to her aid was the outside of enough. Had she been some wide-eyed girl in her first Season, he would not have let his irritation show, but she was not some schoolroom miss in the whirl of her first visit to London. He wondered, suddenly, how it was he had not seen her before, and frowned. He judged that she must have come out at the time he had been dealing with the demise of his father, but that would not account for his not noticing her in the subsequent years. It would serve her right if . . .

'Do not blame me if you are chasing after the unassai—' He gave himself a mental shake. Would he really stoop so low just because a young woman, probably still seething over the ridiculous suitor, was less than gushing in her thanks? The image had been tempting but no, he would not.

'Unassailable? You think so?'

'Unassuming, Collingbourne, unassuming,' lied Sir Lucius smoothly. 'You must have misheard me. The lady does not hold herself up as an object to be admired, I think.' He was still wondering why that was so.

'Yet she is not the coy type. Odd sort of female in some ways, but dash it, very fine-looking filly.'

'Talking of fillies,' Sir Lucius steered the conversation cleverly away from Miss Ashling, 'are you coming along to Tattersall's tomorrow? They are selling Coningsby's breakdowns, and I rather fancy that bay he had off Carnforth last year.'

The conversation turned to horseflesh, and his rash comments upon Miss Ashling were, Sir Lucius hoped, forgotten. He did not see Lord Nuneaton, a few feet to his rear, smiling to himself.

Sir Lucius did not remain late at the ball, and although he stood up with several ladies of long acquaintanceship with every sign of pleasure, and three young ladies whom Lady Chesham feared had numerous vacancies in their dance cards with cool politeness, his mind was elsewhere. Whilst he was perplexed by Miss Ashling, he was more concerned at his own behaviour. Almost unconsciously, he had looked for her in the crowded rooms, and watched her as she feigned her lameness, made conversation with various ladies, and then, rather inexplicably, permitted young Escott to lead her away. No, that was not quite true, for he would swear she was the one leading. Perhaps she was avoiding the fool delivering verse to her in front of too many onlookers. He had followed, he told himself, out of curiosity, but that was not the half of it. He had no faith in Escott behaving with any sense, and thought he might be of use to the lady. He had intervened for that reason, although Miss Ashling had been far from grateful. Why, he asked himself, was he putting himself out for her? She was not so breathtakingly beautiful, she seemed possessed of an uncertain temper and might even be bookish. The truth was that there was some magnetic attraction that drew him to her. He disliked the feeling that it was something outside of his own control, but it was there. He tried to see the positive things in her. She was pretty, if not a diamond of the first water, and he preferred dark-haired women to fair. She had a quick understanding that enabled a joke to be comprehended without laborious explanation, and sometimes without any words at all. She was not dithery, or timid, but assertive. Thus he had been left in no doubt as to her lack of enthusiasm at being 'rescued'. He knew Escott for a fool, but surely he was being as great a fool. It was with that thought uppermost that he finally fell asleep.

* * *

Elizabeth drew off her long gloves, and sighed as she let Ditcham unfasten her gown. She had the headache, and she was also prey to guilt. She had told herself she was immune to the inconsequential frivolities of the Season, that all she wanted was to retire to Dowlands and concern herself with the price of fleeces each summer, and the wheat yield of the home farm, but tonight . . . tonight there had been brief moments as she danced when she had forgotten herself, and revelled in it all. Why had it to have been whilst dancing with the infuriating Sir Lucius Radstock? Why had she had to be observed in that embarrassing situation by him, of all men? If only he had arrived five minutes later, that foolish young man would have been dismissed upon her own terms, and would never have desired to repeat as much as a line of poetry to her again. As it was, and her brows drew together in a frown, he no doubt felt 'oppressed' and filled with some Quixotic gallantry, reserving his loathing for Sir Lucius. Well, he need not bother, for she would do the loathing for him. How dare the man interfere, act as if she were some helpless female incapable of ridding herself of a feckless boy. Did he think so little of her? Or had he followed them, been watching the whole sorry episode, taking pleasure at her discomfiture? Either way, it was insufferable. She told herself this three times, in an effort to believe it. Then she made an exasperated noise, which Ditcham ascribed to the slowness of her fingers.

'There now, Miss Elizabeth, I am going as fast as I can.'

'Oh, I am sorry, Ditcham, that was not directed at you.' She paused. 'Men are horrible.'

'Yes, miss, of course they are,' agreed her maid, shaking her head. 'Clumsy, thoughtless, cruel . . .'

Elizabeth laughed, and groaned.

'You let me finish brushing your hair, and tuck you up nice and comfy in your bed, and then you can forget the lot of 'em. Never was one worth a decent woman losing tears or sleep over, yet we do, drat them.'

Elizabeth wondered at the 'we'. Had Ditcham some distant reason of her own for her condemnation of the male sex? She was too worn to think deeply of it, but it distracted her mind for a few minutes until she did indeed lie in the comfort of her bed. Although she fell asleep quickly enough, her dreams were jumbled, and at one point Mr Escott, his arms full of lurid red roses, turned to look at her and she was falling into a blackness, but was caught in strong arms, and the firm voice behind her said, 'I will not let you fall again.'

CHAPTER EIGHT

Sir Lucius soon became aware that his injudicious and hastily withdrawn epithet concerning Miss Ashling had, most unfortunately, become known. It was one of those things that spread without anyone wondering whence it had originated. It certainly provided a degree of entertainment and interest within the clubs of St James's, and he remained a largely silent observer, although he did manage to quash one gentleman's idea of opening a book on who might be 'first past the post'. It was at this point that he was conscious of a pang of guilt, but tried to assuage it by recalling Miss Ashling's behaviour, even as he sought out Lord Collingbourne, who was the obvious source of its wider promulgation, being a gentleman to whom the term 'discreet' was rarely applied. His lordship was, however, vociferous in denying having breathed a word, and said he would swear an affidavit if his friend so wished. He looked most put out, and Sir Lucius, frowning, begged his forgiveness. Someone, and he knew not whom, must have caught his ill-considered outburst and thought to make it a joke. Sir Lucius could only salve his conscience with the thought that Miss Ashling, a competent and self-possessed sort of woman, ought to be quite capable of fending off her new admirers. What he did not know, other than whose was the loose tongue, was that Mr Escott, convinced that only some devious plot would keep him from winning his Muse, was already convinced that Sir Lucius Radstock was the Hand of Fate. Sir Lucius was thus spoken of as the instigator of the rumour in order that he might keep rivals from the Fair Elizabeth, and then swoop to claim her for himself. How this might be achieved, and indeed why such a complicated plot need have been devised, did not concern Mr Escott. Suffice that Sir Lucius assumed the properties of a dragon, which he, the noble knight, must slay to win his damsel. As a prelude to this, Mr Escott kept to his rooms as much as possible, and devoted himself to writing a poem of epic scope, bloodthirsty imagery and heroic conclusion. The end proved problematic, since the hero dying in the heroine's arms after having saved her appealed to his poetic soul, but made him feel distinctly blue-devilled.

It did not take long to become apparent to Elizabeth herself that she was becoming unnaturally popular, and that popularity could not be put down to her new riding habit, which arrived early the following week. Several gentlemen who were not noted for being of matutinal habits were suddenly seen riding in Hyde Park of a morning, eager to 'accidentally' come across her. Lady Chalford regarded this with some surprise but vague pleasure, and entreated Elizabeth not to be dismissive. She was, in part, obedient to this. What the gentlemen did not realise was that Elizabeth, despite being condemned to ride the Slug, assessed them as much by their own mount and horsemanship as by their address. To those who showed some discernment in the matter of horseflesh she was prepared, to appease her aunt, to be non-committal rather than crushing. Thus Sir Augustus Lasham, indigent by virtue of inheriting from a spendthrift cousin, and hoping to find a wife of sufficient means to restore order to his finances, was accorded a friendly smile and easy conversation, for he rode a cherished, if rather elderly, chestnut by the name of Hotspur. By contrast, Lord Mathon, who had clearly as little interest in matters equine as Lord Chalford, had hired a wall-eyed roan that was also a wind-sucker. Despite his good looks and eligibility, he was treated to imperious aloofness to such a degree that he retired early from the lists, assuring any who would listen that he would be dashed if he would rise from his bed at an unwholesome hour of the morning to trot around the park in company with a woman who treated him with less courtesy than she did her groom.

Elizabeth tried to think of anything she might have done to attract attention, and drew a blank. Her next thought was that her aunt had quietly encouraged a rumour that had inflated the state of her finances, in an effort to provide her with suitors. This Lady Chalford vehemently denied, aggrieved that her niece could have thought, even for a moment, that she would have stooped to such a deceitful course.

'I declare it is most hurtful, Elizabeth. When have I ever tried to push you forward like that? I do not deny that I would be delighted to see you comfortably established with a man of character, but as for this . . . No, do not set this at my door.'

Though Elizabeth apologised most profusely, Lady Chalford was left feeling both hurt at the false accusation, and also as perplexed as her niece. In desperation, she applied to her lord for advice.

'It is most peculiar. Elizabeth is a pretty girl still, but not . . . forthcoming. I never expected more than a handful of gentlemen of taste to show an interest in her, but the last ten days or so she has been courted as if one of the hits of the Season. She is pestered, and I mean the word, by gentlemen, not all blatant fortune hunters, though most interested in a wife with money. This morning she has given in and let Lord Collingbourne drive her out in his phaeton, and she is engaged to ride out with the Misses Overton, whom she scarcely knows, and at the pressing of their brother. What on earth is going on?'

Lord Chalford could give no satisfactory answer, but promised to see what he could find out.

Meanwhile, Elizabeth, in a cream gown and with a very fetching parasol of Brussels lace, was sitting beside Lord Collingbourne, and bitterly regretting her submission to his entreaties. On horseback, he had seemed competent enough, but it did not require Elizabeth to be knowledgeable about driving to tell that as a whip he bordered on the downright dangerous. On several occasions she actually shut her eyes and awaited the splintering sound of wheel against wheel as they passed another vehicle at a reckless pace for the width of the carriageway, and since he had daringly decided to drive in tandem she was given full opportunity to observe just how not to point one's leader.

It was just after the latest close encounter, whilst she was still quite pale, that Sir Lucius Radstock drew alongside them on his big bay. He raised his hat and bowed to Miss Ashling, with a look in his eye that showed remarkable understanding of the situation.

'Good morning, Miss Ashling, Collingbourne. I see, Miss Ashling, that you have taken your life in your hands, and let Collingbourne drive you. Have you offered up prayers in advance?'

There was no possible polite response that Elizabeth could make, but Lord Collingbourne rendered reply unnecessary.

'And you call yourself my friend, Lucius. Miss Ashling is perfectly safe with me, perfectly. I would not risk so fair a passenger.'

'Not intentionally, no,' Sir Lucius replied with a slow smile, and a laugh.

'There, Miss Ashling. You see how he laughs. He is totally heartless. It is all a ploy to destroy my good name with you.'

Elizabeth had indeed seen how he laughed. The mockery in the eyes was still there, but there was also a very genuine twinkle of amusement that was hard to resist. Her animosity towards him was briefly forgotten.

'Sir Lucius,' she said carefully, but with an answering gleam, 'you may be sure that my affairs are all in order. However, Lord Collingbourne has not yet given me reason to think I may not return to Mount Street in good health.'

'Then you do not drive, Miss Ashling.'

'No. I regret that I do not.' She preserved her countenance with difficulty as Lord Collingbourne spluttered. 'However, Lord Easby has offered to teach me, and I believe he is something of a whip.'

'He certainly dresses like one,' responded Sir Lucius, the laugh replaced by a frosty, clipped tone, 'but I have yet to hear his abilities vaunted by any but himself.'

'Oh.' Elizabeth could not prevent herself sounding disappointed. 'How vexatious. I had so hoped to learn from someone who could teach me good habits.' She frowned at Sir Lucius. 'You are not roasting me, are you, sir?'

'Sir Lucius would never roast you on anything to do with horses, ma'am, I promise you,' declared Lord Collingbourne, with conviction.

'Are you a notable whip, Sir Lucius?' Elizabeth ignored the interjection, and gazed at Sir Lucius challengingly, as her disappointment turned to resentment against the bringer of bad news. She hoped she would put him out of countenance. She failed.

'I am not a member of the Four Horse Club, for I find it pretentious,' he answered calmly, 'and I do not claim to be the best whip, but I can feather a corner easily enough, and, unlike Collingbourne, will not threaten to spill you into a ditch.' Sir Lucius paused for a moment. Easby had an unpleasant reputation with women, and it was just possible that Miss Ashling was in ignorance if it. 'Lord Easby can be very . . . persuasive, but I would not trust any sister of mine in his company.'

Elizabeth's eyes narrowed. In fact, she had already had to listen to an agitated warning about the Earl of Easby from her aunt, whom, she admitted, had the right to do so, even if she thought in this case it was unnecessary. Lord Easby showed a refreshing degree of disinterest, even sympathised at her being hounded. Sir Lucius Radstock had no such right, yet she thought he was trying to warn her off.

'Are we still just talking about driving, Sir Lucius?' she enquired.

'No, Miss Ashling.' If she wanted the word with no bark on it, he would give it to her.

'Then I thank you for your advice, sir, but would recommend that you keep it for your sisters.' There was an edge to her voice.

'I have no sisters, ma'am.' He frowned. He had meant well, and had not expected such a rebuff. Yet again, her swift comprehension had brought them to friendly understanding and easy interchange, and then, suddenly, she had become edgy and antagonistic. 'But I shall, of course, refrain in the future from giving you "advice" upon any topic. Your servant, Miss Ashling.' The tone was curt, but he managed a wry smile at his friend. 'No doubt I shall see you at the club, Collingbourne, if you make it back to the stables in one piece.'

Lord Collingbourne, an embarrassed and not entirely comprehending spectator to this exchange, merely nodded and mumbled, and Sir Lucius cantered away. For several minutes Elizabeth fumed silently. Then Lord Collingbourne cleared his throat.

'Good friend, Lucius. Can be a bit forthright. You should

have heard what he had to say about a hunter I had off . . . Actually, not the sort of thing for a young lady's ears . . . I will drive you back very carefully, ma'am.' He sounded contrite, as if a schoolboy caught daring something foolish.

'He is insufferable. And, Lord Collingbourne, I have complete trust in your driving capability.' Until he set his horses in motion once more, this was perfectly true.

Frederick Pullinger, Earl of Easby, was not a man who wasted time in bemoaning his fate, at the gaming table, on the Turf or with women. If his pockets were sometimes to let after deep play at the tables, he worked on the, thus far, accurate assumption that his luck would turn; if a woman tired him earlier than he had anticipated, he cut his losses, shrugged and took up another. After all, blessed with impeccable lineage, ready wit, burnished wavy locks and a charming smile, conquests came easily to him. In fact, the truth was that sometimes he wished there was just a bit more risk of failure, a little more excitement to the chase. That the mamas warned their vulnerable daughters that he was 'dangerous' worried him not at all, since he rarely dallied with *ingénues*, but preferred more experienced game. Widows, and bored ladies with idle or blinkered husbands, were more to his taste. His current flirt, to put it no higher, was in the last category, and it had all been very entertaining, but he was starting to find that her imperious demands were excessive, and the pleasure was beginning to pall. In normal circumstances it would have run its course a little longer, but the elevation of Miss Ashling to the position of unconquerable gave him a new target, and the prospect of all the excitement for which he could possibly wish. He had taken no interest in her at the commencement of the Season, for, after all, she was but an unsuccessful debutante of several Seasons back, and chasing other men's rejects, as opposed to wives, was not his idea of sport. However, once transformed into 'the Unassailable', and with favourable reports of a tidy little fortune, he took in every detail of her. Having had experience of Society, she was not a shrinking violet with whom he would have to tread as if upon eggshells; she had enough money to make it worth his while considering her as a wife; and had expressed a preference for the country, which would enable him to establish her there, should he wed her, and then conveniently forget her as soon as he decided to carry on in his usual vein. Success with the Unassailable would also make him the toast of the Season in the clubs, where those who had failed would admire his skill and envy his success. All in all, it was a prospect that put a spring in his step and set his mind racing to devise the best means of trapping his prize.

He was not going to rush in, for that way lay disaster, and he had little expectation of being beaten to the finishing line by the hasty. Rather, he watched his prey, assessed her weaknesses, formed a plan of campaign that would have won him plaudits in Horse Guards, and then set about putting it into action without making it look as if he had done anything at all.

Miss Ashling would not be won with honeyed words, and so Easby refrained from uttering any. When they were introduced, and he engineered it cleverly, he seemed disinterested, and waited to see if this alone would spark the lady's curiosity. Women were, in general, a curious species, he had found, and few could resist a man who feigned no interest in their pretty frames. Miss Ashling turned out to be of their select number, which only fuelled Easby's own determination. This might, he thought, be a worthwhile chase.

He had observed her in the park, and had made a swift and accurate assessment of her abilities as a horsewoman, whatever her mount. He ensured his exchanges with her, when he encountered her out riding, were short, and his commiserations upon the Slug were understanding but witty. He engineered that they met going in opposite directions, and that after a brief exchange, he would ride on. That this began to be a regular occurrence was not meant to be obvious, either to Miss Ashling or her other admirers. By dint of being merely friendly, and yet increasingly present, Lord Easby thought that he might be more successful than those attempting to win the Unassailable by direct assault.

He certainly lulled her into a feeling of ease and security. She would greet his arrival with a smile, as often as not of relief, and confided some of her displeasure at the attentions she was receiving from other gentlemen. He listened, and laughed inwardly, whilst giving her anecdotes that were both mildly amusing and showed his rivals, ever so slightly, in an even less complimentary light. Unused to such Machiavellian tactics, Elizabeth accepted him at face value, simply pleased to have someone with whom she need not be on her guard all the time. She innocently admitted that she regretted not being able to drive even a pair of horses, and accepted his offer to teach her with genuine pleasure.

'However, you must know, ma'am, that in some circles eyebrows will be raised. I am accounted dangerous.'

The admission was made in a conspiratorial tone, and its very frankness disarmed her.

'Dangerous, my lord?'

'Oh yes, very. Matchmaking mamas lie awake at night worrying that I might show interest in their daughters.' He smiled.

'I do not possess a mama.'

'No. My commiserations, Miss Ashling, but of course it does mean that your acceptance of my offer will not result in anyone suffering insomnia.'

She laughed.

Lady Chalford might not lose slumber over the matter, but she felt it incumbent upon her to draw her niece's attention to the light in which being taught to drive by the Earl of Easby might be seen.

'He is not a gentleman with a good reputation. He . . . philanders.'

'I hardly think he is going to "philander" with me, dear Aunt. He has shown no interest in me at all, for which I am truly grateful.'

'Elizabeth, I know you are not a girl in her first Season, and not as green as dear Amelia, but we are talking about a man of the world. I beg you to consider very carefully.'

'Are you going to forbid me, Aunt?'

'No, my dear, for that would be to throw you into his arms.'

'Into his arms? No fear of that, I assure you. I am not going to be any man's amusement.'

Lady Chalford was only marginally relieved. That Elizabeth was not inclined to regard Lord Easby with particular favour eased her mind, for assuredly he would hurt her, but she would still have to fend off comments from 'wiser' mamas, who would not cease to shake their heads if Elizabeth chose to be seen in his company, and there was also that final statement. Lady Chalford did not want her niece to be upset again, but was equally unhappy to think that she had so set her mind against men that no gentleman might find favour with her, and make her happy.

Elizabeth herself had been left both annoyed and vaguely uncomfortable. She disliked being under such scrutiny, and also disliked upsetting her aunt, though she felt she was being too swayed by the views of others. At the same time, she felt a small knot of concern deep within. Perhaps she ought to give more credence to Lord Easby's reputation than she had previously, for she had ignored it. That it should then be brought up by Sir Lucius Radstock made things all the worse. He either thought her ignorant or foolish, and the small voice in her head that enquired why that should matter was resolutely pushed away. He had yet again made her irritable, and she blamed him for her loss of temper.

CHAPTER NINE

Her first driving lesson allayed her qualms. Nothing could have been less dangerously romantic or more down to earth, and the groom looked the epitome of stolid respectability. Lord Easby made no attempt to sit unnaturally close, or 'guide' her left hand, but rather explained how the reins were held, and then let her tool the pair at the walk along the track. He then had her bring them to a halt, start, halt again, until she felt in control of the vehicle. He exuded calm confidence, and she pushed Sir Lucius's adverse comments to the back of her mind. There was no sign of her teacher trying to take liberties, and what could she learn incorrectly at this stage? There were few to see her feat of skill, since Lord Easby had recommended that they commence before there were too many vehicles upon the circuit. He praised her efforts, and her reading of the horses' temperaments. All in all, she returned to Mount Street in a delighted frame of mind.

Had she seen the smile on Lord Easby's handsome face as he drove the pair home, she might have been less pleased.

Inexplicably, Sir Lucius did not see Miss Ashling out riding until several days after the meeting with Lord Collingbourne. She was trying, without success, not to be jealous of those who could enjoy a decent canter without expending more effort than the beast beneath them, and it was with acute embarrassment that she saw Lord Godmanchester and Sir Lucius Radstock coming towards her. She could do nothing more than acknowledge their greetings, and try to ignore the pained look upon Sir Lucius's face. The sight of Miss Ashling's mount was almost too much for him to bear. Lord Godmanchester had to bite his lip at his friend's mutterings as they drew up. The fact that Miss Ashling was clearly not a timid horsewoman for whom such a beast might just have been appropriate made it all the worse.

'Good morning, Miss Ashling. Enjoying the fresh air, I see.'

'Good morning, my lord, Sir Lucius. The fresh air is enjoyable but that is as far as my pleasure extends.'

'Ah. Your mount does not seem . . .'

'Equine? Quite probably.' She made no attempt to excuse the animal, and sounded thoroughly fed up. 'I am the only female in the family who enjoys riding, and alas, my uncle believes a ladies' hack must be sound in all paces, assuming only that it has but two.'

'My dear Miss Ashling, you have our sympathies, doesn't she, Lucius?'

Sir Lucius nodded.

'You must know, Miss Ashling, that my friend here is just the man you should consult if you want a good bit of horseflesh.'

'Indeed. Sir Lucius appears to be "just the man" one should consult upon so many things.' She flashed him a brittle smile.

Lord Godmanchester threw his friend a swift glance, but Sir Lucius seemed impervious to the barb. He still seemed overwhelmed by the hack's bad points, which were too numerous to list.

'Lord Chalford actually selected this beast? Did you not have any influence upon his choice?' Sir Lucius sounded genuinely bemused.

'I fear that my own preferences count for little.' Miss Ashling coloured. 'He did not consider it reasonable to bring my own hack up from Sussex. Were I to use my allowance to purchase or hire another animal I would risk insulting my uncle.'

Sir Lucius frowned, and glanced at his friend. 'Would Lady Godmanchester not be grateful if Miss Ashling would exercise her hack whilst she is unable to do so?'

There was a pause for a fraction of a second. 'Now that is a splendid idea. Would you permit me to ask Lord Chalford if you might do that? It would be doing us a service.'

'I . . .' Elizabeth hesitated. 'It is very generous of you. I did not know Lady Godmanchester was a keen horsewoman.'

'She has taken up riding more in the country, admittedly.' The Earl smiled a little self-consciously.

'Then, thank you. I would be very pleased if you

broached this with my uncle. But, of course, I will ask Lady Godmanchester this afternoon, myself, if she is happy for me to ride her own horse.' Her smile was very genuine.

Bowing politely, the two gentlemen went on their way.

'And what exactly prompted that, my friend?' Lord Godmanchester looked sidelong at his companion.

'You saw the beast. Good God, Giles, you wouldn't permit your wife to be seen abroad on a screw like that.'

The Earl laughed. 'No, though I am not sure Helen would describe herself as so bold a rider as Miss Ashling. And what hack is this?'

'I shall provide one by tomorrow, never fear.'

'I am more concerned as to what you expect Helen to say this afternoon.'

'Nothing more than she cannot ride, obviously, and would be glad to have the horse exercised by her friend.'

'And if she asks, perchance, details of the animal?'

'It being a Monday, I suggest we take a look in at Tattersall's sale. It should provide a morning's entertainment, and Lady Godmanchester will be able to describe "her" horse with only a very little coaching.'

'And who is purchasing this horse, Lucius?' The Earl raised an enquiring eyebrow.

'I am, but it will be eating your fodder. When Miss Ashling leaves London, well, either you can purchase it if you think your wife might care for it in the future, or I sell it.'

'Your motivation verges on the altruistic.'

'Verges, Giles? It is entirely altruistic.'

'So you harbour no further thoughts than it would be

a crime to force Miss Ashling to sit upon that revolting animal again?'

'Exactly, my friend. The lady is obviously a fine horsewoman. Did you not see her hands? Such a pity she does not drive.'

'She does not? Would you be the man to teach her?'

'Alas, I think that were I to offer, Miss Ashling would, er, jib, and besides, Easby has already offered his services.'

'Easby? But . . .'

'I know. I think if he has aspirations in that quarter, however, he is heading for disappointment. Not easily won over is Miss Ashling. I seem to set up her bristles at every encounter without even trying.'

'She is not the most approachable of ladies, I admit, although I have not found her anything but charming, and she has been a good friend to Helen. I suppose it is natural in the circumstances.'

'The circumstances? You make that sound ominous.' Sir Lucius grinned, but his eyes were watchful.

'But surely . . . Ah, no, of course, you were not in London most of that Season. I am sorry.'

'Since there was nothing that you could have done, being sorry is singularly pointless. But you could usefully tell me what did occur.'

'It was quite simple really. Miss Ashling's father died.'

'As I am well able to vouch, that should not make a difference in the long term.'

'It does if he drinks himself to death and leaves nothing but debt from some incautious scheme or other. Miss Ashling was threatened with the loss of everything, even her home.'

'Unfortunate, certainly, but she is not impoverished now, unless her relatives are all lying.'

'No, but that came later. The thing is that Miss Ashling was on the point of contracting an alliance with Syston, well, Henry Freshford as he was then. According to Helen, she was very taken with the youth, and he with her, though personally I cannot conceive what she found to admire in him. I always thought him a trifle . . .'

'Weak and watery?' Sir Lucius sneered.

'Indeed. Well, you can imagine how little Syston liked the idea of his heir being betrothed to a girl who was the centre of gossip, and dowerless.'

'Syston was ever a warm one when it came to money, and cold when it came to humanity.'

'He certainly had no interest in his son's feelings for Miss Ashling. He forbad him having anything more to do with her, once the circumstances of the death were known.'

'And Freshford would, of course, obey, the spineless puppy.'

'Of course. Miss Ashling left Town with a bruised heart and no future. I'll say this for Chalford, he might not be able to pick a horse, but he worked hard on her behalf with the lawyers for the best part of a year. Then Chalford's brother – do you remember Gerald Chalford? Poor chap died of wounds after Waterloo – left all his money to Miss Ashling.'

'I never realised the army paid that well. What an opportunity you and I must have missed.'

'Hardly. But he had savings, and he got his man of business to buy into Funds when everyone else was selling before the battle. Good move. Pity he never lived to enjoy the fruits of his acuity.'

'But it means Miss Ashling is restored to "marriageable" status in the eyes of society.' Sir Lucius frowned. 'Indeed she might have returned last Season, had she so wished.' His voice dropped almost to a whisper. 'And yet she did not do so. I think, Giles, I have done the unfortunate young lady a great disservice.'

'You, Lucius? But . . .'

Sir Lucius looked grim, and shook his head.

'But you are purchasing her a horse.'

'Indeed I am. How inadequate.'

Lord Godmanchester frowned, but said nothing more and wondered.

Tattersall's was, of course, busy, being both auction and settling day. They took a brief look into the subscription room, and Sir Lucius collected his winnings from a bet he had laid upon one of his fillies, racing at Newmarket. He appeared to be one of the more fortunate, since many more were paying rather than receiving.

'Don't tell me, this is what you are going to use to purchase the hack for Miss Ashling. You are the luckiest of fellows.'

'It wasn't so much luck. I had every hope for Damselfly, and the opposition was not likely to trouble her. The odds were quite short, though, so do not see this all as profit. Oh, and keep your voice down, there's a good fellow.'

Having exchanged greetings, congratulations and commiserations with a number of gentlemen, they made their way outside to the auction. Sir Lucius was in his element, and at his most relaxed, laughing and joking with his fellow horse lovers. He also kept his eyes on the horses being paraded around the outside, and soon had his eye on a promising grey mare. He spoke to one of the auctioneers, took a close look at her as she was trotted up and down, and had a whispered conversation with one of the stable staff.

'She's the one,' he said, quietly, to Lord Godmanchester. 'Good quarters on her, intelligent head. The lad says she has no vices in her but can be a bit lively, and I think our Miss Ashling will enjoy a bit of a challenge after her current mount.'

Lord Godmanchester noted the possessive 'our', but kept his own counsel.

'Right, she's coming up next. Let us see what the opposition will offer.'

The bidding started in a desultory way, but then picked up. Sir Lucius prompted his friend to up each bid, since ostensibly it was Godmanchester's purchase. As the figure rose, Lord Godmanchester gave a muttered 'Are you sure, Lucius?' but obeyed the pressure at his elbow.

Only one other bidder remained, and Sir Lucius detected a falter. 'Keep going; he'll fold.'

He was proved correct, but the hammer price was rather in excess of what Lord Godmanchester had expected, and certainly exceeded Sir Lucius's winnings.

'Are you mad, Lucius?' he whispered, as Mr Ecclesfield patted him on the back and commended his choice.

'No,' Sir Lucius murmured, 'not quite. If you want to

pay straight away, I have enough, I think, above the roll of soft I collected from Damselfly's win.' He took the notes and slid them surreptitiously to his friend. 'You have bought a nice mare.' He grinned.

Lord Godmanchester arranged for the mare to be collected by one of his grooms. She was certainly a pretty ladies' mount, with heavily dappled, steel-grey forequarters, and an intelligent eye. He thought that Helen would love her looks, but, even in normal circumstances, be very nervous about riding her.

'Are you very persuasive, Lucius, or am I easily gulled?'

'Ah. If I said yes to the first I would be insufferably conceited, and if to the second, intolerably rude.' He laughed, taking his friend's arm. 'Let me buy you luncheon at the club to console you.'

'Console me? That means you do think I am easily gulled!' Lord Godmanchester grinned. 'I think I would do better to return to Brook Street and warn my lady wife about her horse, lest Miss Ashling call and we find ourselves in the basket. Join us, then if the questions become too difficult, I can let you answer them.'

'Not so much a kind invitation then as wanting support?'

'You might say that.'

'What are friends for? Thank you, I accept.'

If Lady Godmanchester was astounded to be told that her husband had just 'bought' a horse for her, so that she could let Miss Ashling ride it, she contained it well. The explanation intrigued her even more. Sir Lucius Radstock was a man whom she found slightly difficult to interpret.

He was not openly judgemental, and yet she always felt under scrutiny when he spoke to her. His collaboration in, indeed instigation of, this subterfuge, made her think. She had never heard her husband remark upon his friend being enamoured of any lady, nor even taking a particular interest in one. This determination to provide Miss Ashling with a horse at his own expense was so strange a thing as made her wonder if he was actually attempting to fix his interest with her, yet if the horse remained 'hers' she failed to see how it would advance his suit.

The mare was duly described to her, so that she need not be in ignorance of its qualities if questioned.

'Does she have a name, Sir Lucius?'

'Ever the female mind' – he smiled – 'picking up the "vital" details. No, ma'am, naming her can be your task in this scheme.'

'Well, if she is grey, would "Mist" work?'

'She is rather dark and stormy for "Mist", but it might be short for "Mistral".'

'Oh yes, that sounds as though it has been well thought through. I shall tell her that.' She giggled. 'One should not be deceitful, and yet this sounds rather fun. I do hope I can be suitably casual about it. Now remind me, my lord, you have purchased her for me recently, knowing I will adore her looks, but of course I may not currently ride her, and was about to have her sent to Thornby?'

'Yes, my dear. That fits the bill exactly.'

After luncheon, the gentlemen departed and Lady Godmanchester changed her gown and prepared for callers.

She had hoped that Elizabeth would be the first, but had instead to endure one from Lady Cumnor, whom she found irritating, since she recycled gossip with sufficient inaccuracy to make one wonder what the original story had been but not trust what had been repeated. It was most frustrating.

'And Lady Rendlesham saw them both "disappear", alone, onto the terrace.' Lady Cumnor sounded suitably shocked.

'Oh yes,' lied Lady Godmanchester blithely. 'Miss Ashling told me all about it. Mr Escott had written one of his poems, and she really did not want him spouting truly embarrassing verse in front of everyone. Poor girl, she was faced with the awful choice of public humiliation or having to act in a clandestine manner. When the verse is upon them, you know, poets have so little understanding of the proprieties.'

With this, Lady Cumnor had to be content, though she clearly found the answer disappointing. She then regurgitated several crim. cons. that Helen Godmanchester had known about for weeks. It was as much as she could do not to stare hopefully at the ormolu clock on the mantelshelf. She was, however, glad that Elizabeth did not arrive before Lady Cumnor excused herself.

It was just gone half past the hour when Elizabeth was announced. The look upon Helen Godmanchester's face was one of joy mixed with relief.

'Thank goodness it is you, my dearest Elizabeth. I need cheering. I have just endured half an hour with Lady Cumnor, and schooling my features into polite interest has worn me out.'

'Oh dear. Do you need a cordial?'

'No, just good company. She was so keen that I should tell her that I am definitely breeding, just to confirm the tittle-tattle, but I was not going to give her that pleasure. Oh, do tell Lady Chalford that she can do so, privately of course. That will ruin the gossips' race to get there first.' She giggled. 'Now tell me your news.'

Elizabeth took a sudden decision not to tell Lady Godmanchester about her driving lesson from Lord Easby, though later denied to herself it was because it did not sit easily with her conscience. She was, however, keen to reveal the conversation that she had had with Lord Godmanchester in the park that morning.

'It would be just the thing, Helen, if you are sure you do not mind?'

'My dear, how could I do so. I am prevented from riding, as you understand, and poor Mist was going to be sent back to Thornby to eat her head off for the rest of the year. You would indeed be doing me a favour.'

'Mist? Oh, what a nice name.'

'Well, she is really Mistral, but I call her Mist. She is such a beautiful creature, but' – she dropped her voice conspiratorially – 'I fear my darling husband rather overestimated my abilities. I do find her rather mettlesome, and get nervous when she is on her toes.'

Lady Godmanchester did not think her friend would believe that the horse, as described by Sir Lucius and her husband, would tally with her friend's memory of her riding skills. In truth, whilst the Slug's conformation would not have pleased her, its lack of pace would not have concerned her.

'Lord Godmanchester did say you had become more adventurous,' commented Elizabeth.

'Yes,' admitted her friend, 'but I think he is just a bit disappointed, and tries to imagine me braver than I am, poor dear. You were always the bold rider, and I am sure she will suit you perfectly.' She paused. 'He said Sir Lucius was with him when he saw you.'

'Oh yes,' Elizabeth sighed, and not, thought Lady Godmanchester, in a lovelorn way. 'I think the Slug offended his sensibilities, or perhaps it was just me. He is the most infuriatingly . . . infuriating . . . man.'

'Why?'

'He sees too much. I always get the feeling he is watching me and either laughing at me or condemning me and . . .'

'And . . . ?'

'Oh, I do not know, Helen, but he gets everywhere.'

'He is universally invited, of course.' Lady Godmanchester frowned. 'Why should he not be. He is terribly good ton.'

'No,' Elizabeth whispered, brows knit. 'I did not mean socially. He gets into my thoughts.'

'Oh.' There was no other reply that Helen Godmanchester felt able to make to this admission. It might mean several things, and jumping to conclusions, however pleasant, might mar all.

CHAPTER TEN

Lord Easby took things slowly. Rushing one's fences never led to anything but a sore head, as he had found from bitter experience, and besides, this was a chase worth savouring. Those of a suspicious mind, and Sir Lucius Radstock was of their number, thought he 'prowled', but Elizabeth saw only the hand of disinterested and amusing friendship. For all her suspicion of men, she had very little experience of them, and certainly none of experienced rakes. She did not encourage him, as she thought, but her refusal to send him to the right about fuelled comment, and those with unofficial wagers on his success took heart.

He took her driving, not every day, but twice a week or so, always with a groom, but as she improved, more in public. Tongues wagged, quietly, though impropriety was not mentioned, except by one gentleman, who averred afterwards that he had been more than slightly foxed at the time, and who had been grabbed by the throat so tightly that he thought his windpipe would snap, shaken until his eyes boggled, and informed in no uncertain terms that to make such comments about a lady was not the mark of a gentleman.

Those who pulled Sir Lucius away from the unfortunate fellow thought this might be considered a challenge, but the shaken gentleman was in his cups enough to make forcing the point excessive.

'No, no, Lucius, can't you see the fellow's top-heavy? Let it go. Far more embarrassing to the lady to make it something that is bound to get out.' Lord Bensthorpe gripped his arm.

Sir Lucius's eyes were very hard, and he whispered between lips drawn thin with anger, 'Then get him out of my sight, before I succumb to the urge to break his neck.'

Lord Bensthorpe spoke soothingly, and jerked his head to speed others in leading away the now garrulously apologetic offender.

The incident was witnessed by only a few, but enough of what took place spread about among the gentlemen to give some food for thought. Sir Lucius was not numbered among the 'Forlorn Hope', as Miss Ashling's admirers were becoming known, but he did seem to possess a very guard-dog-like attitude to her wellbeing. A couple of gentlemen decided to become less attentive, and Mr Escott, emerging from his poetic seclusion, was heard murmuring about Nemesis. Lord Easby, when it reached his ears, merely raised an eyebrow and smiled. Lucius Radstock might have a way with horses, but he had never tried to keep a filly in skirts up to the bit. As a rival, he could be discounted.

It was in this mood of superiority that he attended Lady

Manningham's ball. He danced with Elizabeth, just once, though it was a waltz, and was as amusing as always, animadverting upon several nearly innocuous subjects, and leaving her looking almost relaxed.

Sir Lucius, watching, wondered if she would appear so pleased when she danced with him. He had secured the waltz before supper, and had the distinct impression that she would have made some excuse and refused him, had she not been with the Godmanchesters.

Lord Easby, having made his bow to his dancing partner and returned her to Lady Chalford, did not make the mistake of watching her overtly thereafter, but did so covertly, and with a glitter in his eyes. She did not know it but she was weakening. This thought so pleased him that he smiled to himself, and did not notice Lady Rendlesham at his shoulder.

'I had not thought you would be one to join the throng, my lord.' Her voice had a bite to it, and her eyes glittered. 'After all, she is but the failure of Seasons past, wearing the fresh garb of disdain and flaunting her spinsterhood. What could Elizabeth Ashling possibly have to attract you?'

'You mean, my dear, what could she have to draw my attention from you? What a beautifully vain and selfish creature you are, Aurelia. As one myself, I cannot but admire your self-worth. However, you forget two things. The first is purely practical: you are already married.'

'You do not intend, I hope, to spout morality at me. It would seem rather too late.' She looked at him, her eyes half veiled by the heavy lids, her smile very knowing.

'Not in the least. What we had, and I use the past

tense intentionally, was entrancing, entertaining, infinitely amusing. But if you think I would remain single out of devotion, you are deluding yourself, and if you believe I am seeking to play the cuckoo, and see my brats in other men's nurseries, you are sadly mistaken. Miss Ashling is beautiful,' he raised a hand as she opened her mouth to comment, 'and I know how little you like that epithet applied to others, my sweet. She is deliciously dark, not unlike you of course, but she is also wealthy enough to restore my dwindling assets, at least for a time, and single. What more could a man wish for in a mate?'

'If it is money you are after, why content yourself with her, when Lady Maria Gillingham is worth twice as much?'

'That is unfair, to suggest I would pursue such an unappealing prize. She has money, but that is all. A man would have to be drowning in debt to court so plain a face and discordant voice, and I am not that far gone, I assure you.'

'Then why not me, three years ago?'

'Ah' – he smiled – 'but then neither debts nor the march of time seemed so pressing that I should contemplate having to become leg-shackled, a state to which I admit I am temperamentally unsuited. Also, married women are so much more interesting, unencumbered by the veil of maidenly modesty, no longer having to pretend they do not understand one's intentions. You knew mine from the first.'

She coloured.

'Besides, what hope would I have had, a mere earl, against the advantages of Rendlesham, excepting, of course, wit, charm, figure and age. You chose the bed with the best coronet above it, my love, and if lying in it is unexciting, well, you have proved you are not averse to . . .'

'Stop it.' She averted her face.

'Oh no, you are the one who said it was too late for morality, my dear.' He paused. 'And there is the second reason why the Unassailable attracts my attentions: pure masculine pride. The thought of succeeding where so many others fail, of my conquest being applauded by the disinterested and resented by the defeated, is a prospect that fires my ambition.'

'And if she does not crumble before your assault, what then, my lord?'

He shrugged. 'There will be others. I shall forget it and pass on. As you will, my lady. We are remarkably alike.' He paused. 'But you would be wise to provide Rendlesham with an heir, before lying elsewhere. We have sailed close to the wind, you and I, far too close. Husbands can overlook "mistakes", but not if they are like to step into their shoes. I speak from observation, merely. Of course, if he is not capa—'

'I have no intention of discussing my marriage with you,' Lady Rendlesham declared, in a heated whisper.

'My apologies. You are quite right, of course. A woman should never discuss her husband with her lover, or even her former lover. Now there is Marcus Chivers. I particularly wanted to speak to him about something.' He sounded insultingly vague. 'If you will excuse me, my dear?'

He made her a polite bow and turned away, and she was conscious of it being a dismissal. She did not let her eyes follow him, though she knew the urge to do so. She was not crushed, or broken-hearted, for, as he had said, she was very like him. What had been between them was not love, or even affection, but had been 'amusing', and the edge of risk and subterfuge exciting. It had kept her from being bored. What rankled was that he should break with her, rather than she giving him his *congé*. She was not a woman used to disaffection. She understood his cool reasoning, but resented beyond measure that he should be turning from her to Elizabeth Ashling. It was a very thoughtful Lady Rendlesham who let a gentleman so uninteresting as to normally be treated with contempt procure her refreshment.

'My dear Lady Rendleham, has Easby put you out of countenance?' Lord Nuneaton proffered the glass. 'He is not worth a puckering of those divinely arched brows, I assure you.'

'Nothing of the sort, my lord. I am merely perplexed as to why he is chasing after Miss Ashling, who has been given the title "the Unassailable" when she ought to be termed "the Unappealing".'

'Ah, then I must indeed have misheard, ma'am.' Nuneaton gave a sly smile, and she looked at him rather closely.

'Are you telling me it was you who coined the phrase, my lord?'

'Almost. I did, shall we say, ensure it was not lost to Society.'

'Why?' Her question was frank.

'Because I . . . have my reasons.'

'You are very provoking, sir.'

'Yes, she thinks that too, but for different reasons, ma'am.' Nuneaton's smile lengthened the more.

* * *

Elizabeth, despite herself, was happy this evening. Perhaps it was the dancing. Her partners had not proved to have two left feet, and if some were a trifle dull, it meant that she could respond without having to think, and concentrate upon the music. Lord Easby was a competent dancer, and a better companion. He had complimented her upon her gown, but without flowery exaggeration, and sounded, as always, merely a polite man of sense. Lord Foxton was nimble of toe, but not of brain, and Lord Collingbourne had, wisely, been offered only a cotillion. Sir Lucius Radstock, well, she wondered why he had asked her to dance at all, for he had done so with such a serious expression. Part of her wanted to refuse him, and yet she had not done so. He confused her. She wanted to avoid him, but knew that she felt something akin to a ripple of pleasure when they met, even though they usually ended at odds with each other. She did not trust him, and yet felt peculiarly safe in his company.

When he approached to claim his dance, she smiled, but it was a smile with caution in her eyes. A slight frown appeared between his dark brows.

'Miss Ashling, if you wish to cry off . . .'

'No, indeed, Sir Lucius, no such thing.'

'I will not tread upon your toes, if that is what you fear, you know.'

'No, oh no. You dance very well, as I have discovered, sir.' She put out her hand to lay upon his arm, and looked up at the still frowning countenance. 'If you wear that expression, Sir Lucius, it will be said it is you who are unwilling to dance.' She tried to make the comment light, but even as she said it the grey eyes seemed to draw her in, and as he took her in hold they made a peculiarly sombre couple. It was only upon later reflection that she realised how conscious she had been of his guiding hand in the small of her back, of the light grasp of his long fingers. She could not drop her gaze.

'Why do I get the feeling that I disappoint you, Sir Lucius?'

'Disappoint me?' He sounded taken aback.

'Yes, sir. When you look at me it is as if you find fault.'

The frown deepened, and for a moment of silence Elizabeth thought it anger. When he answered, it was in a dazed whisper. 'I can find no fault, no fault whatsoever.'

It was not flattery, not flowery compliment. She felt slightly dizzy, and if she told herself that it was the twirl of the dance, it was a falsehood. She blinked at him. 'I . . . You found fault with me when you saw me riding, and when I was with Lord Collingbourne.'

'No, in either case. I found fault in the beast upon which you were mounted, as you did yourself, and with Lord Collingbourne . . . No fault lay with you.'

She processed this information as they swirled, so effortlessly that she almost forgot they were moving at all. 'You object to my acquaintanceship with Lord Easby.'

'I have no right to "object", ma'am.'

'No, you do not, Sir Lucius,' she retorted swiftly, and then sighed. Why did it always end with them at daggers drawn? There was silence for several revolutions.

'Miss Ashling, my "objection", if you wish to term it thus, was to you being taught to drive by a man whose skills are inadequate to the task.' He paused. 'And, I admit, because Lord Easby is not a man whom ladies have ever had cause to trust. Forgive me speaking so boldly, but I have been upon the Town a good many years, and you . . . are far less experienced.' He sounded sincere.

Her anger dissipated, and she felt her cheeks flush.

'You think me censorious, ma'am, but be assured I only wish . . .' He stopped. How could he tell her he wished for her happiness when it had been he who, however much he had retracted the term on an instant, had set her up to be beset by unwanted suitors? How could he tell her that he wished for something else that, at this moment, he did not comprehend within himself?

'Wish what, Sir Lucius?' It was barely a whisper, scarcely audible over the scrape of the violins, more lip-read than heard.

He swallowed. 'I only wish to be of service.'

It was so much more than he had intended to say, and so much less than he felt.

'I see.' She did not. There were undercurrents, and such things dragged one down into the depths of Charybdis, so she tried to ignore them. 'Then you might serve me by telling me what you think of Lady Godmanchester's grey mare. I will be in the park early tomorrow. You are, as I hear from all sides, the connoisseur of horseflesh, and I would hate to find myself as poor a judge of a horse as I am, apparently, of men.'

She had said it light-heartedly, but her last words brought a stiffness to her that he felt within his grasp. The music had reached the concluding phrases, they were finishing the formalities of the dance, walking from the floor, and without thinking, he was guiding her to the supper room. She made no demur, and Mr Escott, who had watched their dancing in growing indignation, entertained positively murderous thoughts in his head.

Not normally of a bellicose disposition, Mr Escott was being assailed by strong emotions, the mildest of which was a burgeoning desire to plant Sir Lucius a facer. The fact that he had proved a dismal pugilist at school was temporarily forgotten in this desire, which might have overpowered him had he not retained just enough sense of his surroundings to recognise that to brawl in Lady Manningham's drawing rooms would be a solecism so great that people would assume he was wildly inebriated, or mad as Bedlam. Either was social suicide. The trouble was that Miss Ashling, his Muse, without whom he just knew his inspiration would wither, was being kept from him by the wicked Sir Lucius, a man with no poetry in his soul, a man who saw beauty only in terms of four legs and good conformation. This Philistine was out to destroy him, and indeed his anger over the sight of Miss Ashling whirling round the room with him had already wiped away some very promising couplets about Miss Ashling dancing, 'Terpsichore in Mayfair', from his head. Had it not taken him a considerable time to create the careful disorder of his gleaming locks, he would have run his hands through his hair in distraction. He did, however, manage to make himself hyperventilate to the point where the room began to spin, and he felt a little faint. He groped his way to a chair and sat down heavily upon it.

* * *

He was not the only interested observer. Lady Godmanchester, in whose bosom the horse purchase had raised hopes for her friend, had watched the couple closely. Her feminine intuition told her that matters stood as yet in flux, but that neither was impervious to the other. She certainly did not detect any animosity in their body language, nor sign of quarrel. Her husband understood Sir Lucius as she could not, but discussing such things would, at this stage, bring down a charge of being fancifully romantic. Men were such doubting Thomases, demanding physical proof where a woman trusted instinct.

She thought Elizabeth's resolve to keep gentlemen at a distance was crumbling, which would alarm her and make her withdraw as much as possible. She hoped Sir Lucius had the intelligence to make allowances for this, and help her dismantle her defences. Aware of the gossip, but unwilling to broach her concerns with her friend, she also hoped that the Earl of Easby was not using the breach for his own less honourable ends. Three years' experience of London society had given Lady Godmanchester knowledge that Miss Ashling, with not even one full Season behind her, could not hope to possess, for all her natural intelligence and good sense. The Earl of Easby was, in her ladyship's opinion, both dangerous and unpleasant. She could not see how Elizabeth could be blind to his faults, but, from all that Elizabeth said, knew that any remonstration on her part would be regarded as paying too much attention to the old tabbies. He was, Elizabeth had assured her several times, not interested in her and was simply a friend. It was Helen Godmanchester's firm belief that there was nothing at all simple about Lord Easby, and that the concept of 'friendship' with a woman was alien to him.

The object of her disapprobation had also taken note of the last waltz. Lord Easby had been dancing with another young woman, a chattering blonde with the faintest hint of a lisp. The lady found him a little distant, since he was focusing upon what he could detect as he manoeuvred his partner closer to Sir Lucius and Elizabeth. What he saw gave him pause for thought. Whilst he still refused to see Radstock as a serious rival, if the man's word grew to have weight with the chit, he might yet ruin at the least a promising seduction. He himself would have to make some slight alterations to his plans in order to negate this threat, but he was confident that it was quite within his powers. After all, the dismally reputable Sir Lucius would only use fair means to achieve his aim, and he was not similarly constrained. In fact, it might even add a little extra spice to the whole thing.

CHAPTER ELEVEN

Sir Lucius returned home prey to unsettling thoughts. He had not formed any intention of revealing anything of his feelings to Miss Ashling, largely because they were not clear in his own mind, but he now believed that she could not be in total ignorance that he felt some ill-defined inclination towards her. She had not ripped up at him at this meeting, which was an advance, and had made what was effectively an assignation with him in the park for the morrow. This was, on the one hand, a pleasure to be anticipated, but at the same time it presented further risk of him saying too much, far too soon. Perturbed, and trying to unravel complicated knots of thought and emotion, he did not sleep well, but awoke to find that the Heavens had been kind to him, and opened. A summer storm of torrential proportions meant that there would be nobody out riding this morning. He lay back against his pillows as his valet announced this news and declared it a 'poor sort of day', and contradicted him.

'No, Jutton, it is an excellent morning. I shall deal with my correspondence without fear of interruption from callers, and when the rain passes, the London dust will be laid, so you will have less work brushing my coats.'

'Indeed, sir. I had not perceived it in such a positive light, but I see now that you have the right of it. Er, you said last night, sir, that I should remind you of your intention to visit Messrs Rundell, Bridge and Rundell today, though if the weather remains inclement . . .'

'Thank you. I will probably take the carriage anyway.'

His mother had sent the steward with a hamper containing some choice early fruits brought on in the succession house at Paley, as if such things were not purchasable in the metropolis, and a ruby necklace, part of what were termed 'the family jewels' – though they were only purchased by Sir Lucius's grandfather as a wedding gift to his bride – which she said needed cleaning and two loose stones securing. She would be sure to write and ask if he had attended to this, so he had decided to do so before other events might lead him to forget. He was not, he knew from experience, too old to avoid being rung a peal over by his mama.

The morning passed as he had hoped, and he ate his luncheon secure in the knowledge that he had dealt with several important matters and cast his eye over the domestic accounts that had been brought up for his approval. The rain was considerably lessened, but he did take his carriage to Ludgate Hill, not wishing to bear such a valuable burden in the public thoroughfare.

Whilst far from the most illustrious of the clients of

Messrs Rundell, Bridge and Rundell, Sir Lucius's family were always treated with the greatest courtesy. Lady Radstock was known to smile and say it was because the senior Mr Rundell had had a secret *tendre* for her when she was newly married, and it was true that if ever she did visit the premises, he made every effort to attend to her ladyship himself. On this occasion, Mr Rundell had to content himself with asking after her ladyship's health and promising that the 'Radstock Rubies', which grandiose title nearly made Sir Lucius laugh out loud, would receive their prompt attention. With his errand completed, Sir Lucius then gave in to a spontaneous urge, being surrounded by jewels, and undertook a more modest purchase. He selected a small pearl brooch in the form of a ring, which might be thought suitable to nestle in the folds of the stock with a lady's riding habit. It was whilst this item was being wrapped that Lady Rendlesham entered, head held high and as imperious as royalty. She paused for effect and awaited someone to come forward and be suitably obsequious. Sir Lucius gave her the briefest of nodded acknowledgements, and then shook hands with Mr Rundell.

'We will, of course, send to you as soon as the necklace is ready, Sir Lucius. I never like to keep a lady waiting, after all. I am sure it will look as good as when the first bride received it.'

With which he nodded to an underling to open the door and bow Sir Lucius out. Lady Rendlesham raised an eyebrow and smiled to herself. Perhaps Lord Easby was not taking the opposition seriously enough. What was potentially more useful was the opportunity to start a little rumour that might give Elizabeth Ashling palpitations, if it was true that she wanted nothing to do with men.

The rain had ceased by the time that Sir Lucius's carriage reached Piccadilly, and so he directed the coachman to set him down at Hatchards. His mother's letter had made mention of a new novel over which one of her friends was waxing lyrical, and he thought that enclosing her a copy with the letter confirming that he had discharged his errand would please her. Since his father's death, Lady Radstock rarely came to Town, and certainly not for the Season. She contented herself for the most part with good, if dictatorial, works in the neighbourhood, writing to a wide network of friends and reading eclectically, from *Improvements in Horticulture* to far-fetched romances. When he was at home she would be as likely to read him a snippet from the former as the latter when they were alone after dinner, and he never knew whether he was going to hear advice on growing cucumbers or the most lurid details of a Gothic romance. On balance, he preferred the former.

Hatchards was busy, those who had been put off by the morning's rain having now emerged to make their purchases. He recalled the name of the novel but not that of the author and so made his way to the desk to ask for assistance. The young man offered to direct him or to fetch a copy for him, but he chose to find it himself, since browsing the shelves, redolent of the leather-bound volumes, was a pleasant way to spend twenty minutes before heading to St James's to look in at his club. He had not expected, however, to bump into Mr Disley, a gentleman who shared his interest in thoroughbreds. Disley was in a similar position to himself, with a modest little stud in Cambridgeshire. They greeted each other warmly, and for a while the purchase and wrapping of *The Rescue of Lucrezia*, clutched in his hand, was forgotten.

The Misses Ashling, having spent a frustrating, and far less productive, morning, had been keen to get out shopping in the afternoon, so whilst Lady Chalford enjoyed a welcome visit from an old friend, they headed for Grafton House. Their object was to purchase some figured muslin that Amelia had seen a few days previously and had persuaded her mama to let her buy to make a morning gown when the Season was over and she was back at Marden Hall. That Lady Chalford secretly hoped that she would be too busy with wedding preparations to worry about making a gown was something that lady kept to herself.

They made their way down to Piccadilly, the footman carrying the parcel of muslin and some lengths of ribbon that Miss Amelia Ashling could not resist, and they crossed the busy thoroughfare to Hatchards, where Amelia hoped to buy a book of poems for her mother's birthday. Elizabeth had greeted this announcement in mock horror.

'No! Please, not poetry. Your mama might start holding evening readings or press Mr Escott's lamentable suit upon me. Take pity, Amelia, dearest.'

Her young cousin merely laughed.

Standing before several shelves of slim volumes, Amelia began to leaf her way through them, giggling occasionally.

'I think,' whispered Elizabeth, 'the authors generally wish to rouse the reader to joy or tears, but rarely mirth.'

'But Elizabeth,' hissed Amelia, 'this is nearly as "good" as Mr Escott.'

'Oh no! You mean things like that get published?'

'It appears so.'

Elizabeth shook her head and tried to think of something other than imagining the horror of being the subject of printed words. It was then she heard voices on the other side of the shelving. The first spoke indistinctly, but she recognised the respondent instantly.

'No, I disagree. I would give her a year off, not counting any miscarriages. I think it unreasonable to produce every year. Think of the strain upon the system. I know we put them through the risk with the births, but to wear them out young seems, well, unfeeling. Yes, I know you think me too soft, but . . .'

Indignation rose within Elizabeth's bosom. How could Sir Lucius think himself considerate with views like that? 'A year off' indeed! How fortunate that he was not yet married. Pity the poor woman who accepted him and was then treated as some sort of . . .

'And I have no intention of expanding beyond twenty.'

Twenty! Her mind reeled for a second but then Elizabeth put her gloved hand to her mouth, caught between the gasp of shock and laughter. Of course, Sir Lucius must be talking about brood mares. She coughed, and choked slightly. Sir Lucius and a shorter gentleman, some years his senior and with thinning hair, emerged from behind the line of shelves. Sir Lucius smiled.

It was such a simple thing. He smiled. There was no mocking laugh in it, no polite greeting. It was a surprised smile that announced unashamedly that he was pleased to see her, and it sent such a tremor through her that she caught her breath. He bowed.

'Miss Ashling, good afternoon. I regret commenting upon Lady Godmanchester's mare was impossible unless one had developed gills this morning.'

'Indeed, Sir Lucius, but the offer stands for tomorrow if you are free of other commitments.'

'Thank you. Weather permitting, I hope to be there. Oh, I forget my manners. Miss Ashling, may I have the honour of introducing my good friend Mr Disley, who has bred some very successful racehorses at his home north of Cambridge. Horace, may I present Miss Ashling, who appreciates a good horse.'

There was a twinkle in his eye, and she just knew he was thinking of her adverse comments upon the Slug.

'Indeed I do.' She curtseyed politely and extended her hand. 'I am pleased to make your acquaintance, Mr Disley.'

Mr Disley bent over her hand and murmured something, clearly ill at ease in feminine company, and when he straightened was pink in the cheeks.

'Is Lady Chalford not with you, Miss Ashling?' Sir Lucius asked.

'No, Sir Lucius, and it has given my cousin an opportunity to purchase a present for her birthday next week. At least, she says it is for my aunt's birthday. I sincerely hope she is not buying a volume of poetry for mine! By coincidence, her birthday falls only two days before my own.'

Amelia, who had wandered a little to the left, and had been lost in some verse, looked up. Sir Lucius bowed again, and repeated his introduction. Amelia regarded him with a wary eye, as if any innocuous comment might have deeper meaning, but his words were perfectly innocent.

'I hope that you have found something that you think Lady Chalford will like,' Sir Lucius commented politely. 'On which day does your mama's anniversary fall, ma'am?'

'On Tuesday, sir, and,' Amelia added in a sudden burst of confidence, 'I have been desperate to find an excuse to come here without her.' She paused, and then frowned slightly. 'Do you like books, Sir Lucius?'

His eyebrows flew up involuntarily. 'Why, yes, Miss Ashling, but surely since you find me within a bookshop . . .'

'Oh no, sir.' Amelia coloured. 'I meant to say novels, not books. You have a novel in your hand.'

He had almost forgotten *The Rescue of Lucrezia*, which he had found just as he had been hailed by Mr Disley, still in his hand.

'Ah.' He smiled again. 'I have a mama who enjoys lurid romances. Though to be fair, she also enjoys more serious material.'

Amelia had been reduced to blushing silence, and, taking pity upon her, he spoke instead to Elizabeth again. 'Have you come in Lady Chalford's carriage, Miss Ashling?'

'No, sir, for we decided to walk. After all, a little exercise is good for one, and the air is less stuffy after the rain. We have a footman in attendance, I assure you, so you can be sure we do not flout the proprieties.' A defensive note had crept into her voice, as if she anticipated his censure, and resented it.

'No such thought crossed my mind, ma'am, I promise you,' he assured her swiftly. 'It is simply that it has come on to rain again.'

He indicated towards the front of the emporium, as Elizabeth turned her head. Rivulets of water were chasing hurriedly down the windowpanes.

'Oh no! How depressing, and inconvenient.'

'I regret I am without a conveyance, but permit me to hail you a hack when Miss Ashling, Miss Amelia Ashling, has selected her purchase.'

He sounded both solicitous and in an unusually good humour, and Elizabeth could not but smile and accept his offer prettily. When he handed her into a vehicle some minutes later, he did so with a cheerful farewell and, impulsively, lifted her gloved hand to his lips. Elizabeth blushed, and murmured embarrassed thanks. Amelia cast her a sidelong glance but said nothing.

Sir Lucius carried on to his club with a certain spring in his step, which forced Mr Disley to almost trot along to keep up with the long strides. When he arrived, a trifle damp, he cheerfully announced to Lord Foxton, who hoped he would not catch cold, that the rain was in fact very refreshing.

Lady Rendlesham had been busy. Upon reflection, she had decided not to warn Lord Easby of his rival directly, thinking he would put it down to mere spite on her part.

Far more enjoyable would be to stand back and watch him discover it through the web of rumour, the first threads of which she set humming during several morning calls that took up her afternoon, enabling her to return to her house in eager anticipation of the results.

The rumour was easy to start by simply giving the truth of what she had seen and heard but with a particular emphasis. After all, Sir Lucius Radstock had been in the jeweller's, and Mr Rundell himself had been overheard to say that the item, clearly of family significance, would be ready shortly in as good a condition as when presented to the first bride for whom it had been purchased. It needed but the additional information, supplied sotto voce, that Sir Lucius had appeared in a very good humour and had purchased, significantly, another item of ladies' jewellery, to intimate that he was clearly about to make some lady an offer, and that he had every expectation of being accepted.

Rumour, like flame, had tongues that spread quickly, and by the evening's end there were a number of ladies who could be said to have looked with interest to see if Sir Lucius Radstock was singling out any young lady in particular, and some had clearly already come to the correct conclusion that Miss Ashling might be the object of his gallantry. However, they were disappointed if they had hoped to see them together that evening, since Sir Lucius was engaged with the Duke of Grafton and several other members of the Jockey Club, and was not present at Mrs Goodison-Thorpe's party.

Elizabeth was conscious of being observed, but at a loss

to think of any possible reason, until old Lady Killingholme placed a gnarled hand upon her arm and fixed her beady eye upon her.

''Bout time too, I say, my dear. Don't be missish and say you need time to think, for gentlemen do not, whatever some ninnies may say, like to be kept dangling.'

'Ma'am? You mistake, surely.' Elizabeth frowned in perplexity. 'If you are intimating that I am about to be made an offer, I can only assure you that I am entirely unaware of it. I think, perhaps, you might have heard something concerning my cousin, who is, confusingly, also Miss Ashling, though I would hasten to add that I do not think—'

'I may be old, but I am not senile, my girl, and I know the difference between you and Maria Chalford's chit. I can also vouch that the girl would not be the sort to trap Lucius Radstock. Never saw him as much as glance at a child of her stamp.'

Elizabeth felt the room reel about her.

'I repeat, ma'am, I am unaware of any,' and she stressed the 'any', 'gentleman with an intention of making me an offer.'

'Well, I don't know about that. Seems to me to be a whole parcel of 'em keen to fix their interest with you. None of them a patch on Lucius Radstock, however more elevated their titles. I knew his father, a good, fair man.' The old lady's eyes twinkled for a moment and her mouth pursed in a myriad of lines. 'Not half as well as I knew his grandfather, mind you, before he was wed. He was one of the bucks who came to watch me dress.'

Elizabeth was momentarily diverted from her shock. 'Dress, ma'am? Goodness.'

'Oh yes, mind you we did not go about in the flimsy rags you have clinging to you today. We had petticoats and panniers and stiff brocades and . . . Once the underdress was on, it was permitted for gentlemen to see the toilette, hair powdering and rouge and . . .' She sighed reminiscently, then jerked herself back to the present. 'But that was nigh on forty years ago. What I am saying is you are a lucky chit.'

'I am sure Sir Lucius has no intention—'

'Rubbish. Why else have bride jewels refurbished or buy a ring, and go about looking like the cat that got the cream?'

The rumour had already begun to take on a life of its own.

Elizabeth felt sick. Was that the reason he had been so engaging today? She had felt happy in his company, but was his happiness based upon the arrogant assumption that all he had to do was make her an offer and she would fall upon his manly bosom in relief and say yes? Indignation rose in her. What cause had she given him to believe such a thing?

Lady Killingholme watched her as her eyes grew angry, and spoke more gently.

'My dear, I am an old woman, so I can give you advice. Sometimes a man don't see that his intentions have been understood, and acts hasty. Don't cut up rough with him for it, and don't put him off until you are sure you do not care for the idea. Many a good marriage has been based on far less than the namby-pamby languishing that girls call love nowadays. Men of his ilk do not make pretty speeches, but words are just words when all is said and done. He's a real man, not like that milksop poet who has been dangling after you.'

'Mr Escott,' replied Elizabeth, through almost clenched teeth, 'is only interested in me in as much as he finds me inspirational to his poetry, ma'am.'

'Nodcock. His mother is a die-away female full of silly notions. You take my advice and think hard before you refuse a good man, and one whose interest in you is far more red-blooded than a milksop who thinks you his poetic muse.'

Elizabeth blushed, and nodded rather mechanically, but was a prey to so many conflicting emotions that no further response was forthcoming.

CHAPTER TWELVE

Amelia noticed how *distraite* her cousin appeared. Her friend Julia, with an acute ear for gossip, had been swift to tell her what was being whispered, and, with the afternoon uppermost in her mind, she wondered why Elizabeth seemed not in alt, but confused. Sir Lucius, whilst clearly not an unattractive man, was rather too dry and complicated for her taste, but she thought, even in her novice womanhood, that he and her cousin seemed made for each other. There was some indefinable spark between them, though had she mentioned it, Elizabeth would no doubt have laughed and said it was a spark that led to outbursts of wrath.

Such a thought was in Elizabeth's mind. That she was finding herself inexplicably drawn to the man was, reluctantly, undeniable, but that it existed at all made him untrustworthy. Men let one down, but could she say that if he was about to offer for her? Would not everyone say this was proof to the contrary? The voice of experience told her to be wary. A man might still break one's heart even if he slipped a wedding band upon one's finger, but even as she told herself this she knew Lucius Radstock was not a man likely to betray a wife. So why was she filled not with delight, but rather a burning sense of indignation? She tried to be objective about this at least, and discovered that it was the shame of having absolutely no inkling of his intentions, and yet him being apparently so confident that all he had to do was ask and she would fall into his hand like a ripe plum. Well, if you picked fruit too early it would be tart, and if Sir Lucius did propose that would be what he would discover.

Yet Lady Killingholme's words had been sensible. What if she rejected the man and then realised over time that it might have worked? No man would ask twice, she was sure. The answer might be to put off any declaration until such time as she might know her own mind. This would mean damping down those instincts that wanted accord with him, and giving free rein to her inclination for verbal jousting, which both irritated her and yet had a frisson to it. At this moment being annoyed with him was easy, so she had little doubt that holding him off would not be difficult. The old lady had also, with the lack of embarrassment common to the aged, talked of him as 'red-blooded'. As she took to her bed that evening Elizabeth was prey to wicked thoughts of what it might be like to be kissed by Sir Lucius Radstock. She blushed, and hid her head under the bedclothes in the same manner she had as a child hiding from monsters. However, this was not a monster but a temptation, and since it inhabited her head, the covers gave no protection.

* * *

It was with a combination of trepidation, excitement and intentionally fanned flames of outrage that Elizabeth took to the saddle the next morning. The mare, sensing her ill ease, was equally fractious, and diverted her thoughts for the first ten minutes or so of her ride, choosing to be spooked by such previously ignored things as the cry of a pie vendor in the street, a lady opening her parasol and a pigeon. She coped with this wilfulness in a manner that, had he seen it, would have drawn Sir Lucius's admiration. However, by the time that he approached her, most of the mare's jitters had been worked off. He greeted her with a friendly ease that simultaneously gave her a warm glow of pleasure and an equally warm glow, smouldering, of affront.

'Good morning, Sir Lucius.'

'The weather has not beaten us a second time, Miss Ashling, I am glad to say. The mare looks very fresh this morning.' He was admiring the picture she made, the soft grey and deep red of her habit complementing the deeper greys of the horse. They made a fine pair.

'She has given me an interesting few minutes, I admit, but I feel confident that she knows who is in control, and who would wish to crawl about as I had to with the Slug.'

It was the first time that he had heard her actually name the hired hack, and it brought a sharp crack of laughter, which made the mare toss her head.

'An apt name, for it was assuredly not a real horse. It did you no justice, Miss Ashling; that much was apparent from the first.'

She told herself that the man was being patronising, though his tone did nothing to indicate it, and thereby fuelled her resentment. Her smile became fixed and her eyes, which had been unconsciously bright and laughing, grew cold. Her voice lost the intimacy.

'It seems, Sir Lucius, that your opinion is highly sought after when it comes to the purchase of horses. I wonder, perhaps, if you advised Lord Godmanchester upon the purchase of Mist here, for his wife?' She looked at him speculatively.

'Godmanchester would not buy a poor animal, but yes, I was with him at the time.' He wondered what had suddenly happened to make her withdraw from him without warning.

'And were not silent?'

'No, not silent, ma'am.' He would not lie to her direct.

'Then you must think me foolish to invite you to come and view an animal of whose points, good and bad, you are already well aware. I must applaud your, shall we say "joint" choice, but I do wonder that you selected such a spirited mare. I recall Lady Godmanchester as a competent rider, but not a daring one.'

As if to confirm this, the grey mare curvetted, and Elizabeth took some moments to bring her back alongside Sir Lucius. He watched, apparently unconcerned, but ready, should he be needed, to grab her bridle above the bit. He need not have worried, and could even admire her skill.

Miss Ashling was in no way discomposed, and even seemed to relish the mild tussle of wills. She smiled naturally again, and patted the mare's neck. 'You see, sir, she really is no novice ride. To be honest, she is a bit of a handful, but with a lovely soft mouth, and very responsive. All she needs is firm handling.'

Sir Lucius did not reply instantly. Miss Ashling, the reserved, chilly Miss Ashling that had reappeared for a moment, was once again so different a being. There was a slight flush to her cheek now, a genuine smile on her lips, and when she did the beauty that had stirred his interest but mildly was transformed.

'I, er, let Godmanchester be the judge of his wife's abilities as a horsewoman,' he lied, laying any misjudgement at his friend's door. 'However, I think it fair to say that you, Miss Ashling, find her just in your style.'

'Indeed. At home, in Sussex, I have a chestnut mare, Pallas, who is of a not dissimilar temperament, but has learnt who is mistress, as this one, as yet, has not. But neither has an ounce of vice; it is all spirit and eagerness. My uncle, who is himself not particularly interested in horses, approached Lord Egremont, who obviously is, and has his stud at Petworth. He obligingly found Pallas for me. She has Gohanna as her sire, and I am terribly proud of her. I think Lord Egremont found her a trifle disappointing, having hoped she might make a good brood mare, but felt she was a little short in the back for perfection. However, she is a lovely mount.'

Sir Lucius blinked. It was unusual to meet a young lady who knew anything at all about the best thoroughbreds, unless it was the latest winner of the Derby, and then it would be merely the name, and perhaps what colour it was. There were ladies who attended the races, but most were older, and married to gentlemen who frequented the meetings.

'Forgive me, Miss Ashling, I did not know that you were

acquainted with Lord Egremont.' Sir Lucius was a little surprised.

'Ah, not very well, Sir Lucius. My papa was a friend of his many years ago, but my aunt would not permit me to go to Petworth, though it is not far from either Marden Hall or Dowlands, in view of Lord Egremont's, er, unusual domestic arrangements. She says his house is "overrun with doxies and children of shame" and no decent woman should enter its portals. I have, however, met him at the races at Goodwood, of course. My uncle attends the meetings there, and I have joined him occasionally. I fear he is more interested in the company than the horses, unlike Lord Egremont, whom I found to be a very nice old gentleman, and a fount of knowledge. I think he picked Pallas for me because of my father.'

'I myself own two mares bred from the Petworth stud, and breed on a modest scale.'

Elizabeth coloured, remembering the overheard conversation and the misinterpretation of his words.

'So Lady Godmanchester informs me, sir.' She lowered her eyes, and he frowned, thinking she objected to the mentioning of such a matter. It seemed odd.

'If I have offended you by speaking of—'

'Good grief, sir, do you think me so poor a specimen, having such exaggerated sensibilities?'

'No, ma'am, but . . .' His voice trailed off.

'But it was easy to think it?' She glowered at him.

He was getting confused. She seemed to be blowing alternately hot and cold with him, and he could not, for the life of him, think why. 'What have I done, Miss Ashling?'

'Done, Sir Lucius?' She tried to look as if she had no idea of his meaning.

'Yes. It is not, was not, my intention to irritate or anger you, and yet you seem to harbour some animosity towards me today that, forgive the impertinence, was not there when we met yesterday. Has someone so traduced my character to you, Miss Ashling?' He tried to speak lightly, but there was a frown in his eyes.

She felt his sense of hurt, and it made her feel guilty, and in her turn she blamed him for making her feel that way. She could not shout at him that she was angry because he took so much for granted.

'No, Sir Lucius. I have never heard anything that would cast your character in a bad light.'

'Then what is it?'

'You presume, sir, perhaps more than exists, has existed.'

'Is a presumption of friendship too much, Miss Ashling?' His voice was low and quiet, and very sincere.

She looked him in the eye. He deserved that much. 'Perhaps, at this moment, sir, yes. I . . . find it difficult. Please, do not press me.'

He did not more than half understand, but saw that she was troubled. 'I will not press you, Miss Ashling, but when you find it in yourself to admit friendship, be sure that mine will be waiting for you.'

She wanted to answer him, but her throat felt tight, and so she nodded, biting her lip. He was conscious of a feeling of protectiveness, so strong that it was almost a physical thing. Its intensity took him by surprise. He did not want to part from her like this, but it had created a tension between them.

'Shall we canter, ma'am, and perhaps this . . . difficulty . . . can be set aside for a while?'

They did so, and she let her mind empty. The big bay had a longer stride, and drew ahead slightly. She watched the straight back of Lucius Radstock, and only the depth of her fear held her back. After all, the more one felt, the worse the betrayal.

Sir Lucius rode home a troubled man. The image of Elizabeth Ashling, beautiful and at ease upon the horse that he had chosen for her, made his heart rejoice, and he acknowledged it, fair and square. When she looked at him with barriers down he felt that they had a natural affinity, that there was no more comfortable and yet exciting place in all the world than at her side, that things that he found ridiculous she would find so, and what interested him would interest her. He could imagine her galloping shoulder to shoulder with him, discussing his horses with him whilst watching one of his mares with a foal at foot, sitting in contented domesticity at the breakfast table with him at Paley. There were other thoughts, thoughts of shared intimacy, which revolved within his brain, nebulous, but with occasional tantalising glimpses in sharp focus. They seemed so close, and yet she kept pulling away, fearful. He wanted to reassure her that she need not distrust him, that he would not be as Freshford had been. Now he knew something of her story he regretted the half-uttered epithet, regretted it most bitterly. In one foolish half moment he had been the one to start men, men like Easby even, chasing after her. That he had immediately attempted to limit the damage exculpated him not at all. How could he have been so insensitive as to not even to consider the poor girl might have her reasons for keeping men at arm's length? His half-declared irritation had caused her distress, and now, whether she could feel about him as he did about her or not, he would do his utmost to defend her, protect her, even if his actions remained unknown to her.

Yesterday he had bought the little pearl brooch upon a sudden whim, for Lady Godmanchester had mentioned that her friend was about to celebrate her birthday, and he had hoped to discover the exact date from her. Fortuitously, he had learnt it via Miss Amelia Ashling, and had parted from the two young ladies with the idea of presenting the gift in person, hoping to see Miss Ashling's face light up with pleasure. In view of this morning's encounter, he considered, regretfully, that he would have to send it with a note, lest she felt cornered further. Of course, if she was relieved of the attentions of other men, that too would ease her mind. He would have to set about steering them in other directions.

What Sir Lucius failed to see was that what he considered a gentlemanly act upon Miss Ashling's behalf looked suspiciously like clearing a path for himself to other aspirants to her affections. A couple of the less committed merely laughed, and shook their heads over the heretofore impervious Sir Lucius falling so heavily for a chit well past her first Season, and who was proving poor sport, but in two breasts, at least, less charitable emotions were roused. Lord Easby smiled a little grimly, and Mr Escott was appalled, viewing Sir Lucius's 'pursuit' of his Muse, and the clear intent to persecute him should he continue to be inspired by her person, as malevolent in the extreme. He wondered whether he should write a poem about it, but, after some considerable thought, and failed attempts at quatrains, he opted for action. After all, without poetry he was nothing, and this man was going to deprive him of his poetry. He was the next best thing to a murderer.

That any physical remonstration with Sir Lucius was unlikely to go in his favour did occur to him, but he had to face the ogre. That Miss Ashling would need to know of this courageous deed was obvious, and so he spent much of one night's hours of darkness, after attending a party where Miss Ashling was notable for her absence, in composing suitable lines to convey his intentions. It took five sheets of paper screwed into a ball and cast into the oblivion of the fire before he achieved his aim, but when he finally sought his couch it was in the pleasant certainty that he had created stanzas worthy of Byron – in fact, probably better.

Elizabeth had been feeling low. Lady Chalford looked at her heavy eyes and put the lack of sleep down to too many parties. Perhaps Elizabeth did not possess the stamina she had thought. It was therefore easy to persuade her to permit her niece to remain quietly at home for a couple of evenings, accounting for her absence with the excuse of a summer cold. Amelia, encountering Lord Carbrooke, almost by accident, was a little more honest, and put it down to weariness.

'Done to a cow's thumb, no doubt, poor lady. She has not your youthful vigour, Miss Ashling.'

'She is not in her dotage, my lord,' murmured Amelia, colouring deliciously at his compliment.

'But you always look so wonderful—' He caught himself up for being too open. 'Wonderfully, I should say, fresh and full of life. You remind me of a leaf.'

'A leaf?' Amelia was not sure this was so complimentary.

'Yes. A new leaf, just unfurled, all bright green and delicate and . . . I am sorry, Miss Ashling, fancy words are not in my line. You need poets for those and I am no poet, I assure you.'

'I am glad, sir' – she giggled – 'for my dear cousin is beset by a poet, and most uncomfortable she finds it.'

'But I thought ladies liked flowery compliments.' Lord Carbrooke frowned slightly, and Amelia found it rather fetching. There was an almost puppyish innocence, which appealed. It made her feel very grown up in a womanly way.

'We like compliments, yes, but it is nicer if they are meant,' she explained. 'The flowery ones are somehow all show. Pretty, but not real.'

'Oh.' His lordship digested this information, and then brightened. 'Well, since I cannot do "flowery" . . .'

'Just leafy,' interposed Amelia, with a giggle, and their eyes met, full of laughter.

She really was a dashed pretty girl, sweet-natured too, thought Lord Carbrooke, and determined to get his mama to pay a formal call upon Lady Chalford as soon as she returned from aiding his sister following her recent confinement. He had previously dismissed any idea of him becoming a tenant for life, but the golden-haired Miss Ashling had given him cause to reconsider his position.

He had been a little worried that she was so social a girl as to want to spend as much time as possible in London, since at heart, barring the odd spree, he hankered for his estates. She had favoured him with her artless confidences, however, and one of them was to declare that though she was, obviously, having a wonderful time going out every evening to glittering functions, she really rather missed evenings at home, playing spillikins with her younger sister, and entertaining on a more modest scale. Had Lady Chalford been aware of such sentiments being expressed, she would have been horrified, but Lord Carbrooke's very low-key wooing of her daughter seemed to have gone comparatively unnoticed whilst that lady had focused her eyes upon every nuance of word and gesture that marked Lord Nuneaton's more florid and now aborted 'pursuit'.

Amelia, who had found Lord Nuneaton's compliments so objectionable, was positively delighted by the youthful Viscount's rather more tentative efforts. Lord Carbrooke did not make comments that put her to the blush, and if his initial fraternal manner had become rather less brotherly, it blended respectful admiration with hints of ardour that did not in any way frighten her. He had held her hand for slightly longer than a dance might necessitate, or let it rest upon the hand she laid upon his arm if he led her into supper, but his restraint was admirable. Only in the moments before sleep, when doubts assailed her, did she wonder if that meant he felt less for her. Otherwise, she was happy.

CHAPTER THIRTEEN

Amelia was still in a light-hearted mood next morning, and managed to make an appearance at the breakfast table. Elizabeth was buttering toast and discussing the likelihood of rain for the afternoon's military review. She smiled at her cousin, who nearly bounced in, and received a quelling look from her mama.

Ribston brought in a salver, which he presented to Elizabeth. On it was a letter, which made her groan when she saw the script.

'Ooh, is it from Mr Escott?' Amelia giggled. 'What fun! Do read us his latest gem.'

This time it was her cousin whose look spoke volumes. Tempting as it was to discard any missive from Mr Escott without deigning to peruse it, she unfolded the sheet of paper and read. The expression on her face was not as expected, and Amelia grew silent.

'Is he mad?' whispered Elizabeth to herself, paling.

'If he has written anything indelicate or offensive—'

began Lady Chalford, with a belligerent snort.

'Not indelicate, no. Dangerous, yes. I must warn him.'

'That what he writes is dangerous?' Amelia was confused. 'Is it seditious?'

'But it is difficult to broach.' Elizabeth was still talking to herself, ignoring her cousin. 'Oh dear, what should I do?'

'Elizabeth, may I see what is written, my dear?' Lady Chalford held out her hand, and Elizabeth gave her the sheet of paper. Lady Chalford scanned it, her eyes narrowing. 'Foolish man!'

'Am I right to be concerned, Aunt?' enquired Elizabeth, frowning.

'I am not sure. It is not such a situation as one might have foreseen. He is not what one would consider a violent man.'

'But volatile, ma'am. I think the least I can do is warn Sir Lucius Radstock, for I know of no other men in Town bearing the name. If I write to him . . . what if he was hurt?'

'I daresay Lucius Radstock can rebuff and repel any attempt by young Mr Escott, Elizabeth, without resort to excessive violence, but I am more concerned that if they do meet, there will be scandal. No, Sir Lucius is experienced enough to avoid that I think, I hope.'

Elizabeth's hands were to her cheeks.

'What does he say?' Amelia could contain herself no longer.

Elizabeth took the poem from the table.

'O fair Divinity Sublime, let not
The curlèd lip and jealous eye so green,
Nor Persecution that I face persuade

You that my love is less, My Beauteous Queen.
For burning is my tortured heart
When Malice raw keeps us apart.

'Persecution!' She sniffed derisively. 'In what manner does he think himself persecuted?'

'Perhaps,' offered Amelia diffidently, 'he saw you with Sir Lucius in attendance.'

'In attendance? But you could not describe . . . we rarely . . .' Her voice petered out.

Whilst Sir Lucius Radstock had not made any 'push' for her, and often seemed, she thought, to regard her with some amusement as if she were a diversion, it was true that he was often close enough for their eyes to meet; and though it meant nothing, obviously, perhaps so biased a mind as the poet's might read more into it.

'It is ridiculous,' she huffed, but defensively. 'Sir Lucius does not haunt me, not like Lord St Loe, Mr Chorley or Mr Browndown, who do not have any real interest in me.'

Amelia was bold enough to look sceptical at this last remark.

Elizabeth continued, hurriedly.

'I cannot bear to suffer long, and so
Would rather face my Fate, though it might be
That in the noble cause of Love I fall
To rise no more, yet you must surely see
'Tis violence of Philistine
Keeps me from that which is all mine.

'All his! What insufferable presumption! Does he expect me to be moved by this?'

She continued.

'But hold! If fair Melpomene shall sleep,
And tragic death is not my destined way,
Calliope may aid this poet's hand,
More Lucifer than Lucius shall he slay,
By word and deed, and shall I thus
Release You from this Incubus.

'Oh, this is terrible. What if he genuinely means violence? Excuse me, Aunt, I must let Sir Lucius know of this as soon as possible.' She rose from the table, shaking her head. 'I would never have thought of anything so awful.'

She went to the green saloon, and seated herself at a small, walnut escritoire. She drew out paper and pen quickly, but then paused, unsure what to say. She looked again at Mr Escott's poem. Would Sir Lucius think her fanciful? Well, better he do so and laugh at her if it was but bluster, than he suffer an assault from a man who might be deranged. At the same time, what could she write?

In the end she enclosed the poem, not wishing in any case to retain it, and added what she thought sounded urgent but not hysterical.

Dear Sir Lucius,

The enclosed was delivered to me this morning, and I am disturbed enough by its contents to send it straightway to you in case Mr Escott's mind is unhinged. The verse is execrable, but the sentiment within it positively dangerous. Might I beg you to take care if approached by Mr Escott, whom I can understand you would normally dismiss. I am compelled to say, had you permitted me to give him every reason to dislike me for cruelty when you watched us on the terrace, this situation would not have arisen. The deed is done, however, and I am saddled with a man who assumes blithely that I would accept him out of duty as his 'muse', without considering the real me at all, and who has turned you into some looming villain for no reason.

Please do not dismiss this as female feebleness, and be upon your guard.

She wondered in what manner to conclude and, finding formality too ponderous, simply subscribed it *Yours, Elizabeth Ashling.*

It was sent with some urgency, though Ribston showed not by so much as a twitch of a facial muscle that he wondered at her sending a missive of an urgent nature to a single gentleman.

It was only after he had returned from riding with Lord Godmanchester that Sir Lucius received Elizabeth's message. He had just come downstairs from changing his raiment to something more suitable for heading to his club, when his butler, Sansom, brought it in to him. Miss Ashling's hand was unknown to him, and he broke the seal with a slight frown of puzzlement. The poem fluttered to the floor like a desiccated autumn leaf. He bent to pick it up, and then held it and her note in his hands, looking from one to the other. Her missive was in a neat script, though clearly written in some agitation.

His first reaction was a sneer that Escott could even contemplate violence on a poetic plane, let alone in reality, but then he grew angry, angry that whatever he intended, the feckless poet had severely upset Miss Ashling, which he counted as unforgivable. The fool, he had obviously had no thought of how she might react to the aggressive intent. Sir Lucius fumed. He did not think he stood in any great danger, but would keep a wary eye open in case the poet made a scene that might be laid at Miss Ashling's door, and also because he did not think her prone to hysteria.

He read the note again. She had signed it 'Yours'. It would be madness to read too much into that, but it struck him how much he wished it was true. Would she have written to any man she thought at risk? Yes. Had it made her realise that he had been near her more than she had realised? Possibly. The reproof in the note was clear enough, but need not, he told himself, mean that it would rankle with her. He screwed up the results of Mr Escott's tortuous late-night efforts, but placed the note in a small drawer in his desk, and sauntered off to his club for luncheon in a thoughtful frame of mind.

Whilst Miss Ashling herself remained uppermost in his mind, he had no concerns about Mr Escott, since he was not a member and would hardly storm into his club to accost him. He discussed the likely outcome of the Derby with Lord Ebbsfleet, ate in the company of Lord Collingbourne and Sir John Hemsworth, and, upon his departure along Piccadilly, turned off into the shade of Green Park, where the glare of the sun was less intense. He wanted to think, needed to think, and indoors was not the place to do so this summery afternoon. The park was quiet. The regiments of nursemaids giving their little charges an airing of a morning were but a memory beneath the trees, and it was far too hot and sunny an hour for ladies to promenade, even under parasols. There was some degree of solitude, therefore, with nothing more disturbing than the occasional flap of a pigeon, disturbed in the boughs, and a few twittering sparrows on a pathway.

Sir Lucius was wondering how he ought to proceed with Miss Ashling upon their next meeting. She would be embarrassed, and yet for him to make no reference at all to her warning would be both ridiculous and offensive. Broaching it would therefore be a delicate matter. He wanted to assure her that he had taken the contents seriously, without having been excessively worried by the perceived threat, and also to make it clear that what she saw as interference on Lady Chesham's terrace had been undertaken from an honourable desire to rid her of a man who was causing her distress. He had to achieve this whilst not giving her the impression that he was trying to fix his interest with her, even though, he admitted, that was his ultimate intention. In the dappled light he lost himself in his thoughts.

'You!'

The cry brought Sir Lucius up short. Coming along a path at ninety degrees to him was Gregory Escott, his face unnaturally flustered, even for the weather, his lavender-gloved fists clenched by his sides. Sir Lucius was not particularly concerned. A true madman might attack without warning, but if Escott was going to come up to him face to face, he had absolutely no doubt that he could neutralise any threat he might pose.

That this showed in his expression only drove the enraged Mr Escott to an even higher level of frustrated anger. So 'the Wicked Sir Lucius', who sought to ruin his life, thought him no more than a worthless fribble, did he? Well, he would find out just how wrong he was.

'You!' he repeated, half an octave higher.

Sir Lucius merely looked bored. 'That is a singularly pointless observation, Escott. However great the excess spleen from which you are suffering, please do not waste my time by venting it upon me. The afternoon is too warm and I have more important things to consider.'

'Yes, no doubt. How to seduce my Muse.'

'I take it that you are referring to Miss Ashling. You are wrong in both assumptions, both that I have any reprehensible intentions towards that lady, and that she in any sense is "yours". Both are also insulting to me and to Miss Ashling, and if you repeat them in public I shall have no compunction in knocking you down.'

'You need not call me out, for I shall call you out, Villain.'

'Stop being histrionic. If you want to behave like that you should be on the stage.'

'You cannot refuse to meet me and call yourself a man of honour,' goaded Mr Escott.

'Not only could I do so, but the reverse is true. If you

think meeting a feckless greenhorn like you at dawn would show me in an honourable light, you are far off the mark. For goodness' sake, grow up and behave like a sane man, if that is possible.'

'You don't understand.' Mr Escott sounded petulant.

'No, I probably do not, but it does not make my words less true.'

'I cannot write without her,' wailed Escott.

'It is my opinion that not writing would do you the world of good.' It could not be said that Sir Lucius was going out of his way to be placatory.

'You have no poetic soul,' bemoaned the tortured poet, almost wringing his hands.

'No.'

'She is perfection. She is inspiration. She is—'

'A young woman who does not deserve that you make her acutely embarrassed,' Sir Lucius observed.

Gregory Escott was nearly hopping from one foot to the other, and looked like a cat preparing to pounce. Sir Lucius appeared unconcerned, but was fully prepared.

'Philistine!' cried Mr Escott, rocking on the balls of his feet.

'I say, you can't go around shouting things like that, Escott.' Lord Bensthorpe, who had turned into Green Park to take the shady route to a meeting of the Patrons of St George's Hospital at Hyde Park Corner, spoke most reprovingly. He had espied Sir Lucius and the irate poet, and approached, frowning.

'This is no matter of yours, my lord,' Escott declared pompously.

'Dashed well is if you start insulting my friends, and if,' Lord Bensthorpe announced, noting Mr Escott's pugnacious stance, 'you think you can start a mill in Green Park then you are very mistaken. Terribly bad ton. Ladies might see, if,' he added honestly, 'there should be any about. That is, they would see Lucius draw your cork within seconds. Not nice. Might faint. The ladies that is, not Lucius.'

Sir Lucius watched, amused, as Mr Escott digested this slightly confused speech.

'Escott, you have no knowledge of Miss Ashling whatsoever. All you have is an image in your head, and upon which you let your over fertile imagination feed.' Sir Lucius drove home his point. 'What was at first merely mildly embarrassing is fast becoming unsavoury and unpleasant. If you have any feeling towards the lady at all, you will desist in this theatrical and highly unbecoming pursuit of her, and keep your muses purely imaginary.'

'Thus leaving the way open for yourself, Sir Lucius.'

Sir Lucius scowled. 'You know, despite Bensthorpe's sound advice, I may just plant you a facer anyway, you impertinent cub.'

'Best not, Lucius.' Bensthorpe laid a hand upon his friend's sleeve. 'Not seemly here. Come with me to St George's.'

'I am not a patron, Bensthorpe.'

'Er, no, but it is a devilish good cause so perhaps you might become one,' offered Lord Bensthorpe, with a hint of desperation.

Sir Lucius laughed. Mr Escott found himself suddenly sidelined and was prey to mixed emotions. Part of him, obviously, wanted violent action, but a good upbringing gave him a voice within his head that acknowledged the Awful Truth, with capital letters. There seemed no easy way to withdraw from the encounter without considerable loss of face. He caught Lord Bensthorpe's eye, and there was some sympathy in the gaze.

'Not quite up to snuff yet, Escott, dear boy. Everyone makes mistakes, so best put this down to experience and toddle off like a good fellow. No point in making a cake of yourself, eh?'

Mr Escott looked almost beseechingly at Sir Lucius, and gabbled some incoherent phrases in which an apology was at least indicated. Then he raised his hat and stalked away with as much dignity as he could manage, which was not a lot.

'Looby,' muttered Sir Lucius.

'No real harm in the boy, Lucius, and we have all suffered calf love at some point in youth.'

'Oh, this was not love, but "poetry". He thought I had unpoetic designs upon his muse.'

'Miss Ashling. Mmm, well I daresay he will not be the only one to wish you uncharitable thoughts in the near future.'

'What do you mean?' Sir Lucius frowned, bemused.

'Miss Ashling and yourself, Lucius. Can't say I didn't fancy a tilt in that direction myself, but she is a difficult girl to get close to, and it all seemed a bit like hard work in the end. But I wish you well, truly I do.'

'But there is no understanding between Miss Ashling and myself.'

Lord Bensthorpe blinked. 'As of this moment, perhaps

not, but I mean, if you have got as far as the purchase of a ring, then—'

'A ring? What on earth are you talking about, Bensthorpe? Burgundy or claret, was it, last night?'

'No, no, my dear fellow, not bosky at all. Couldn't have been. Heard it from my mother, and I wouldn't be sitting there with her if I was on the go, now would I? Besides, this has been common knowledge for days. Everyone knows you are about to make the Unassailable an offer. In fact, some fellows were wondering why you were delaying, afraid to put it to the touch, perhaps. She can be quite daunting, the Unassailable.'

Sir Lucius's expression was one of horror. 'But this is ridiculous. My mother asked me to take a family piece to be cleaned, after which I made an insignificant purchase, certainly not a ring, and even if I had, what cause would there be to assume I was going to propose to Miss Ashling?'

'No idea how the ring came up, but you know, everyone has noted how you have become a bit like a guard dog about the Unassaila—'

'For Heaven's sake, stop calling Miss Ashling that, Bensthorpe. She is not a bastion.'

'Well, no doubt poor Escott, who is clearly dicked in the nob, as poets so often are, believed every word, saw what he thought was true, and was overwrought. Old Farncombe is going to have to take him in hand, or he'll be clapped up in Bedlam. You can't have fellows dashing about Town threatening violence like that. Dear me, no.'

Sir Lucius was by now only half attending. He was thinking, and the results of his cogitations were not pleasant.

The rumour had sprung from a half truth, so someone had seen him with Mr Rundell. Lady Rendlesham's arrival came to mind. Yes, she was the sort of woman who would enjoy mischief, and he had little doubt she knew the truth to be different. She was also reputed to be Easby's most recent flirt. Why she should advance Easby's cause by putting a spoke, as she would see it, in his own wheel . . .

'Oh my God, that was why she was like that in the park.'

It was Lord Bensthorpe's turn to look perplexed. 'Who, my dear fellow?'

Sir Lucius merely shook his head, his brows drawn together in a frown. 'Try and keep what passed here to yourself, Bensthorpe, for the sake of old Farncombe, and also the lady.'

CHAPTER FOURTEEN

Declining Lord Bensthorpe's repeated invitation to the Board of Patrons of St George's Hospital, Sir Lucius continued home, a frown of concentration upon his brow. In view of the circulating rumour, he was surprised that Miss Ashling had been civil to him at all in the park, and the very fact that, at times, she had been on more comfortable terms, yes, friendly terms, gave him reason to hope that she was not impervious to him.

However, the current problem was their next meeting. He had to persuade her, by being perfectly friendly but un-lover-like, that he had no thought of making her an offer, even though that thought, which would have seemed ridiculous even a fortnight since, now loomed large in his mind. The more he saw of Elizabeth Ashling, even when she held him off as now, the more he knew no other woman would do. He found her beautiful, yet it was not her beauty that enthralled him. There was simply some magical 'something' within her that called to his soul. He laughed mirthlessly at himself. That sounded far too like Escott. However, the closer he got to the lady, the more she was likely to shy away like a nervous thoroughbred. Well, rattling a bucket of oats would not bring this filly close enough to halter. He coloured at having made such an analogy, but, since he knew far more about thoroughbreds than women, perhaps it was natural.

Lord Easby, by contrast, knew an awful lot about women and far less about horses, but the gossip that reached him, which declared confidently that Radstock was about to put things to the touch, gave him cause to think. He had dismissed Sir Lucius Radstock as a rival, largely because of his inexperience with the weaker sex, and to Easby they were weaker. What he had failed to consider was that the simplicity of his approach might find favour with a woman such as the Unassailable. He himself had been tangential, hunting without fear of alerting his prey, while Radstock had blundered in so boldly that perhaps she had not realised anyone that obvious could be serious, until he had got so close that his rather mundane honesty slipped past her guard.

She was an unusual female, and in truth, he could not judge whether Sir Lucius's offer might be accepted. He thought not, and if so Radstock would have no further chance with her, but she was so unpredictable there was always a chance she might, out of sheer perversity, say yes. It was a risk, but Lord Easby decided, logically, that it was one he could do little about, unless he could engineer time alone with Miss Ashling before the declaration was made. Frustratingly, she had cried off his last invitation to go driving, and been absent from several parties where he might have hoped to encounter her. He would therefore have to work on the assumption that Radstock would be rebuffed, either by her alone, or with the benefit of his 'encouragement'. He would have to become a little less subtle, and start to hint at more than friendship, or the prize might slip through his fingers.

Miss Ashling proved elusive to both gentlemen for the next few days, but it might be said that Sir Lucius had the advantage, because he knew the day of her birthday, and because it was he, rather than Lord Easby, who frequently interrupted her thoughts.

Lady Chalford was not of an age when birthdays were celebrated except very privately. She had come to find the day depressing, although her husband never failed to remind her, very cheerfully, that she should be rejoicing at living another whole year. He did, however, sweeten this by remarking how beautiful she still looked to him, and presenting her with some expensive trinket.

This year she had had so much to keep her mind busy that she had almost forgotten the anniversary altogether. She had every hope that Amelia would end the Season betrothed, and to a man whose position would mean comfort and social elevation. Amelia shared the aspiration, but with an entirely different gentleman in mind. Blinkering herself when it came to Lord Carbrooke, whom she dismissed as a 'mere boy', he being no more than twenty-five, Lady Chalford had once cherished hopes of Lord Nuneaton. These had been quite dashed when he had overstepped the mark, and he had withdrawn from the lists. However, unbeknown to Elizabeth, he had approached Lady Chalford but three days previously at an evening party, and been abject in his apologies, and, he said, was desperate to make restitution. He had, he claimed, been so smitten with Miss Ashling that he had not known how to make himself agreeable to her, and having not sought out a young lady in many years, went about it in entirely the wrong manner. He sounded so desirous of absolution that her ladyship had relented, and granted that he might again ask her daughter for dances. If he was prepared to grovel, and Lady Chalford felt this was so, he must be very keen. Hope was rekindled in her maternal breast.

With regard to Elizabeth, she had initially despaired of her niece's disinclination to put herself out in any way to be appealing, and then been surprised by that damsel's popularity. Most of the gentlemen who were inclined to court her were, in Lady Chalford's opinion, unworthy, but there were a handful she would not think a bad match. When her daughter had nonchalantly mentioned how Sir Lucius Radstock seemed so frequently in her vicinity, she had at first dismissed the idea as girlish over-optimism, but she had paid more attention. He did not act like an aspiring lover, but then, perhaps it was the aspiring lover in men that put Elizabeth on the defensive. When Amelia reported the rumour of Sir Lucius's impending proposal, she quite rightly chastised her for listening to gossip, but hastily sent an invitation to him for the party that they were holding in

Mount Street to celebrate Elizabeth's coming of age. What better occasion for him to request the pleasure of a private interview at Elizabeth's earliest convenience.

Elizabeth herself was unaware of these machinations. She felt oddly out of sorts, and flitted about the house unable to sit still long enough to set more than a few stitches, or turn a few pages of a book and thereafter have no idea what she had just read. She told herself that it was the sultry weather, that it was being cooped up indoors, which was Sir Lucius's fault, since she was having to avoid him – any reason except the truth. That truth was so disturbing to her mind as to be banished to a dark recess, from which it clamoured to escape. Giving in to it, admitting just how much keeping herself away from him cost her, how easy it would be to let herself be carried away with the idea of placing her future in his hands, was against everything she had learnt in the past decade. Her heart ached to trust him; her head cried 'No surrender'.

She tried to set aside her confusion and look to her cousin's *affaire de coeur*. Amelia was exhibiting every sign of, at the very least, infatuation. Excepting in the presence of her mama, she spoke frequently of Lord Carbrooke, and Elizabeth noted that 'Lord Carbrooke says' was now more frequently used than 'Mama says'. Part of her wanted to warn her of the dangers of giving her tender heart into another's keeping, but the girl was so innocently happy that Elizabeth could not bring herself to disabuse her of her happy ignorance. She was very fond of Amelia, and wished her nothing but joy. From what she could tell of the young Viscount, he was perfectly genuine in his affection and clearly held Amelia in the highest esteem.

The morning of her birthday dawned to rain, which Ditcham berated as she drew the curtains as if it had fallen just to disrupt her mistress's day. Elizabeth was unconcerned by it, but laughed.

'My birthday will be much the same whether the clouds are grey or not, Ditcham.'

'That's as may be, Miss Elizabeth, but I know as how you like your ride, and it would be nice if you could get out this morning, having kept indoors a few days.'

Elizabeth sighed. She thought of Mist, eating her head off in Lord Godmanchester's stable, and resented her enforced seclusion.

'Will you be wearing the sprigged muslin this morning, miss?' repeated the maid, seeing her in a brown study.

'The . . . Oh yes, please, Ditcham. I do not intend going shopping this morning, unless Miss Amelia is set upon it, and if we do, then the mulberry spencer will suffice with it.'

'And tonight?'

'The pale lemon silk with the silver trimming, if you please. I will wear Mama's diamonds with it, for the occasion, the grande parure.'

When she came down to breakfast, her uncle was finishing his repast. He had clearly enjoyed a hearty meal and the servants were clearing a plate showing signs of cold beef, and slices of a fine York ham. The ladies of the household ate far more sparingly, and Lady Chalford frequently shook her head at her spouse's adherence to what he termed 'setting up for the day'. He rose at her entrance, beaming, and came forward to envelop her in an avuncular hug.

'My favourite niece. My sincere felicitations, my dear. I was hoping you would come down early, so I lingered over breakfast.'

She smiled at him, and her eyes twinkled. 'I do hope that this lingering did not lead you to overindulge, Uncle. I am sure I have heard my aunt say that if you ate too much she would put you upon a restricting diet.'

'Your aunt, bless her, fusses too much. A man needs to keep his strength up.'

'Indeed, sir.'

'Minx.' He patted her cheek, and then took a package from the seat of the chair beside him. 'Upon the occasion of your coming of age, my dear.'

He handed her the slim parcel. She unwrapped it carefully. Within a case with the name of Phillips, New Bond Street inside it, lay a delicate necklace of topaz stones, and a matching bracelet.

'Oh, Uncle William, they are beautiful. Thank you.' She hugged him. 'I was going to wear Mama's diamonds tonight, but I can . . .'

'Oh no, my dear, tonight is just the night for your poor dear mother's jewels. I shall not be offended, I assure you.' He planted a kiss upon her cheek. 'You are a good girl, Elizabeth, and I am as proud of you as your father would have been. Now, before I get maudlin, I will be off.'

He left her in solitary state, but it was not long before Amelia peeped round the door, gave a giggle and rushed to embrace her.

'Happy birthday, my dearest, dearest cousin.'

'I am your only cousin, to my knowledge, barring those awful connections of your mama, who descended upon us last summer, and they were second cousins, I am sure.' She grinned.

'Well, you would still be my dearest cousin if I had a positive regiment of them,' declared Amelia. 'And I have a present for you.'

'Not one of those knotted purses you made for Aunt Risborough last year, I hope.'

'No such thing.' Amelia giggled. 'So wait here.'

She rang the bell, and Ribston, clearly primed, entered with a soft package upon a salver. Beaming in a positively paternal fashion at Elizabeth, he held the tray so that Amelia might take the parcel and hand it to her cousin.

'What is it?'

'Open it and find out, go on.'

Untying the ribbon and folding back the tissue paper revealed a scarf of ecru ribbon lace.

'Oh Amelia, just such a one as we saw at Grafton House. You clever puss, that is just the thing.' She hugged the blushing Amelia.

'I was, of course, tempted by a book of verse, but in the end . . .'

'Wretch!'

'Perhaps I could do as well as Mr Escott? Let me see. Um, "Cousin fair, I want to say, On this, your very special day, I hope your hours are filled with joy, And" . . . Oops, what rhymes with that besides "boy" and "toy"?'

'Coy?' suggested Elizabeth, failing to keep a straight face.

'But none of them fit,' bemoaned Amelia, with an exaggerated pout.

'Ahem.' Ribston coughed in a polite manner. 'Might I suggest "Nothing shall your peace destroy", miss?'

'Oh. Well, it sounds a bit like a hymn, but jolly good, Ribston. Better than I could manage, anyway. I fear, Cousin, that Ribston and I lack the muse.'

'Thank goodness for that.' Elizabeth began to laugh, and they were both still laughing when Lady Chalford entered. Whilst uncontrolled hilarity would normally have drawn a frown of disapproval, her ladyship merely raised an eyebrow, and recommended that Amelia wipe her eyes carefully so as not to redden them.

'Happy birthday, my dear,' she murmured, taking Elizabeth by the hands and pressing a small box into them. 'I hope you have a special day.'

This echo of her own words sent Amelia into another paroxysm.

Elizabeth untied the ribbon and opened the box, revealing a silver vinaigrette with an enamelled lid, painted with violas in purples and yellows.

'I know you are not one to have need of a vinaigrette in most circumstances, but you never know when one might be useful, and, as one gets older one, is less able to cope with shocks.'

Ignoring the idea that, having reached the age of twenty-one, she must now be on a slow but inevitable decline into mental, and probably physical, enfeeblement, Elizabeth smiled, and kissed her aunt fondly.

'It is delightful, Aunt, thank you.'

The three ladies then sat down to discuss the minutiae of the day over breakfast. They were about to disperse, Amelia to go for a drive with Julia Wingate and her mama, Elizabeth and Lady Chalford to write letters, when Ribston entered once more, bearing what was clearly another gift.

'Oh, I wonder if Helen Godmanchester has sent me a present? I had thought since she is paying me a call this afternoon . . .'

Elizabeth unwrapped the small parcel, and opened the velvet box within in a mixture of anticipation and curiosity. A pearl ring-brooch nestled on a ground of sapphire-blue material. The note, which had nothing poetic about it, was written in a neat hand and folded within. Sir Lucius had not wished Miss Ashling to discover the giver and then refuse to open the gift, for any reason. Once she had seen it, he thought it less likely that she would reject it, for that would be petty, and he did not think her petty.

She read out the message.

Dear Miss Ashling,

Being aware of your natal day, I hope you will accept this small gift as a token from one who would count himself honoured to be, in your eyes, a friend. I thought it would look appropriate in the cravat of your riding habit.

LR

She took the brooch, carefully, from its blue bed, and gazed at it with a tremulous smile. It was not an extravagant present, not embarrassing, but both touching and thoughtful. It was certainly unexpected.

'What a pretty gift, Elizabeth. It shows taste. How kind of Sir Lucius. I wonder how he knew the date?'

Elizabeth ignored her aunt's immediate comprehension of the identity of the giver.

'Most likely from Lady Godmanchester, though I must confess that I unwittingly offered some indication of its proximity. Might I accept it, Aunt?'

'Accept it? Of course you may accept it. It is gauged to a nicety as a gift. Now, oh, look at the time, I really must be about writing to send condolences to Sarah Embleton on the death of old Lady Steyning. No more dancing for her Harriet this Season. How vexatious for them, especially when she shows to such advantage in the ballroom.'

Lady Chalford left, shaking her head at the perversity of elderly relatives who departed this life at inappropriate times.

It was mid-afternoon when Lady Godmanchester arrived to congratulate her friend. She had suffered a particularly trying morning, and still looked a trifle pale, but had decided that moping at home and feeling sorry for herself would do no good at all, and that Elizabeth would undoubtedly distract her from the vague feeling of nausea that persisted. She brought with her a Norwich silk shawl, delicately fringed, and a request to drive out with her in the park for an hour.

'Fresh air is good for one, though not the heat, of course, and this morning's rain has cleared the air wonderfully. You won't mind sitting with a pathetic creature like me for an hour as entertainment, will you?'

'Pathetic? Hardly. I wonder how you manage to be out and about so much in your condition.'

'Partly desperation,' admitted Lady Godmanchester, with a conspiratorial smile. 'Later on one becomes terribly sluggish, and being withdrawn from society to the greater extent jades one's spirits. Until it becomes obvious, or I simply find it too exhausting, I do want to remain part of the social whirl.'

'But you do take enough rest, Helen?'

'Oh dear, you sound as fussing as my lord. He positively refuses to hear of me getting up in the morning before ten thirty, if I have as much as stayed an hour at a function the night before.' She sighed. 'He is so very considerate, even if inclined to wrap one in cotton wool. Now, enough of me and my delicate state. Do tell me what gifts and congratulations you have received. I do not suppose Mr Escott is aware of the significance of the date, or else he would have written a sonnet in your honour.'

'I sincerely hope not!' Elizabeth shuddered, and described the presents she had been given. Finally, to the list of family offerings, she added, in as off-hand a manner as possible, that Sir Lucius Radstock had sent her a small, and she stressed 'small', brooch. 'Just a token, you understand, since he had overheard it was my birthday.'

Helen Godmanchester nodded, and kept her thoughts to herself.

* * *

The evening party was not going to be a society squeeze, but a rather more select affair, limited to no more than fifty persons, with supper, and, since Elizabeth enjoyed dancing so much, a few impromptu sets after supper. Those invited were closer acquaintances and friends. Lady Rendlesham was most certainly not invited, nor had Lady Chalford sent a card to Lord Easby. Lord Nuneaton had been favoured, however, and, at Elizabeth's request, Lord Carbrooke and Mr Southram, because, she said, they made her laugh. Most of the guest list had been of her aunt's devising, and she did not know of the addition of Sir Lucius. Without any anticipation of awkwardness for the evening, Elizabeth dressed in a happy mood.

The lemon silk was new for the Season, her mother's diamond set sparkled about neck and wrist, and in her dark hair, and she knew herself to be looking her best. Ditcham was patting the single curled lock of hair before each ear when Elizabeth, upon a whim, reached for the little blue box upon the dressing chest.

'What on earth do you be wanting to wear that for, miss? It will scarcely show on this gown and with you glittering with diamonds . . .'

'An indulgence, Ditcham. I simply feel like wearing it tonight, and placed so' – she pinned it centrally at the neckline of the bodice – 'if any remark upon it, it may be taken as part of the dress, since there are seed pearls among the silver embroidery on the sleeves.'

Ditcham sniffed, but said no more. At least her mistress looked better tonight than she had for several days.

* * *

Elizabeth stood to receive the guests, secure in the knowledge that she could be at ease. There were none of her unwanted admirers, nor the ladies of Lady Rendlesham's circle who clearly despised her. She was more than a little taken aback when Sir Lucius Radstock was announced, and felt slightly breathless as she watched him climb the stairs towards them. He bowed over Lady Chalford's hand, and then Elizabeth's, and as he straightened, his eye caught sight of the pearl brooch. He looked up, clearly surprised, and their eyes met, his questioning, hers full of confusion. Belatedly, he let go of her gloved fingers. Lady Chalford watched indulgently. Rumour must surely be true.

'Sir Lucius,' Elizabeth murmured, blushing. 'I have to thank you for your generous gift.'

He wanted to tell her that she need not thank him, that the sight of her wearing it was greater thanks than he would have dared to imagine, but he was not a man used to pretty words.

'It is but a trifle, ma'am. I am only delighted if it was received in the spirit with which it was sent.'

The blush deepened, and Elizabeth murmured something indistinct before she had to move on to another arrival. That might keep her from him for a while, but she knew that in a gathering of this size it would be impossible to avoid him all evening.

In fact, Sir Lucius was being very circumspect. He wanted nothing more than to have the chance of conversation alone with her, but gauged that to appear over-keen would ruin all. He therefore watched her, covertly, as she stopped here and there, received compliments and congratulations, laughed softly at some witticism of young Southram's. He felt as if only she remained in focus, and everyone else was vaguely blurred. With planning worthy of Lord Easby, he positioned himself so that he might approach her in time to lead her in to supper, although their conversation would have to be superficial under the eyes of many. However, he was beaten to this pleasure by the unexpected presence of Lord Nuneaton, who, having just failed to secure Miss Amelia Ashling, descended upon her cousin. That she would far rather have declined his arm was clear, and for a brief moment her eyes met Sir Lucius's, and he saw the embarrassment and, yes, disappointment within them. Was it disappointment because she did not like Nuneaton, or that it had not been himself leading her in to supper? He told himself not to read so much into it, and went to ask a slightly shy-looking young lady to take his arm.

It could not be said that Elizabeth enjoyed supper as much as she had hoped, despite the well-chosen repast. Lord Nuneaton chose to treat her to his uninhibited manner, secure in the knowledge that in such a public place she might not do anything about it. It was an appropriate revenge, so he thought. She found him offensive more from the intimate tone he adopted than his actual words, but itched to slap the self-satisfied pink cheeks. By the end of supper she could feel her own anger marring her visage. It was not, perhaps, the most propitious time for Sir Lucius to approach her, and her eyes flashed as brilliantly as the diamonds at her bosom.

'I must apologise, Miss Ashling.'

'Apologise, Sir Lucius? For what?'

'For failing you in your hour of need. Had I not been distracted by Lady Micheldever, I would have pre-empted Nuneaton's request to lead you in to supper.'

She looked at him, the angry fire glowing. He understood so much, and yet he understood so little if he thought her his for the mere asking.

'You feel you had the right, sir?'

'No. Not the right, but every chivalrous instinct.' He looked very serious, and his voice was calm. If she expected him to fan the flames of her wrath for her, she was mistaken.

'Oh.'

'Miss Ashling, might I beg a few minutes' conversation with you, somewhere a little more private?'

'No. I mean, it would be remarked upon, Sir Lucius.' She looked flustered, nervous.

'I think we are at cross-purposes, Miss Ashling. I wish to speak to you in order to correct a misapprehension that owes everything to malicious rumour. If you would but indicate a chamber where we might be private, you might slip away first and I would follow some minutes later, if you are concerned about gossip.'

She frowned. He sounded very reasonable, and very dispassionate.

'I am not sure . . .' she faltered.

'Be sure.'

She looked at him, and trusted. 'There is a small withdrawing room on this floor, at the back of the house, adjacent to the room where supper was laid out. I will meet you there.'

He bowed and walked away to exchange pleasantries with

an acquaintance, and Elizabeth, feeling very clandestine, slipped out, unaware that Lady Chalford had watched the interchange and was smiling benignly at her.

The withdrawing room was a peaceful haven, but Elizabeth felt more as though she was entering a lion's den. She sat, then stood, then walked up and down in agitation, and when the door opened, and Sir Lucius entered, she was gripping the back of a chair as if it were her only support. He noted it.

'Thank you for seeing me, Miss Ashling. I shall not insult you by beating about the bush. I fear that you have been made aware of a rumour that' – he paused for a moment – 'that I had the temerity to be about to propose marriage to you in arrogant confidence that you would accept me on the spot. This is so?'

She nodded.

'The rumour, and it was merely that, was started by a lady who is partial to malice. She observed me in a jeweller's where I took a minor heirloom to be cleaned, upon my mother's instructions. The unfortunate phrasing of one of Mr Rundell's remarks might have led to supposition. However, the lady must have been very aware that my other purchase was simply a small brooch, the very brooch that I sent to you today.'

Elizabeth felt a wave of relief, that was yet tinged with something else, run through her.

'So you are not about to make me an offer, Sir Lucius.' She tried to sound light-hearted, but the smile was a little awry.

'Not about to, Miss Ashling, and if I should ever do so,

be assured it would not be with any insufferably puffed-up assumptions as to your answer.'

'I see. Thank you for your honesty, sir.' She was as calm as he was now.

'I am only sorry that any breach of . . . trust, existed between us. Lady Rendlesham has much for which she should answer.'

'Lady Rendlesham? So it was she who . . . How very typical of her. Yes, I see now. I too am sorry, Sir Lucius. You have been open and honest with me, and' – she extended her hand suddenly, and he took it – 'I must have seemed inconsistent and rude. Forgive me.'

He held the hand firmly, though from choice he would have kissed it. 'There is nothing to forgive, ma'am, I assure you.'

'And I have not thanked you properly for my birthday gift.' Her other hand went to the brooch at her bosom.

'You wore it.' He could say nothing more without betraying himself entirely.

There was an awkward silence, but not a silence of emptiness, rather one in which many confused thoughts jumbled and jostled until none could be understood.

'Will you ride with me tomorrow, Miss Ashling?' Sir Lucius asked, seeking to lessen the tension with normality. 'Weather permitting, of course? If we were to meet at the Godmanchesters' stables at, shall we say ten o'clock?'

'I . . . Yes, Sir Lucius, that would be a pleasure.'

'Then I shall leave you now. Thank you for hearing me, and' – he smiled, though it was a slightly lopsided smile – 'happy birthday, Miss Ashling.'

He bowed and was gone, and Elizabeth took a deep breath, easing her fingers, which were stiff from clutching the back of the chair. She wanted solitude but knew she must return to what was in many ways 'her' party. With a sigh, she gathered herself together and went back to the throng.

CHAPTER FIFTEEN

Lady Chalford was agog to find out what had passed between Elizabeth and Sir Lucius, but it was clear at the end of the evening that Elizabeth was yearning for her bed, and had no intention of recounting anything without questioning. She did not look miserable, nor yet angered, but Lady Chalford doubted that she had given Sir Lucius a firm answer. When he had left the party he had thanked her politely and without any trace of emotion. A man rejected might well have shown disappointment, even chagrin. She was perplexed, and blamed a disturbed night upon that rather than an overindulgence in crab patties.

Come the morning, however, and Lady Chalford was early in the breakfast parlour, and prepared to wait for Elizabeth's arrival. She had little doubt that her niece would be down earlier than her daughter, who had not sat out a single one of the dances after supper. Elizabeth herself had not lacked partners, and had clearly enjoyed the dancing, but her aunt caught her several times looking preoccupied.

When she came in, that slightly distant look was again present, though she greeted her aunt with a calm smile.

'So, my dear . . .'

'So, Aunt?'

'Now do not, for pity's sake, try and tell me that nothing passed between you and Sir Lucius Radstock last night. I saw you slip away, yes, and saw him do likewise. Did he make you a declaration, Elizabeth?'

'No, he did not.'

'But' – Lady Chalford looked confused – 'then why did he want to speak privately to you, at a party?'

'That is easily explained, Aunt.' Elizabeth bit into a piece of toast, and never before had her aunt wanted to tell her to rush her food. When she had swallowed, she turned an innocent smile to her aunt and said, 'You see, he thought it imperative to tell me that he was not making me an offer.'

Lady Chalford's mouth opened for speech, but no words came. She stared at her niece as if she had spoken in an unknown foreign language. Slowly, the words sank in, and in consequence her ire rose.

'Not going to make you an offer? How dare he arrange a meeting in a room alone and not propose marriage. It is outrageous. My poor Elizabeth.'

'Poor? Why, no such thing, ma'am. I was heartily relieved, and it showed Sir Lucius to be a man of honour and integrity.'

'Relieved, Elizabeth? Are you mad, child?'

'Not at all. I disliked the idea that any man should be under the impression that all he had to do was snap his fingers, so to speak, and I would instantly fawn at his feet in gratitude.' Her tone had a bite to it.

'Do you not like Sir Lucius?'

'I' – she paused – 'like him well enough. Indeed, we are engaged' – she left the word hanging just long enough for her aunt's eyes to widen – 'to go riding this morning.'

'I do not understand you, Elizabeth. Do you tell me you simply do not want to be married? My dear, it is not' – she coloured, and sought in vain for the right word – 'frightening, I assure you.'

Elizabeth looked at her plate. Had she not spent several hours in the night asking herself that question? She had been relieved, as she said, that Sir Lucius had not proposed, expecting her acceptance, but there had been a sigh of disappointment in her heart, a heart that whispered that of all men, Sir Lucius was the one she could trust, the one who could make her life joyous. She had tossed and turned, as the whisper became a clamour in the silent hours, and her dispassionate head not been able to respond.

Lady Chalford watched her niece's face. She had never quite fathomed why Henry Freshford's defection had made Elizabeth turn away from men permanently. After all, she had not been wildly in love with him from the first. It had taken some persistence on the young man's part to win her over, and only then had she gained the bloom of young love. That the heart of the problem was an earlier desertion, Lady Chalford had failed to see. She would have probed deeper had not a note been presented to Miss Ashling. Elizabeth would normally have winced at the handwriting, but this morning a letter from Mr Escott was an ideal distraction.

She had expected a poem, but found instead a letter, so confused in composition that she was forced to read it twice before she could make any sense of it whatsoever. It was a twisted mess that was quite possibly a combination of an apology, an exculpation and a diatribe against the cruelty of women. It was also no less impassioned against the soulless inhumanity of Sir Lucius Radstock, whom he could not bring to meet him in honourable combat, for which last Elizabeth offered up a silent thanks. She gave the gist of the missive to her aunt.

'At least, I think that is what he is saying. To be honest, it is such a mish-mash, and scattered with obscure classical references, that I am hard pressed to be sure. The only certainty seems to be that he no longer sees me as his muse and thinks I may therefore be guilty of robbing the world of untold poetic gems, unless he finds a replacement.'

'Well, and a good thing too, I say, but he is right upon one point. Sir Lucius Radstock is inhuman if he does not offer for you.' Lady Chalford was still outraged, and her niece vouchsafed no response.

Elizabeth was glad to escape into the fresh air. She arrived in Brook Street a couple of minutes after Sir Lucius, who had dismounted from his big bay and was murmuring endearments to Mist, who seemed decidedly jumpy. The groom looked at her very seriously.

'You'll have to watch her this morning, miss. She's already kicked over a bucket, dragged a lad about the yard and run me ragged just getting a saddle on her. Being cooped up has got her on the fret, good and proper.'

'Thank you. I shall be careful.'

Sir Lucius made his bow, and before she could demur, offered himself to throw her up into the saddle, which he did as if she were as light as swansdown, which she knew she was not. The grey mare chewed on the bit as if meditating what to do next, and rolled a sapient eye at Sir Lucius.

He took his own horse from the waiting groom, mounted in a single fluid movement and left the yard, close to the grey so that she could not sidle into traffic. Effectively penned against the edge of the carriageway by the bigger horse, Mist showed her disapproval by throwing her head about, presumably hoping to pull Elizabeth's arms from their sockets, but found that her rider simply let her toss as much as she wished.

'I think we would be better trotting, Miss Ashling. The sooner we are off the paved highway the better. I get the feeling the mare is like a rocket this morning, just after lighting the blue touch paper.'

'She does feel very pent up, I agree. Poor girl.'

Elizabeth did not have to provide much urging for the grey to break into a bouncy trot, and once they had crossed Park Lane onto the track about Hyde Park, the mare threw up her head, nostrils wide, and proceeded to try and buck Elizabeth from the saddle. It certainly gave Sir Lucius the chance to admire her skills as a horsewoman, although it precluded conversation. If he knew a few moments of concern, he did not let them show, nor the readiness in which he held himself to act if the mare tried to bolt. Elizabeth had too much to concentrate upon to pay him attention, but after a few minutes the worst of the mare's agitation passed.

'Well, that was exciting,' commented Elizabeth, rather breathlessly. Sir Lucius tried to gaze at her face and not the rapid rise and fall of her bosom beneath the muslin folds pinned with his brooch.

'I think when we saw her for sale, she had been exercised. I confess that, had I seen how mettlesome she was, I would have not recommended her as a ladies' mount.' He sounded quite concerned.

'Fiddle! She just needs a firm hand. However, unless Lady Godmanchester has become infinitely more at home upon a horse, I fear that for her she is too difficult a mount. I am only glad that for a few months, at least, I will have had the opportunity to ride such an animal.'

The serious look remained.

'You think me foolhardy, sir?'

'No, ma'am, for you have just given an exhibition of your skills as a horsewoman, had I not guessed them previously. It does not mean, however, that I think the mare best suited to a lady, and especially not to Town, and busy streets.'

'I will concede that she would be far better for a good gallop, and the streets are somewhat of a concern.'

'Might I ask, Miss Ashling, that if the mare is not at least exercised by a groom for a day or so, that you let me accompany you. Chester here is big enough to keep her from cavorting in front of other vehicles.' He saw her scowl. 'You think it presumption, I can see, but I feel in some measure responsible.'

He was not using this as an excuse. It was no ploy, and had he not said that he was not intending to make her an offer? The sense of being under his protection increased, and Elizabeth was surprised to find that she did not object to it.

'In that case, Sir Lucius, I accept gladly. The poor weather prevented Lord Godmanchester's grooms from taking her out, no doubt.'

'Or perhaps they were not so doughty, ma'am.'

She coloured at the implied compliment, and tried to steer the conversation away from herself. He regretted the comment almost as soon as it left his lips, guessing her reaction, and made no attempt to stop her, but was surprised that she immediately chose the subject that had arisen on their last, and intermittently awkward, ride.

'I was wondering, Sir Lucius, about your horses at your country residence. I am sorry, I do not know whereabouts that is situated. Do you get the opportunity to get back and see your new foals during the London Season?'

'We live in Berkshire, at a place called Paley Court. I can get back and spend a night there, easily enough.'

'We?'

'My mother rarely comes to London, since my father's demise, except for new hats, and a visit to her dressmaker, and then she enjoys all the benefits of seeing her friends. Otherwise, she is a prolific correspondent.'

'Is Lady Radstock interested in your horse breeding?'

'No, my father was a friend of Sir Charles Bunbury, and a member of the Jockey Club. He was more interested in the racing itself, and owned a few good winners in his time. I suppose I have the interest in, er, my bloodline.'

He smiled, and she laughed softly, her eyes lit by the emotion. The mildly depressing thought that she felt able to do so because she saw him, at least temporarily, as non-threatening, he put aside.

They rode in companionable silence, the groom at a discreet distance behind them, and when they cantered, the mare, in competitive spirit, lengthened her stride to match the bay's.

'Oh, for the chance to gallop,' bemoaned Elizabeth, though she looked happy enough, and her cheeks were tinged with colour. Sir Lucius glanced at her and thought how very beautiful she looked, but even in that brief look the life went from her face and the mask fell into place. The voice that hailed them gave the reason, and they slowed to a walk.

'Miss Ashling! How glad I am to see you are no longer indisposed. Radstock, your servant.' Lord Easby raised his hat, and the look he gave Sir Lucius was not amicable, though the smile remained fixed to his lips. 'Fair lady, you will now be able to resume our driving lessons. I have to say my mornings have not been the same without you.'

Sir Lucius was conscious of a deep-felt urge to wipe the smile from Easby's face, and it clearly showed, for that smile lengthened. For his part, Lord Easby had been most put out to see Miss Ashling in company with Sir Lucius, but the gentleman's scowl gave him relief. Had Radstock been accepted he would have the triumphant pride of the victor, not beetling brows. Hope remained, and he had every intention of exploiting it to the full. Taunting Radstock was merely an additional pleasure. He therefore set about being most agreeable, largely inconsequential and with just a hint of the seducer that the innocent Miss Ashling would fail to see, but of which the increasingly irate Sir Lucius would be fully aware. If the lady did not seem as responsive to his tone as previously, he would not worry. It was fair to say that Radstock had stolen a march on him, but the next move was his.

'You know, Miss Ashling, I do not think Sir Lucius appreciates my presence. In fact, I think he would dearly like to put an end to my existence at this precise moment. Would it not make you feel important to have gentlemen meet at dawn over you?' The tone was teasing.

'No indeed, sir. I can think of nothing more foolish, nor embarrassing for any woman,' Elizabeth replied, with acerbity.

'There, Radstock, if you want to meet me, we will have to keep it hushed or the divine Miss Ashling will frown upon the victor.' He laughed, but Sir Lucius was not laughing.

'Your funning is in poor taste, Easby.'

'Is it?' Lord Easby raised a quizzical eyebrow. 'I wonder if I am funning.'

The animosity crackled between the two men, and Elizabeth, aware of it, sought only to send Lord Easby upon his way as soon as possible. 'Your driving lessons, my lord, are they still available?'

'For you, ma'am, of course.'

'Then would tomorrow morning be convenient, at eleven o'clock?'

'I am, entirely, at your service, Miss Ashling. I will present myself in Mount Street at that time, and look forward to imparting . . . what skill I possess to you.' With which, and raising his curly-brimmed beaver once more, he trotted off.

'What skill he possesses, indeed!' Sir Lucius nearly ground his teeth. 'That would take no more than half an hour all told.'

'Is your dislike of Lord Easby of long standing, sir?'

He could not admit it coincided with that gentleman's interest in her. 'I dislike his manner with ladies, he has a far too elevated idea of his own worth and he drives badly.'

'The last being of greatest importance?'

'Only when he is driving you, ma'am.'

'Yet you do not exhibit such antipathy to Lord Collingbourne, who seemed far more likely to throw me into a ditch.' Her tone was light, for she wished him to come down from the boughs.

'Ah, but I did ensure he did not take you driving again, ma'am, and on the first two points he is unimpeachable.'

'In all seriousness, Sir Lucius, am I at risk with Lord Easby?'

He looked her straight in the eye. 'I fear you will take umbrage if I tell you the truth.'

'No, Sir Lucius, not if it is simple truth. I ought to say that I already have reason to know that you have taken it upon yourself to "dissuade" another gentleman from pursuing me. Mr Escott has decided that I have toppled from my pedestal as his muse, not least because if I so remained it would be injurious to his health, which latter part stems from you. He also said that you would not meet him over me, for which you find me grateful rather than affronted.' She smiled lopsidedly. 'Are you thinking to do the same with his lordship?'

'Escott is an appalling cub, of whom you are well rid, ma'am, but no threat to you.' His tone remained serious.

'Unlike Lord Easby?'

'I doubt he will overturn a vehicle with you in it, so in that sense you are safe. However, beyond the veriest basics he is likely to teach you bad driving habits. He does not feel his horses' mouths well, for a start. You would be wise to consider what he tells you very carefully.'

'And we are still talking about driving, Sir Lucius?' She recalled the last time she had asked the same question.

'No, Miss Ashling' – his gaze held firm – 'we are not. You may still think that an impertinence, but . . .'

'No, Sir Lucius, I accept it for what it is, this time: your honest opinion.'

When first Lord Easby had become known to her, his disinterested manner had seemed so genuine that tittle-tattle was ignored. However, over the weeks it had become clear that it was not all tittle-tattle, and there was a dark past to his lordship. Helen Godmanchester disliked him intensely. Having agreed to let him teach her to drive, Elizabeth was reluctant to admit her mistake, and continued out of bravado, and with the knowledge that she would not be taken in. Had she not thought dropping him now would give rise to more gossip as to the reason, she would have quietly given up driving with him. She was frowning.

'Miss Ashling, I did not seek to distress or frighten you.

Being aware of the danger, if you will accept the term, you are far less at risk.'

'And bad driving habits, Sir Lucius?' She fought to control the rising blush. 'If I learn any, perhaps you would permit me to drive you one day, and you could show me my failings.'

For a moment he could not answer. It was more than just an olive branch.

'You would accept correction, from a friend?'

'Yes, Sir Lucius, from a friend I would.' Instinctively, she held out her kid-gloved hand and he took it in his larger grasp, quite solemnly, as if a pact were being made.

They rode back to Brook Street with little said, each contemplating the crossing of an invisible barrier that had lain between them. He escorted her to her uncle's door, bent over her hand, and walked away with a spring in his step that several friends who encountered him put down to good news from his head groom at Paley.

Elizabeth hurried upstairs, not wanting to speak with anyone. She had committed herself so much more than she had ever thought possible. It would be wrong to say she regretted it, but it made her feel quite odd inside, like contemplating riding a new horse, excited but also just a little nervous. She rang for Ditcham, and removed the grey hat with its jaunty cockade.

Ditcham found her mistress quiet, but there was a smile playing about the corners of her mouth, and the fretfulness of the previous night was gone. Whatever the cause, the maid gave silent thanks for it.

* * *

Sir Lucius gave the footman who opened his door a cheery thanks, and also went to change his raiment. She had offered him her friendship, offered it, not had it wrung from her, and the look she had given him, the shy trust, made him hope as never before. From friendship and trust he could show her affection, have her accept the love he felt for her. The impossible now seemed the attainable, as long as he did not rush headlong. He was conscious of a feeling of exultation, one that even the knowledge that she was to go driving with Easby on the morrow could not diminish. The thought that he might ride a little later himself, and thereby, perhaps, encounter teacher and pupil, made him smile. That smile would have died had he access to Lord Easby's intentions.

CHAPTER SIXTEEN

Mindful of Sir Lucius's warning, it was a slightly frosty Miss Ashling who was handed up into Lord Easby's equipage next morning. She sat very upright, and though her answers were perfectly civil, her body language was uncompromising. Lord Easby took note. So Radstock had warned her, had he? Well, he was sure that he could thaw the icy Miss Ashling in the course of an hour tooling the pair about the park, and if the best Radstock could offer her were frowns and admonitions, he would find her most unlikely to accept any offer he should make her. That Radstock would propose, Lord Easby now had no doubt. It forced his hand somewhat, and meant that he had to abandon his previous disinterest rather suddenly. He decided to face one issue, at least, squarely.

'You are stiff this morning, Miss Ashling, and it shows in your hands. I must assume either that something has occurred to make you displeased with the day, or that the watchful Sir Lucius has indeed persuaded you that I am a dangerous fellow. Well, I told you on our first outing that I was accounted a Bad Man, so I see no good reason why the growling mastiff should have made such a difference.'

Like it or not, the description of Sir Lucius as a growling dog was rather amusing. A muscle twitched at the side of her mouth, though she kept her eyes gazing firmly between her leader's ears. Lord Easby relaxed. One only had to apply warmth and ice melted.

'Sir Lucius is a worthy man,' he declared, making 'worthy' sound a damning fault, 'but he can be tempted to interfere where he has neither the right to do so, nor the information to make a sound judgement, and he is terribly judgemental.' He drew a bow at a venture, and continued. 'I have no doubt he has told you I am cow-handed as a whip, and that you risk ending up turfed into the greensward.'

'Not quite, my lord. He actually said that the latter was most unlikely.'

'How surprisingly generous of him,' sneered Lord Easby.

'Do you find worthiness and generosity so dull, sir?'

'My dear, what a question. Would you prefer a polite lie, or the wicked truth?'

If he hoped to shock her, she had already decided he would find it difficult.

'I am not afraid of truth, my lord, be it never so wicked.'

He smiled, in a lupine way. Not meek and mousy was the Unassailable. Perhaps he had approached her the wrong way in the past, and she might actually respond positively to a more daring attitude.

'Then I make so bold as to tell you, ma'am, that vice is so very much more entertaining than virtue.'

'But more harmful.'

'To one's self, oh, perhaps, but worth it for the excitement.'

'I was thinking it more harmful to others.'

'Oh, but I rarely think of others, Miss Ashling.'

'That is not particularly edifying.'

'Ah, but I said "rarely", ma'am. For you, I make an exception.'

'Do you know, my lord, I fail to find that edifying either.'

'Touché, Miss Ashling.' He laughed, but was stung. So the cat had claws, had she? 'Are you so very nice in your requirements, ma'am?'

'My requirements?'

'Why yes. Not for nothing are you termed "the Unassailable". Many the man has turned back at the flash of your eyes, the haughty upturn of your rather beautiful nose, the disdainful curl of your equally delightful lips.'

Elizabeth coloured. 'We are not alone, sir, and those comments are not seemly.'

'No, alas we are not alone, ma'am, but I only employ the most discreet of servants. Being a Bad Man, I find it prudent. Lambton is very deaf, when asked to be so. And as for "seemly", why, I thought you said you were not afraid of truth.'

Her cheeks grew even more red. She now realised her predicament. Her hands were full with reins and whip, and making a scene in public almost unthinkable.

'So you see, I am compelled to assume that your requirements in a man are very precise. Clearly looks are not everything, since Templecombe is quite an Adonis, but remarkably boring. So a degree of wit is on the list, which really ought to discount the worthy Sir Lucius, who is merely dry.'

'Stop this,' Elizabeth commanded sharply.

'Why, my dear? You see, I simply think that you have not had that additional element to make a man deserving of you. I am not as handsome as Templecombe, not as worthy as Radstock, but I do have a certain dangerous quality that adds intrigue. Women so like a mystery, and I can be very mysterious.'

He slid a hand beneath the light driving rug and set it just above her knee. She jumped, which made him laugh. It was more than he had intended to do, but he had thrown caution to the winds, for this conquest had become more important to him as Radstock had become a greater threat. He did not wish to be bested by either him or the lady.

'How dare you, sir. Remove your hand this instant.'

'What will you do, my dear? Scream? I think not. So public a place, even if at this moment there is nobody close enough to—'

He did not finish, for she struck him in the face with the butt of the whip and dropped her hands. The pair broke into a canter, and Lord Easby, his lip split and bleeding, had to grip on to prevent himself being thrown back off the seat. Unconsciously, his hand gripped her leg more tightly, though it was for balance rather than from passion. Elizabeth had not handled the pair at speed, and had to concentrate as they took a corner, which was thankfully a comparatively gentle curve. It was at this point that she saw Sir Lucius trotting towards them. She began to pull up, more practically than with style, the horses agitated.

She was flustered, Easby had blood on his lip and his hand was still hidden beneath the rug. Sir Lucius had all the information he needed in a single glance. He rode calmly alongside the box, raised his hat politely to Miss Ashling, replaced it, and then, out of the blue, grabbed Lord Easby and pulled him off to fall and roll through the dust and into the grass.

Instructing the groom, curtly, to hold his horse, he dismounted, removed his hat and gloves, and dragged the dishevelled Earl up from his knees.

'Miss Ashling has an aversion to duelling, so I will not call you out, Easby, but I will do what I have longed to do and you deserve.'

With which, having taken the trouble to haul Easby to his feet, he promptly knocked him down. Dazed, Easby lay still for a moment, then shook his head to clear it, and looked up into the belligerent face.

'Oh, take a damper, Radstock,' he muttered thickly, a bleeding nose now added to his injuries. 'It is hardly abduction.'

Sir Lucius looked undecided as to whether he would like to repeat his performance, or just kill the man. Elizabeth, calling the groom to stand to the horses' heads and let her take Sir Lucius's mount, clambered down from the vehicle.

'Enough.' She laid a hand upon Sir Lucius's arm and looked up at him.

'I apologise, Miss Ashling. This was hardly suitable for a lady's eyes, but—'

'I appreciate your concern, your intervention even, sir, but I beg of you to go no further. I think Lord Easby has been made perfectly aware of my . . . disinclination to receive his advances in any form.'

'To take advantage, under the pretext of—' Sir Lucius began, frowning, but was interrupted by the unwanted suitor.

'Yes, yes, Radstock, go on, by all means, and enumerate my ungentlemanly failings if you must, but do so after I have had the opportunity to depart, bloodied and conceding the error of my judgement.' He looked to Miss Ashling as he fumbled for a handkerchief. 'My profound apologies, ma'am. I can only say that I permitted my inclinations to get the better of good breeding. I accept that my behaviour was unpardonable, yet crave your pardon nonetheless, and your permission to withdraw.'

Miss Ashling, feeling somewhat overcome by events, nodded dumbly, and Lord Easby staggered to his feet, sketched an approximation of a bow, and commanded Lambton, in a testy tone, to drive him home.

'Sir Lucius, yet again you have thought fit to rescue me from a situation from which I had hoped to extricate myself unaided.' Elizabeth's words admonished, but the tone was one of gratitude.

'His behaviour was unpardonable.'

'Indeed, I do not deny I was shocked by it, but the horses were not likely to bolt, and I still had the whip, should I have needed to use it again.'

'Again? So that is how he got the split lip,' murmured Sir Lucius appreciatively, rubbing his grazed knuckles.

Elizabeth saw the action, and put out a hand in sudden concern.

'Your hand! Oh dear!' She seemed about to take it in her own, but pulled back at the last moment, as the tip of her gloved fingers touched the skin.

'It is nothing, I can assure you, ma'am. Of no importance.' He paused. 'I have no doubt Lord Easby will prefer this episode to remain private, and there were no bystanders, but we are faced with a predicament, Miss Ashling, since I cannot offer you my horse without drawing attention, and circumstance forces us to walk unattended.'

'I thank you for your concern, but think perhaps a version of the truth might suffice, Sir Lucius. If we should meet anyone we say that Lord Easby's carriage suffered an accident, and it was impossible for him to escort me home.' She saw his scepticism. 'I know it is not perfect, but as long as we are not observed by anyone of Lady Rendlesham's imaginative curiosity, it may serve.'

She then bent to retrieve his hat and gloves, and handed them to him, with the reins of his horse. He thanked her, and offered his arm, which she blushingly declined. They set off at a strong walking pace, certainly not that of a couple enjoying a clandestine meeting. The park was not busy, for which both were thankful, and by chance the first carriage they encountered contained the Misses Bosworth, who were friends of Amelia, and their sister-in-law, Lady Ackford, who exclaimed at seeing Miss Ashling on foot, and accepted the reason without giving it any great scrutiny. They immediately offered her a place in the landau, and Sir Lucius handed her up into it. She attempted to thank him without revealing the nature of the service that he had rendered her. In other circumstances, he would have been highly appreciative of her confusion, but contented himself with an almost imperceptible squeeze of her fingers before he let them go, and a promise to present himself in Mount Street in the near future, to ascertain that she had sustained no lasting upset. He bowed, mounted and trotted away, and Elizabeth resolutely kept herself from watching his receding figure.

The young ladies were eager to find out details of the accident, and Elizabeth invented a broken trace and a lamed horse. Thankfully, none of them enquired why Lord Easby had given the escorting of her home to Sir Lucius Radstock, and Elizabeth made much of requesting that they did not spread the tale to spare poor Lord Easby further embarrassment over an incident that, she said, with truth, had caused him acute discomfort.

Her being set down in Mount Street in a different vehicle from that in which she had departed was bound to cause a stir, but was unavoidable. Lady Chalford had happened to be looking out of the window, and complaining at the raucous cry of a chair mender, when the landau drew up, and Elizabeth was handed down from it. She went out onto the landing to intercept her niece as she came upstairs, and instantly observed her serious face.

'Elizabeth! What has happened? Was that Lady Ackford's carriage I saw you in?'

Elizabeth smiled weakly, overcome by a lassitude that owed everything to the strain of the last hour. 'Yes, Aunt, it was. Do but let me change my dress and I will give you explanation.'

Her aunt frowned, but nodded. 'And I shall call for tea. I will be in the morning room.'

She had, perforce, to wait some twenty minutes before Elizabeth, tidily attired and with her hair rearranged after being crushed by her hat, stepped into the morning room. She had had a little time to compose herself and decide just how much of the tale she would relate. Honesty might be admirable, but the incident was over, and no good would come of agitating her aunt. She therefore told her that Lord Easby had attempted to show off a piece of rather fancy driving and that in consequence, the vehicle had come to grief, and Lord Easby sustained a very minor, but bloody injury. She herself, she assured her aunt, was unhurt, and merely rather shaken. Lady Ackford had been so kind as to take her up. She would have preferred to keep Sir Lucius's name out of the tale entirely, but if he was going to pay a call, that might be awkward. She therefore acknowledged that he had 'seen' the occurrence and waited with her until a vehicle had approached in which she might be conveyed home. If Lady Chalford found this in any way significant, she wisely refrained from comment, but concentrated instead upon Lord Easby's failings.

'How foolish of him, and how wrong to offer himself to teach you to drive when he is not competent. You know, my dear, that I never liked you going driving with him. I doubt his motives, truly I do.'

'You need have no fears on that score, Aunt, for I shall most certainly not go driving with him again. It was a most unpleasant experience, and one that I have no desire to repeat, be he never so apologetic.'

'I think that very wise, Elizabeth, very wise. There is something I cannot like about the man.'

Elizabeth could have given a long and detailed list of 'somethings' but did not. And she had been fool enough to imagine him a disinterested acquaintance from whom she had nothing to fear. The perfidious male of the species! If her heart omitted Sir Lucius from the generic condemnation, her head tried to ignore it. She told herself that she would have simply driven to the point nearest to Mount Street, halted the horses and dismounted, to stalk off in high dudgeon. That she had given the swine a swollen lip pleased her, but there was, she had to admit, something particularly uplifting in seeing Sir Lucius knock him to the ground, however much, as a lady, she should have thought it repellent. She was, naturally, not conversant with the pugilistic art, and could not comment upon Sir Lucius's 'science', but thought he had made it look very easy. His poor hand, though, how that must have stung.

Sir Lucius's grazed and slightly swollen knuckles were unimportant to him, at least until he tried to retie his neckcloth and found them stiff. He regretted, in part, that Miss Ashling had been present when he had taken retribution upon Lord Easby, but the look of concern on her face when she saw his hand was surely not indicative of any anger towards him, even though she had restrained his desire to beat the offending Earl to within an inch of his life, which was wise if unpalatable. Her expression had been all concern; she had surely nearly taken the injured hand in hers in a gesture of compassion. They had parted too publicly, and his decision to visit Mount Street had been taken in the moment. Upon reflection, he could see that there might be an awkwardness if he simply sought admission to see that all was well. Miss Ashling might not have chosen to reveal everything that had taken place in Hyde Park to her relatives, and his blithely asking questions in front of Lady Chalford might create untold difficulties for which Miss Ashling would most certainly place the blame upon him.

He sat for some while considering the problem. What he needed was another excuse to gain admission, one that would arouse no suspicion. Unfortunately, he had no close association with the Chalfords that would make that a simple matter.

The clock upon the mantelshelf chimed the half hour, and he recalled with a start that he was engaged with Giles Godmanchester for luncheon. He set his concerns temporarily to one side and headed off to Brook Street. Lady Godmanchester did not join the two gentlemen, feeling, as her lord described it, 'rather fragile today', so they ate alone, companionably, though Lord Godmanchester had several times to repeat remarks before receiving a response. He noticed the right hand also, but did not say anything. At the end of the meal they adjourned to the billiard room for a quiet game, and there, amid the clink of ivory upon ivory, Sir Lucius unburdened himself to his best friend.

'Good God, what a commoner Easby is, to be sure. And he actually had a hand laid upon her?'

'Almost certainly. She had clearly delivered a very neat

blow, with the butt of the whip as it turned out, and you may be sure she would not have taken such violent action without extreme provocation. That she had set the horses to a pace she was not yet fully competent to handle says much also. I tell you, it was as much as I could do not to strangle the life out of him for frightening her so.'

'Well, I am sure he will lick his wounds in private, and emerge to seek entertainment elsewhere. Personally, I cannot see what it is about him that attracts the fair sex.' Lord Godmanchester paused. 'Do you think it possible that Miss Ashling, er, was in any danger of being taken in by him?'

'No, certainly not. Well, certainly not this morning for I . . . we . . . had discussed him and his driving lessons but yesterday, and I would swear that Miss Ashling had no thought but to keep him at arm's length.'

'Which might have been the spur that set him off?'

'Oh, I do not know, Giles, I really do not. The thing is, I handed Miss Ashling over to Ackford's wife and sisters, pretending all was very normal of course, but promised to look in at Mount Street to see she was none the worse for the misadventure, for she did look quite shaken. The deuce of it is, I cannot go barging in and revealing all, and cannot think of a reason to call upon Lady Chalford and the young ladies.'

Lord Godmanchester paused, cue in hand, and rubbed his chin. Suddenly, he smiled. 'My friend, I have just the thing. What happens next week?'

'Next week?'

'Yes. Goodness, Lucius, your brains must be addled

by this. The Derby meeting. Say you are getting a party together. Helen and I will expect invitations, of course. It won't be considered in the least havey-cavey.'

'Giles, you are a genius.'

CHAPTER SEVENTEEN

However much Sir Lucius might have wanted to visit Mount Street that very afternoon, he controlled his natural inclinations. It was thus the following afternoon when he handed his card to Ribston, with a request to see Lady Chalford and the young ladies, should they be at home. The response, had he been privileged to see it, would have both amused him and given him cause for hope. When Ribston presented the card for her ladyship's perusal, Lady Chalford read out the name and smiled enigmatically, Miss Amelia gave an involuntary squeak and dropped her copy of *Moral Tales* over which she had been yawning, and Miss Elizabeth ran her embroidery needle into her finger, and was heard mumbling agitatedly whilst sucking the injured digit.

When Sir Lucius was announced and entered the room, all signs of these actions were gone. Lady Chalford rose regally to greet him, and the young ladies set aside their respective activities with cool deliberation and made their curtseys. Only the tinge of colour in Elizabeth's cheeks betrayed her internal agitation. The one glance she gave Sir Lucius, as he bowed to her, was of warning.

'I am come to enquire after Miss Ashling after yesterday's "mishap", though I can see that she looks very well.' He gave her the ghost of a smile as he was invited to take a seat. 'But also to ask whether you might consider joining a party I am putting together for Derby day next week.' He paused as Lady Chalford blinked in surprise, and played his masterstroke. He was well aware that neither Lady Chalford nor her daughter were interested in horses so he had to make the day appeal to them as a social event. 'The Godmanchesters are engaged to come and Lady Micheldever and her daughter, Miss Wingate, and both Lord Nuneaton and Lord Carbrooke hope to join us.'

Sir Lucius knew a moment of panic. If Lady Chalford declared they were otherwise engaged, he had spent the last twenty-four hours scrambling around to make up a party of persons, excepting the Godmanchesters, whom he barely knew. The potential for a disaster hung in the air. Elizabeth looked unashamedly delighted at the prospect, but her approbation was not what counted.

Lady Chalford had her own idea why Sir Lucius had bothered to put together a party, and understood far more than Sir Lucius might either suspect or wish, and was happy to promote his cause. Whilst she foresaw a day of limited interest to herself and Amelia, she applauded the way in which Sir Lucius had hit upon just the thing to cast Elizabeth into transports. That he had thereafter gone to the trouble to invite persons that she and Amelia would be happy to spend a long day with showed both his intelligence, and the lengths to which he would go. He had even invited Lord Nuneaton, and she would have given her new hat to see the look on his lordship's face when approached, since she doubted very much that Lord Nuneaton and Sir Lucius had exchanged more than common civilities until now.

'That is a very generous offer, Sir Lucius.' She waited, enjoying the moment. 'I believe we are not engaged upon that day, and it would be a high treat for the girls. Assuming the weather is not terribly inclement, we will be delighted to come. Do but tell us the hour by which we must be ready.'

Details were given, and Amelia and Elizabeth added their thanks. Sir Lucius, fighting the urge to gaze only at Elizabeth, addressed Amelia, recommending she bring some pin money so that the gentlemen might place small bets on her behalf.

'Oh, but I will need guidance, I am sure. One horse looks much like another to me. It is Elizabeth who will make educated choices, based upon their grandmother winning something in Yorkshire, or whether the turf is too bouncy for them.'

Elizabeth smiled and shook her head. It gave Sir Lucius the opportunity to look directly at her, and for a moment he thought the smile in her eyes deepened, though whether it was from more than gratitude for the promise of a day out, and his circumspection over the incident in the park, he was unable to judge.

'I will be interested to hear your selections, ma'am.'

'Oh dear, I fear my cousin has given you a false idea of me, Sir Lucius. I am not some Delphic oracle of the Turf.'

She did not look very perturbed, but blushed delicately.

'I will limit myself, therefore, to hoping you are not a Cassandra, who will tell me that every horse I have backed is doomed to be boxed in on the final turn, or stumble at the vital moment.'

'Ah, to do that, sir, would be both pointless, since the bet would already be laid, and ungracious, since we owe you so much,' and she gave a slight stress to the phrase before adding, 'for arranging the expedition.'

She could not thank him openly for his services the day before, and hoped he understood her covert gratitude; she thought that he did. The constrictions upon them, which she would until so recently have welcomed, now chafed as fetters.

'I assure you, Miss Ashling, no thanks are needed.'

Amelia frowned slightly, hearing yet not understanding the subtext. Her mama, with years of experience, made a decision, and when, after a few minutes of polite but non-committal conversation, Sir Lucius rose to take his leave, she waited until he had just left the room and then exclaimed, 'Oh no!'

'Mama?'

'I forgot to tell Sir Lucius that we must definitely be home before eight in the evening. Elizabeth, my dear, do go after him and make sure he knows.'

Elizabeth got up and hurried to detain Sir Lucius as he went downstairs. He turned at her voice, looking up at her, his expression surprised but pleased.

'My aunt says that I must tell you that we have to be back by eight in the evening, Sir Lucius.'

'Oh yes, that will be no problem.'

Elizabeth was now at his side, and dropped her voice. 'I could not say, could not tell you how truly grateful . . .'

'Please, Miss Ashling. As I said, no thanks are necessary. I am only sorry that you were exposed to upset.'

'And your hand, sir?'

He held it for her inspection. The swelling had largely disappeared, but there were still red grazes. She reached out to touch it with her fingers.

'You see, nothing of note.'

'It looks sore to me, Sir Lucius.'

He could not say he did not care how sore it was if it meant the touch of her hand. They stood for a moment, then the spell broke and she pulled back her hand as if scalded.

'You should put salve upon it, you know.' She tried to sound practical and matter-of-fact.

'I will bear that in mind, ma'am,' he answered, as formally, hearing the butler's approaching tread in the hallway.

They continued down the stairs, at the bottom of which Sir Lucius made his bow, and was shown out by Ribston, who concealed his interest admirably. Elizabeth returned upstairs, and informed her aunt of the successful delivery of the message before seating herself once more with her embroidery. Lady Chalford noticed, with satisfaction, that she actually did not set many stitches, and that she frequently had difficulty in controlling the urge to smile.

It was only an hour later when Lady Godmanchester paid a call, and she too noticed a change in Elizabeth. Lady

Chalford, aware that confidences were best exchanged in private, absented herself after the first few minutes under the pretext of a slight headache, and sent Amelia for her hartshorn. Left alone, Helen Godmanchester raised an eyebrow.

'Well?'

'Well what?'

'No, do not pretend with me, Elizabeth. Godmanchester was irritatingly cryptic yesterday evening, but I gather Lord Easby was in some manner offensive, and that Sir Lucius possesses a sore fist. Now am I, or am I not, your best friend?'

'You are, Helen.'

'Then tell me everything, from the beginning.'

Elizabeth did, diffidently at first, fearing her friend might say 'I told you so', but Helen Godmanchester was a true friend and did not. Gradually, she forgot herself and let out the emotions she had pent up in her family's presence: the outrage, the anger, fear and then relief, when matters were taken into Sir Lucius's capable hands.

'I know that I would not have come to serious harm, Helen, because, after all, we were in Hyde Park, and he could not have made off with me. But his behaviour; it was repellent. To take advantage of a lady in such a way! I am sorry if I sound heated but . . .'

'No, no, I quite understand. How awful for you.'

'At least I took some action in my own defence. His lip bled quite profusely when I hit him with the butt of the whip.'

'Brava!' Lady Godmanchester actually clapped her hands.

'Helen!'

'I think it admirable, oh I do.'

'Well, it was not as effective as Sir Lucius's knocking him to the ground. I actually thought for a moment that he might take him by the throat and shake him as a terrier does a rat.'

'That would have been appropriate, if nothing else,' remarked her ladyship unsympathetically. 'Ghastly man.'

'I . . . Sir Lucius . . .'

'You like him, do you not?'

'Lord Easby? Why of course not!'

'No, ninny, Sir Lucius.'

Elizabeth looked at her hands, which were working in the fringe of her shawl and frowned, though her mouth twisted in a smile. 'I should not, I know.'

'Why "should not", Elizabeth?' Lady Godmanchester looked puzzled and perturbed. 'Surely you know nothing to Sir Lucius's detriment? I am sure I have never heard anything other than good things about him as a man.'

'But that is the nub of it, Helen. He is a man.'

'Er, yes, obviously.' The confusion was more pronounced.

'In the end, men let you down. You let yourself love them and they desert you.' Elizabeth looked at her friend sorrowfully. 'I am sorry. I know you will not understand. You have been so very fortunate.'

'You mean like Henry Freshford? But surely you can see Sir Lucius is not at all like him? And your heart cannot still be broken over that.'

'Oh no, he is not, and my heart is not.' She paused. 'I thought it might be, but it was but the memory of pain and disillusionment.' She sighed. 'I do like Sir Lucius. I tried so hard not to.'

'My dear friend' – Helen Godmanchester laid a hand upon her arm – 'you said you "let" yourself love, but love is not something that requires permission. It happens, or it does not. You cannot make yourself love someone for whom you feel nothing, nor feel nothing for someone whom you love. Oh dear, that sounds terribly profound, but it is true.'

'No.' Elizabeth shook her head. 'It is true for you, Helen.'

'It is true for you also.'

'But I will end up hurt again, if I give in to it. History proves it so. Papa, then Henry.'

Lady Godmanchester felt tears prick her eyes. 'Oh Elizabeth, I am so sorry, I never thought . . . Your father . . . of course.' She squeezed Elizabeth's arm. 'But you must not let the past determine your future. Sir Lucius, I am convinced, entertains the most honourable and tender of feelings for you.'

'I have wondered. He . . . Helen, sometimes I think he does, and yet . . .'

'I am not sure a man who was not interested would have been so bellicose, my dear. Mr Escott, for instance . . .'

'Oh, Mr Escott has clearly found his "goddess" is but a graven image. He wrote me a most confused letter and then I saw him in the street but a few days since and he barely even acknowledged my presence. It is a matter of extreme relief to me.' Elizabeth smiled wryly.

For a moment, Lady Godmanchester was distracted. 'Truly? Well, how fickle of him. He would have written a ballad about you, had you been his muse still, rather than acting on your behalf.' She shook her head. 'So much for poetry.'

'Indeed.'

'But Sir Lucius is no poet.'

'Oh no, he is not.' Elizabeth smiled more broadly, remembering him pulling Lord Easby from the box.

'He is not a man who will betray you, I am sure of it. Think about that.'

'I will,' she sighed.

Elizabeth had little time over the next few days in which to give serious consideration to her feelings for Sir Lucius, climbing into her bed so late that his presence was solely in her dreams. She hoped to catch sight of him in every crowded room, but failed to do so, and was dimly aware of feeling vulnerable without knowing quite why. She certainly did not fear the reappearance of the Earl of Easby. That gentleman kept within doors until such time as the injuries to his face were not so visible as to cause comment, and when he did, he betrayed neither by word nor look that anything untoward had occurred between himself and Miss Ashling.

He wrote her a letter of apology, profuse in its self-blame, and hoped that she would at least read it. Whilst he was not confident that it would restore his position with her, he did think it would prevent her giving him the cut direct, and thereby fuelling just the close scrutiny he wished to avoid. He was in luck. Elizabeth's every instinct was to tear the letter into pieces as soon as she saw the author, but there was an element of curiosity. How could a man who had betrayed himself as so base find any words that might exculpate him?

It seemed Lord Easby was not even going to try. He accepted his fault, and her right to outrage. He did not throw himself upon her mercy, for he was a man of pride still. Instead, he made it plain to her that to treat him as she might wish would be detrimental to her own position and good name, since prying would undoubtedly discover the truth of what had passed in the park. However blameless, he was terribly afraid that scandal would be attached to her fair name, and the less generous would condemn her for placing herself in such a vulnerable position. His own character, he said, was sunk so low in the estimation of many that it mattered not, but he felt this last service he might perform for her 'in friendship and humility'.

She scoffed at his words, but reluctantly saw the sense of them. She so wanted to denounce him, though at least he had never sought to seduce innocents in their first Season, and would no doubt revert to 'playing' with bored wives and dashing widows, but she realised that she must appear at ease with him, as if he were as unthreatening as he had seemed before. She schooled herself so that when they did meet she was able to smile, however falsely, and even offer him a country dance, during which they discussed nothing more alarming than the violins being a fraction flat in tone. Having performed this 'duty', she relaxed.

Sir Lucius himself was out of Town, ostensibly simply paying a visit of a couple of days to his mother and to his brood mares. In the comparative peace of Paley, he came to his decision – not that it was a hard one to make in itself, but he had told Miss Ashling that he was not about to propose only a few days since, and here he was contemplating just that. The incident with Easby had advanced matters faster than he had thought possible. Her subsequent reaction led him to believe that her own feelings were engaged, and that she would not reject him out of hand, at the very least. The Derby outing would prove too public for any declaration, and he thought that if she enjoyed herself as much as he hoped she would, then the following day might be a propitious time to make her an offer. She was technically now of age, but out of courtesy Sir Lucius felt he ought to approach Lord Chalford and ask his permission to pay his addresses. It was exceedingly unlikely that Chalford would have any objections whatsoever, and indeed Lady Chalford was more likely to fall upon his neck in relief.

He broached the matter with his mother in initially general terms, announcing, as they sat together after dinner, that he thought it about time that he settled down.

'Settled down? Lucius, you scarcely live a life of idle dissipation. I take it that you mean you have at last found a young woman who fulfils those requirements that you must have held in your mind these five years since.'

'I would not phrase it quite like that, Mama, but I have certainly discovered a woman without whom I am increasingly sure my life would be incomplete. I think you will like her too.'

'If she makes you happy, I see no reason why I should not. Do I know of her?'

'That may depend upon the depth of detail you receive from your sources in Town. Her name is Miss Ashling.'

'Not Chalford's chit, surely. Just out the schoolroom, and hardly your style, I would have thought.'

'You are up to snuff, Mama! But no, not Miss Amelia. I have an eye to her cousin, Miss Elizabeth Ashling, who is a few years her senior.'

'The one they are calling "the Unassailable"?'

He coloured. 'Unfortunately, yes.'

'And is she?'

'No. I believe not, but she has her reasons not to trust men, and persuading her of one's bona fides has not been easy. However, I think that her feelings are engaged, and intend to make an offer for her hand next week.'

'Not immediately upon your return? That sounds very restrained, Lucius.'

'I think she might be in the best frame of mind then.' He grinned. 'She is a fine horsewoman and I have planned an outing to the Derby, which I think will please her greatly. In the aftermath, I think my chances very good.'

'Then I wish you well, and look forward to meeting her. Horses! I should have guessed!' She smiled at her son.

CHAPTER EIGHTEEN

Whilst Lady Chalford viewed the expedition as a social opportunity, and Amelia secretly looked forward to viewing Lord Carbrooke far more than any colt in the paddock, Elizabeth found herself genuinely excited at the prospect of the day for its own sake. It was the first event of the Season that had her hastening Ditcham to complete those finishing touches without which that redoubtable individual would have felt her mistress unfit to be seen abroad.

Elizabeth had surprised her maid by selecting an ensemble that, for once, was not designed to make her fade into the background. Her gown was a pale old gold, with several flounces about the hem, worn with a claret-coloured spencer, which showed off her colouring to perfection, and a hat with broad ribbons tied in a jaunty bow beneath her left ear. The dress had not been worn for several Seasons, but Elizabeth merrily declared that any lingering odour of lavender bags would be blown away by the breeze upon Epsom Downs.

'Should you be taking a shawl, miss, in case of it being too cold?'

'Oh no, Ditcham, I will be sure to trail the ends in the dust the moment I get involved with the racing, and the weather looks ideal, neither too cold nor too hot.'

'Indeed, miss, though I would suggest you take a parasol to protect your face from any glare.'

'Oh.' Elizabeth giggled. 'And there was me thinking in terms of it making it less likely for the horses to sweat up.'

'"Sweat up"! Now, miss, don't you go talking stable talk in front of everyone, I beg of you.' Ditcham shook her head, and pursed her lips, but knew she might as well hold her breath. If anything was going to animate her mistress, it was horses, and she would forget the ladylike veil of mild disinterest in seconds. She only hoped she did not bounce up and down with hoydenish excitement in the final furlong.

It was Elizabeth who was ready first, and inclined to look down from the drawing-room window for the first sign of Sir Lucius's carriage party. Her only disappointment was seeing Lord Godmanchester, seated beside Sir Lucius in his phaeton, but no sign of Lady Godmanchester. This was explained by his lordship, when he made his bow to Lady Chalford and offered her his hand to assist her into the barouche.

'I regret, ma'am, that my wife has to send her apologies. She finds herself a trifle indisposed this morning, and could not face the long drive or exertion, but she begs me to tell you to avail yourself of her barouche, that her absence must not be a cause for concern, and bids me pass this note to Miss Ashling.' With which he drew a letter from within his coat and handed it, smiling, to Elizabeth. 'She would not have you enjoy your day the less, I promise, but it can wait until we are upon our way, for I doubt Lucius wishes to keep the horses waiting.'

'Indeed not. Thank you, my lord.'

At that moment Sir Lucius himself made his bow. He had been in some discussion with Lady Micheldever over the seating within the two carriages, since he had utilised the barouche that rarely left his stables unless his mother was in Town.

'Lady Chalford, ladies, your servant. I was wondering if Miss Amelia would care to travel to Epsom with Lady Micheldever and Miss Wingate, and Lord Nuneaton, and Lord Carbrooke could travel in this barouche with you and Miss Ashling? Then, upon the return, we could mix the parties up once more, since it is quite a drive, and conversing merely with those whom one spends much of the time would be less entertaining.'

This idea found instant favour with Lady Chalford, although Amelia was clearly disappointed. She cast a glance at Lord Carbrooke, who was being given advice upon some subject or other by Lord Nuneaton himself. They stood together, and the comparison did Lord Nuneaton no favours. He was half a head shorter than the youthful Viscount, and his features were showing the first signs of becoming fleshy, although he was certainly not corpulent, and Lady Chalford looked upon him as a perfectly good figure of a man. Lady Chalford was, however, nearer forty-five than forty, not seventeen. Only the thought that she might yet spend the return journey in the more appealing company enabled Amelia to smile sweetly, and acquiesce without complaint.

Whilst the seating arrangements of the carriages were put into effect, Sir Lucius took the opportunity of exchanging a few words with Elizabeth. He had never seen her look so enchanting, but wisely forbore telling her so. Instead, he smiled down at her and asked if she had been teaching her young cousin what to look out for in a likely winner.

'Amelia?' She laughed softly. 'I fear I would be wasting my breath if I did, Sir Lucius. Amelia will pick the horse with the prettiest features or the most entertaining name.' Elizabeth's tone was confidential, her normal aloofness entirely forgotten. 'And my aunt will make her decision upon how well she knows, likes or dislikes the owners.'

'Remind me, then, to let Nuneaton or Carbrooke lay any bets upon their behalf, for fear I should lose all my credibility.'

Their eyes met, they understood each other, and a small, secret bond seemed forged between them. He handed her up into the carriage, still with the smile upon his lips, and only Lord Godmanchester calling him away broke the spell. Elizabeth was conscious of feeling bizarrely happy, which she resolutely put down purely to the excitement of a day at the races, despite the whisper in her heart that murmured that Sir Lucius himself had quite a lot to do with it.

The journey itself was entertaining, at least for Elizabeth. First of all she read the note from her friend.

Dearest Elizabeth,

Such a feeble creature as I am, I fear that this morning the contemplation of a long carriage ride to Epsom and back is too much for my disordered constitution. I send my beloved lord to act for both of us and enjoy what promises to be an exciting day. I beg you, do not think of me laid upon my sofa, ailing! Seriously, I do hope Godmanchester has his mind taken from my 'ailment', because his worry is actually worrying ME.

I am sorry I cannot be with you, but I am sure you will have a lovely day, and I do hope you return positively weighed down with your winnings. If you do, you may purchase a yard of that lace trimming we saw and I considered for a baby gown.

Your Affectionate Friend,
Helen

She noted, with approval, how Lord Carbrooke did not let his eyes forever stray to the following carriage, and how his manner towards Lady Chalford was pitched to a nicety, being both respectful and charming. With Elizabeth, he let his guard drop very slightly, and there was a twinkle in his eye that she thought quite infectious. He was enjoyable company, and Elizabeth began to see just what attracted Amelia, with her own optimistic nature, to him. For her own part, Elizabeth only once looked past the coachman upon the box and regarded the two gentlemen in the phaeton. Sir Lucius generally kept his eyes upon the road, but at that moment his face was turned towards his friend and he was laughing. Elizabeth chastised herself for wishing she might also know the jest. For all she knew it might be something entirely unsuited to a lady's ears, and yet there was that kernel of curiosity.

They arrived in good time, though there were already a good number of people and vehicles seeking good positions. Before the racing commenced, Sir Lucius regaled his guests with champagne and delicacies from a hamper that he had brought in the phaeton. He then established that, after a brief promenade to indicate their presence, Lady Chalford and Lady Micheldever would prefer to watch events from the barouche, or more accurately, spend the afternoon in exchanging gossip and the latest *on dits*. He shepherded his party to the ring and watched as Nuneaton, as he later commented to Lord Godmanchester, 'made a cake of himself', and tried to explain the finer points of a winning racehorse to Amelia Ashling, whilst selecting an animal as an example that was surely cow-hocked. He saw Elizabeth Ashling bite her lip, and at that moment turn, so that their eyes met. Hers were full of unholy amusement. He had seen her transformed from an elegant icicle in the ballroom into an intelligent and vibrant young woman when upon a horse, but never had he before seen her so plainly and simply happy. He realised that whether his selections won or lost, whether the races were tightly fought classics or disappointing five-length romps, today was a success because he had made Elizabeth Ashling happy. Hard upon that thought came the one that said that wanting to make her happy every day had become his sole aim in his life. It took him rather unawares, though he knew that it had been lingering, unacknowledged until now.

Lord Nuneaton was now trying to inform Elizabeth Ashling's decision, and she was politely refusing his advice.

'I think, Amelia, that I would prefer to place my shillings upon the bay, Pedagogue.' Elizabeth avoided responding directly to Lord Nuneaton. 'His dam is Teacher's Pet, it says in the race card, and so he ought to be a good stayer.'

Lord Nuneaton appeared vaguely shocked.

Lady Chalford grimaced, and laughed, rather mirthlessly. 'My lord, I fear my niece might have you think she peruses the form books.'

Elizabeth coloured slightly. 'No indeed, I do not. It was merely a comment based upon some knowledge. I saw Teacher's Pet win at Goodwood the last season she raced.'

'I would gladly place your bet for you, Miss Ashling,' Sir Lucius interjected, with a bow, 'though I myself might give the edge today to Waterboatman, in view of the ground.'

'Thank you, Sir Lucius. I am much obliged.' She bestowed a preternaturally bright smile upon him, and took five shillings from her reticule. 'Behold, how I dare so much.'

She dropped the coins into his gloved hand, and he withdrew to place her bet.

Lord Easby was regretting that the previous evening he had lingered so long over the tables in a select establishment in Pall Mall, to which he had withdrawn after a galling encounter with Aurelia Rendlesham. He had risen over a thousand pounds down, and with a presentiment of a bad head on the morrow, which had been fulfilled. His 'setback', to put it no higher, with Miss Ashling, compounded by the fact that Lucius Radstock looked in a good way to winning her hand, had made him maudlin, and from maudlin he had gone on to a feeling of failure. Miss Ashling was therefore the cause of his misfortune.

The chance of replenishing his empty coffers upon Epsom Downs had drawn him out of Town and gave him other things to think about than Miss Ashling as some form of Nemesis. It was therefore somewhat of a shock to see her, although logic said that anybody who adored horses would be delighted to attend this particular race day.

The sight of her dropping coin into Sir Lucius's hand galled him unnaturally.

It was at this moment that he felt a movement of his gold fob, and shot out a hand to grasp the scruff of a very small and grubby pickpocket. His lip curled in distaste. It was a very malodorous child.

'You picked the wrong victim, you slippery-fingered urchin. The constable will be pleased to see you, as might yet the hangman.'

'Nah, me lord, I wasn't doin' nuffin', jest passin' by. Don't go an' give me to no harman.'

'With your fingers at my fob. Indeed. I wonder how many other people you have relieved of items of value this day?' He paused, and a speculative look came into his eyes. Most men would have accepted that they had no chance remaining with Miss Ashling, but despite his seeming nonchalance to Lady Rendlesham, he loathed being beaten. He had an idea that might put himself back in her good books. 'However, I might be persuaded to, er, overlook your criminal tendencies, if you were to do something for me.'

The child stopped wriggling, and eyed his captor with suspicion.

'You see the young lady over there, beside the lady with the big green bonnet?'

'The swell mort? Course.'

'Er yes. Well, if you take her purse, and then let me catch you . . .'

'Wot, an' be taken off jest the same to—'

'Listen.' The voice of authority stilled the boy to a whimper. 'I will drag you away, but release you, and even give you a shilling, which is far more than you deserve, since that would be transportation at the least.'

'And I keeps the bung?'

Easby frowned.

'The purse, guv'nor.'

'You most certainly do not. I return it to the lady. Now, off with you, and do not try to disappear in the crowd, because I will be sure to find you and raise a hue and cry.'

He released the infant thief, who paused for a moment, indecisive, and then shrugged and, like an eel, slipped silently between the throng to where Lady Chalford was recommending that Amelia take Lord Nuneaton's advice. How it was that Amelia's reticule was slipped from her wrist, she could not say, but she felt the tug, as was intended on this occasion, and gasped, then cried out. Lord Nuneaton blinked, and stepped backwards, treading on the toes of another gentleman, who made vociferous complaint.

In the meantime, Lord Carbrooke, who had been about

to offer his own services to lay Miss Amelia's bets and was in the process of removing his hat, dropped it and hared off after the thief like greased lightning, successfully grabbing the frayed collar, just as Lord Easby had hoped to do. Amid some outcry and bustle, Lord Carbrooke, breathing just a little faster than normal, frogmarched his prisoner back to the side of the parade ring, where Miss Ashling – who had only moved a few paces to get right to the parade ring rail – had returned, and was trying to calm both Lady Chalford and a tearful Amelia.

'Miss Ashling,' Carbrooke addressed Amelia, who was clutching his dropped hat in a manner that might do permanent damage to the brim, and tore the purse from the grip of the thief. 'Do not be distressed. Your purse is safe.'

Amelia took a sobbing breath and looked up into Lord Carbrooke's eyes with such adoring thanks as quite took what breath he still possessed from his body. Easby, realising the error made by his unwilling minion, had no desire that the urchin should reveal all in an attempt to gain release, and therefore stepped up promptly and spoke with calm authority.

'Good man, Carbrooke. Might I suggest you let me take this object to the constable or whoever is in authority here, whilst you calm the young lady's natural, er, alarm?'

Lord Carbrooke was still mesmerised by Amelia's wide eyes, and let the child be taken from him without so much as a murmur. Lord Easby dragged the miscreant away, and, when sufficiently out of the way of onlookers, shook him until his rather gapped teeth rattled.

'Fool. That was the wrong lady.'

'Wot abaht me bord? Yer promised me a bord.'

The noble lord clipped him sharply about the ear. 'That is all you will get from me, and think yourself lucky for it. Now, disappear, for if I see you here the rest of this day, you will end it in irons, understand?'

Rubbing his ear, the child nodded, sniffed and made himself scarce.

Meanwhile, Elizabeth was making every effort to prevent an embarrassing scene. Lord Nuneaton was still involved in an altercation with the man upon whose toes he had so heavily trodden. Lady Chalford was wavering on the verge of mild hysteria, and Amelia and Carbrooke were gazing at each other as if each were the recipient of a revelation. Elizabeth first addressed the problem of Lady Chalford, asking Lady Micheldever whether she possessed any smelling salts within her reticule and, when these were produced, wafting them gently beneath her aunt's nose, which made that lady gasp and blink.

'Be calm, Aunt. Nothing dreadful has happened and all is resolved.'

At that moment, Sir Lucius and Lord Godmanchester returned from placing bets. One glance at the tableau before him was enough to give Sir Lucius a very firm idea of the situation, and he immediately took control. He whispered to his friend to sort out Nuneaton, and took Lady Chalford's arm in a sustaining manner, speaking very calmly and leading her back towards her carriage. Elizabeth pushed Julia Wingate, who was looking at Amelia and Lord Carbrooke, in the back, and suggested that she and Lady

Micheldever should also retire to the carriage, from whence they might view the racing itself in safety.

Amelia finally blinked, and with a shy smile offered her hero his hat. 'You were so fleet, I scarcely had time . . . So brave . . . No words . . .'

Lord Carbrooke blushed, and swallowed rather hard. He wasn't used to being looked upon in an heroic light, let alone by a girl with whom he was fast falling headlong in love. 'Not heroic . . . Just a scrubby urchin.'

'But he might have been part of a vicious gang,' whispered Amelia, her eyes becoming even more saucer-like as she imagined the peril into which her champion might have put himself.

Lord Carbrooke had not considered this, but swept it aside with aplomb. 'For you, any price would be worth paying.'

Had Elizabeth heard this declaration she would have undoubtedly sneered, but Amelia was no cynic. Her lip trembled, and unconsciously her hand went out to lay upon his arm. He closed his fingers over it. Godmanchester, not wishful of seeing a scene worthy of *Romeo and Juliet*, whispered in Lord Carbrooke's ear that he was drawing attention and would be better to take Miss Amelia back to the carriages. He then returned to smoothing relations between Lord Nuneaton and the man of the trampled toes.

By the time Sir Lucius and Elizabeth returned, Lord Godmanchester was able to give them a wry smile, and announce that Lord Nuneaton had been persuaded to seek some refreshment.

'And we have missed the race, just to complete our delight.'

'Oh well, I wonder who won?' Elizabeth retained some interest.

'Waterboatman, by a short head.'

'From?' Sir Lucius raised an eyebrow.

'Pedagogue.' The smile broadened. 'You only just lost your shillings, Miss Ashling.'

'At the risk of sending good money after bad, I shall risk another two on the next race, and hope to be more fortunate.'

There followed a very good-hearted argument between Lord Godmanchester and his best friend concerning the merits of Triplicate over Do-As-You-Wish, in which Miss Ashling sided with Sir Lucius. They both put their money on the former, though the odds were quite short, and it dutifully won. Miss Ashling, holding ten shillings in her palm, was delighted with her success. Sir Lucius, whose bet had been considerably larger, was delighted not so much with his winnings as with his companion. It was as though she had finally sloughed off a skin of suspicion and caution, and the Elizabeth Ashling he had glimpsed upon Mist was revealed in all her golden glory. Lord Godmanchester kept his thoughts to himself as he watched them, and hoped his news would please his poor Helen upon their return.

Lord Carbrooke had persuaded Lady Chalford that his close attendance upon Miss Amelia would render it safe for her to watch the parade of the horses before the Derby itself, and it was a glowing Amelia who met her cousin as the thoroughbreds were duly walked around the paddock. A couple were on the fret and on their toes, showing signs of sweating and agitation. Elizabeth studied both the animals and their ancestry, but could not make a firm decision between her final two.

'At the risk of sounding patronising, Miss Ashling, the only thing you have not considered is the trainer. Merrymaker is a fine animal, but Azor is a Selim colt and trained by Robson, who has already trained four Derby winners, his last being Whisker, two years ago. If the two look equal to you, add that into the equation. And I also spoke to Payne, the owner, last month and he said that he thought Azor would be at the peak of his form about now, though I know Robson thinks his other runner a better bet. I might also add that Azor would give you very good odds at fifty to one.'

'Oh dear, I do so hate vacillation, but it is very difficult. My head tells me to go with what you say, Sir Lucius, but my heart tells me to be wilful and independent, and with things equine I will listen to my heart.' She paused, looking him straight in the eye, and what she saw made her suddenly drop her gaze and a frown appear between her brows. 'I will trust you,' she whispered, and it seemed to cost her much to say it. Then she took a deep breath and looked up again, holding out her hand. 'And in token of that trust, here are my winnings to go upon Azor.'

Lucius Radstock had never wanted a horse that was not his own to win as much as he did Azor, as the field thundered round Tattenham Corner. Azor had taken an early lead but gradually the rest of the field was catching him up. Beside him, he could feel Elizabeth's excitement, see her little, gloved hands, clenched with tension. Into the last furlong Elizabeth was convinced Azor would fade, despite her hopes. As the colt passed the post first by half a length, she gave a little jump and turned a face wreathed in smiles to him.

'He did it!'

He felt that at that moment, were it not for the very public nature of their position, that she could have kissed him, and he knew that he wanted so very much to kiss her. Godmanchester clapped him on the back, but it was the brief touch of her fingers upon his arm that he felt. Her eyes shone, and then, as if a cloud passed in front of the sun, that delight was occluded by a doubt, a wariness and a sudden sadness. His look questioned, but he said nothing, and he led her without further speech back to the carriages, where Amelia was happily bemoaning losing her coin upon an also-ran called Wishful Thinking.

When Sir Lucius returned with her winnings, which amounted to the impressive sum of twenty-five pounds, Elizabeth was clearly delighted by the success, but that mystifying air of sadness remained beneath the public face of victory. She pleaded over exertion and did not do more than watch the last two races from the carriage vantage point, and when, for the return journey, Amelia and Lord Carbrooke accompanied her and her aunt in the barouche, she added very little to the conversation, and she was content to listen as Amelia chattered away with the hint of a blush, and Carbrooke fought the urge to gaze solely upon those soft, pink cheeks.

In the phaeton, Sir Lucius was also rather quiet. Giles Godmanchester looked sideways at him.

'A good day's sport, Lucius. How much did you put on Azor?'

'A pony.' Sir Lucius smiled, as Lord Godmanchester gave a low whistle.

'Either you were very confident or very lucky. That will keep your stud in oats a decent while. You know, I really thought Manfred would beat them all.' He sighed. 'I am glad you won, though.'

'I am not convinced,' remarked Sir Lucius, feathering a corner with precision, 'that I have yet won at all.'

With which cryptic utterance, Lord Godmanchester had to be content.

CHAPTER NINETEEN

However much Elizabeth might have cautioned the clearly entranced Amelia to keep her views upon Lord Carbrooke to herself, it would have been impossible for her young cousin to bottle them within, and besides, her looks and demeanour were those of a young lady quite carried away. She had, as she had confided to Elizabeth already, a distinct preference for him over other admirers, and his presence aroused feelings in her maidenly bosom that the more experienced would sagely ascribe to being smitten. His actions, both in rescuing her property, and thereafter looking after her, had elevated these feelings to an open admission that he was the most perfect of men and that she loved him. This last she did not actually declare in front of her mama, but she scarcely needed so to do. From the moment that he handed her, tenderly, down from the barouche, in which she had spent the past couple of hours in intoxicating proximity to his person, made his polite farewells, thanked Sir Lucius for an outstanding day and walked away with a spring in his step, Amelia had let her emotions have free rein. Her own thanks to Sir Lucius were prettily put, and he accepted them with due seriousness, though his eyes twinkled at her choice of words. The expedition, she said, had been one of the best days 'ever' and she could not thank him enough for his kindness. This, as he remarked wryly to Lord Godmanchester, as he drove him back to his house in Brook Street, was from a young lady who had no interest in horses, and could not tell one anything about the day's events upon the racetrack, even the name of the winner of the Derby itself.

'It would seem you have, unintentionally, acted as Cupid, Lucius.'

'Not a role to which I have ever aspired, I promise you.' Sir Lucius's lip curled. He seemed only half attending, and it was not because of negotiating the traffic.

'Nonetheless, I would be very surprised if Carbrooke doesn't offer for the chit.'

'Lady Chalford clearly has high hopes of Nuneaton.'

'I think "had" is more accurate now, my friend. His behaviour today did not show him in a good light at all, and to be honest, I do not think he would walk into parson's mousetrap after all these years. He has admired her, yes, as a pretty object, but he showed absolutely no interest in how that bungled theft affected her at all. No, Lady Chalford ought to be very pleased with her offspring forming an attachment with Carbrooke. He might not have the wealth, but he is a good-hearted young man, who will no doubt be very steady once married.'

'I cannot pretend to have made a study of his good

points, and I know little more of him than he is an admirer of Chalford's daughter, and was a good way of guaranteeing her presence in my party, but I will say this: he can run well.'

'A sprinter not a stayer, though, eh, Lucius.'

'I wouldn't set him over more than five furlongs, no.'

'And' – Godmanchester grinned, returning to his subject – 'he plainly dotes upon the girl.'

'Plainly. I only hope the sight of them did not make Miss Ashling feel queasy on the journey back.'

Sir Lucius sounded almost bitter, and his friend, sensing that Lucius found the sight of another man's courtship coming so easily towards a successful conclusion was hard to bear when his own remained in the balance, dropped the subject.

Having deposited his friend at his house, Sir Lucius made his way back to his own residence in silence, prey to jumbled thoughts. When he handed his matched bays over to the groom, he did so with courteous thanks to him, and to those who had driven the barouche, but with his mind elsewhere. Once indoors, he withdrew into his library, and sat at the desk with his chin resting on his long, steepled fingers, and a pronounced frown.

The day had been most successful but the morrow still filled him with trepidation. Ironic as it was, he had fallen for the woman least likely to want a declaration among all the single ladies of his acquaintance. He had supposed, vaguely, that one day he would see a woman he admired, would find his feelings, of whatever depth, reciprocated, and life would continue smoothly in the married rather than single state. He had seen men in the tangled passions of love and thought himself immune from their anguish. Now he saw the error of his self-assurance.

Elizabeth Ashling had a sort of serene, dark beauty for which he had a natural preference, but he had seen plenty of far more obvious dark beauties before and never felt as he did now. He tried to analyse those feelings, and found himself more, rather than less, confused. She was not meek and amenable, and had frequently snapped at him, which had made him wish to retaliate in kind, but he knew she was not shrewish. She was quick-witted, independent, yet desperately vulnerable, and he wanted to protect her, take whatever burdens she carried from her, chase away the demons that seemed to haunt her. When they had first met he had heard her say, bitterly, that she would grant men nothing, and her subsequent behaviour had marked her simply as a natural man-hater. Yet no sooner than she been placed in the awkward position of having men pursue her, and from his own foolish intemperance, he had begun to see that whilst she distrusted men, she distrusted herself more. At parties she was always aware of her position as 'prey'. She was fearful of attention, but at heart, more afraid of giving anything of herself.

Despite this, in the saddle she had forgotten her sex, and been confident, one human being engaging with another. He had learnt that there was so much more to her than the defensive spinster. When she forgot to be afraid, he found her a kindred spirit who could understand his passion for bloodstock, who could spar light-heartedly with words, seemed happy in his presence, and yet, as today, she would suddenly pull up short, shy away from him. She had been laughing, eyes shining, excited and vital, and then this chasm had appeared between them, a chasm he could not explain, and the camaraderie, the closeness, disappeared into it. He wanted that closeness; he wanted her as she had been when watching the racing; he wanted to shield her from whatever blackness it was that descended upon her. She put him at arm's length, and it frustrated him. When she withdrew he had no belief that if he offered his protection, and yes, he admitted it, his love, she would accept it. Rather, she was likely to draw back from him entirely. It hurt his pride that she would not trust him, but it hurt his heart more, and he was unsure how to overcome her reluctance. If she had the slightest *tendre* for him, and there had been evidence of it, surely it was possible? And if she had not, what else might he do to win her?

The clock upon the mantelshelf chimed the hour, and he sighed, ran a hand through his now slightly disordered hair, and went upstairs to change.

'Was it not kind, Mama, of Lord Carbrooke to promise to come round to Mount Street tomorrow to see that we are all recovered from our exertions?'

Lady Chalford winced. She had seen her hopes of Lord Nuneaton dashed, and in truth, was most displeased with the man for his abysmal attitude. A reasonable woman, she could understand Amelia's *tendre* for the handsome Viscount, and the loving mother in her was delighted that her affections had found, seemingly, reciprocation. However, her matchmaking mama side had too raw a wound in Nuneaton's failure to, as yet, rejoice in the likely declaration of the lesser 'prize' of Carbrooke.

'. . . and he said that he rather thought he might be making up a party of his own to visit Astley's, and . . .'

'We heard, Amelia. Now do, I beg of you, go upstairs and change your gown, and leave me in peace. I fear I have a sick headache coming on, and I think that I will take but a little supper in my room.'

Amelia was immediately apologetic, but it was Elizabeth who gave her aunt her arm up the stairs to her bedchamber. Lady Chalford bade her come in for a moment, and sat heavily upon her daybed.

'He will offer for her, of course.'

'And when you are less wearied, dear Aunt, you will be delighted.'

'Perhaps. She could have achieved a better match if she had applied herself, though; I am sure of it.' Lady Chalford sighed.

'Better in terms of position and wealth, possibly, but they will deal extremely well together and she will be happy. Is not that far more important?'

Lady Chalford nodded, but sniffed, whether at the thought of the lost brilliant match or the realisation that her daughter would actually be leaving her for a household of her own, it was impossible to judge. Elizabeth had little doubt that a rest, and a rather more substantial meal than she had suggested, combined with some sound good sense from her lord, would see Lady Chalford's spirits revived with the new day. Elizabeth left her, keen to have the solitude in which to consider her own situation, but this was again denied her, since, as she passed Amelia's room, that damsel peered out, and beckoned her within.

Amelia had discarded her gown for it to be brushed down by her maid, and was only attired in her petticoats and a rather fetching pale apple-green dressing gown. Her cheeks were still slightly flushed and her eyes sparkled. 'What a day we have had, to be sure. I never thought it would be that exciting.'

'No indeed. That first race was so close too.' Elizabeth smiled, teasing, as Amelia blinked. 'Oh, were you not referring to the horses?'

'I . . . Oh, you wretch! You know I scarcely saw nor cared about the horses, except that race where Lord Carbrooke took me to stand by the rail. Were not the horses fast?'

'Yes, thankfully. I would not care to have to watch a race of slow horses.'

Amelia pouted, but her eyes betrayed her. 'It is not right that you should mock me so. Just because you care for nothing that does not stand on four legs.' Amelia did not notice the sudden twist to her cousin's smile. 'He is wonderful, isn't he, and do not ask if I mean the horse that won the Derby.'

'I will not, Amelia, and he is certainly a very nice young man.'

'And so fast! I had barely time to exclaim and away he went . . .'

'Like a greyhound after a hare.'

'Like a . . . No. How could you? He was brave too, for the thief might have had accomplices.'

'Possibly over four and a half feet tall also.' Elizabeth held up her hand. 'Yes, I know that he did not know whom he might encounter, or rather, did not consider his own safety, Amelia. It was the thoughtless act of a young man, "thoughtless" of himself and thinking only of you.'

Amelia blushed rosily, and tears came to her eyes. 'I have never met anyone like him, Elizabeth, never.'

Elizabeth forbore to tell her that she had not met that large a number of people in her seventeen secluded years. Part of her wanted to warn her in her innocence that, in the end, she would find her 'god' had feet of clay, and yet there was nothing that she could think of that might occasion Carbrooke doing what Henry Freshford had done to her. Had she been this ecstatic? Looking back, she thought that just before it all fell apart, she had. Initially, she had been healthily sceptical of the attention paid to her by gentlemen. After all, what they professed could be proved false by deed and time. However, Henry Freshford had got under her guard, a guard she had thought unbreakable, and once he did, then she had become as uncritical as Amelia was now about the Viscount Carbrooke. She had let herself be swept away on hope and anticipation, casting the voice of experience into the shadows, and paid the penalty for her folly. She would not, could not do so again, could she?

'And he says that they make pyramids of riders, and they ride six horses abreast.'

Elizabeth realised she had let Amelia's conversation flow over her, and that 'what Lord Carbrooke says' was now going to replace 'what Mama says' as Amelia's watchword in every circumstance.

'Oh.'

'I am sure you will want to come, since there are so many horses involved. You will want to come, won't you, Elizabeth?'

The pleading note in Amelia's voice was childlike, and just as it would seem cruel to withhold a treat from a child once it had seen what it was, so Elizabeth knew that she could not deny her cousin.

'Of course. I am to be the sop to chaperonage, am I?'

'No.' Amelia dimpled. 'Well, not entirely. I think Julia's brother is coming down from Oxford next week and he could come with us, with Julia, I mean.'

It did not strike Elizabeth that her evening would be one of unalloyed delight.

'Elizabeth?'

'Sorry.'

'If he, if Lord Carbrooke were to . . . Papa would not refuse him, do you think? Mama was not quite pleased when we got home, was she? If I was told I might never speak, or correspond with him again, I think I might just . . . die.'

'That, Amelia, is histrionic.' Elizabeth sounded suddenly unflinching. 'You would no doubt be rather miserable for a while, but you would not die, nor go into a decline, nor any other of those things that only happen within the covers of lurid romances. This I promise you.' She saw the desolation upon her cousin's face and softened. 'But it is nonsensical to speak of such a thing. Your parents will, I am sure, be most receptive if Lord Carbrooke makes an offer for your hand. They only want the best for you.'

'He is the best for me.'

It was a simple statement, said softly, but Amelia meant it honestly and completely. Elizabeth squeezed her hand.

'Indeed. Now, do not be a goose and shed tears, but rather look your best and most dignified for dinner. You do not want your papa to think you tardy and silly, and your mama did say he was dining at home tonight.'

Elizabeth was almost monosyllabic through dinner. She had tried to be logical and sort her thoughts whilst she washed her hands and face, and changed her gown, but it was too serious a process to do with Ditcham fussing about her, and Ditcham had fussed, sensing something untoward, yet not being able to ask outright what it might be. She responded to everything as if there was a delay before her mind could process what was said, and her eyes held trouble. Well, from Ditcham's long experience, that meant some man had upset her, but if that was the case, why was she neither distraught nor angry, more puzzled?

Lord Chalford was in a good humour, and in a mood to be pleased. His daughter fulfilled his wish, rattling on about the expedition and how enjoyable it had been, and if he might wonder, at one point, if she had even seen a horse beyond the ones pulling the barouche, he did not make overmuch of the degree to which Lord Carbrooke figured in her narrative. His wife, who had indeed recovered enough to come down for dinner when reminded that the chef was preparing turbot, was more thoughtful than usual, and he anticipated her seeking him out once he had enjoyed his port in lonely state. He thought that Elizabeth should have had an excellent day, and indeed she did assure him that this was so, and that Azor had proved a worthy winner, but thereafter she looked at her plate in the manner of one struggling, unsuccessfully, with the quarterly accounts. When the ladies withdrew he knew the urge to make a bolt to his club, thereby avoiding anything that smacked of a 'scene', but reluctantly admitted to himself that he had a duty as head of the house, and thus appeared in the drawing room whilst his lady was extolling the virtues of Lord Nuneaton in a half-hearted manner.

'Good enough fellow, Nuneaton,' he announced, adding his mite to the conversation, 'though he can be a dull dog, and snores. You should hear him in the club after a good luncheon.'

Lady Chalford threw him a look indicative of disapprobation. It had been hard enough to sound enthusiastic after Lord Nuneaton's performance at Epsom, but this was hardly likely to make Amelia think of him in a better light. She had consoled herself during her rest with the idea that Nuneaton might still offer for Amelia, and that if she could be prevailed upon to be obedient to her parents' greater wisdom, she might accept him. This was a fiction born of desperation, as Amelia's dinner conversation had shown, but she stuck resolutely to her plan.

Elizabeth let it flow over her. She could not think properly, yet needed to do so, desperately. It was a relief when the tea tray was brought in and she could shortly afterwards retire. Only lying in the dark, alone at last, could she give herself up entirely to the knots within her thoughts.

She had enjoyed her day, so very much. Had she enjoyed it simply because of the thrill of watching fleet thoroughbreds and exciting finishes, or had most of that enjoyment been because Lucius Radstock had been at her side? Her cynical head told her that it was the former. Her treacherous heart, however, insisted that it was his particular being there that had transformed the expedition, and she was inclined to believe it.

So why had this man, with whom she had frequently argued, been accepted by her heart as, at the very least, a friend? She knew a deep-seated longing to trust him, and let herself give in at last to the part of her that said 'love him'. Yet that was what she had done before, given in, loved, though her feelings for Henry Freshford had been far less intense, and the result had that time been desertion and heartbreak. She was no longer teetering on the edge, she knew it, and there was nothing to save her. Sleep, when it came, was interlaced with weird dreams of falling, and the wry smile of Lucius Radstock, which metamorphosed into a sneer.

CHAPTER TWENTY

Having spent a disrupted night, trying to work out how he would actually propose, and with so many versions revolving in his head that they eventually merged into gabble, Sir Lucius arose restless rather than rested, and at an unseasonably early hour. He therefore went for a ride, earlier than nearly everyone in the park other than a troop of the Life Guards. Riding cleared away the muzziness that fogged his brain, but did not, unfortunately, make the words fall into place. Chester's ears flicked back as his rider tried various phrases, though none seemed right. The tone was soothing, and the bay at least seemed to appreciate them. After an hour and a half of exercise, Sir Lucius returned home, and took such care with his apparel and the tying of his neckcloth that anyone who had seen him might have thought he had suddenly decided to join the dandy set. Thankfully, his only audience was his valet, who was surprised, but knew that his master was, as he later described it, coughing delicately, to the butler over a glass of port, 'not quite himself'.

He made his way to Mount Street feeling peculiarly light-headed, only to be greeted with the information that his lordship had just departed on a two-day visit back to his estates in Sussex. Sir Lucius's sense of disappointment was acute. Having worked himself up to taking the plunge, he was to kick his heels for two whole days, two days that would seem interminable. He went to his club, feeling distinctly 'unclubbable' and disinclined to socialise, and found himself a quiet corner with the *Morning Post*, behind which he hid. However, when he came to the Court and Social page and found the announcements of engagements, he tossed the paper aside and called for a bottle of claret.

It was two glasses later that Lord Godmanchester found his friend staring at the wall, and sat down in the neighbouring chair, in some concern.

'Not like you, Lucius, to broach a bottle so early.'

'Hmm.' Sir Lucius was clearly not in loquacious mood.

'Might I take a glass?'

'Help yourself, Giles.' Sir Lucius was still staring at the wall, and twiddling the stem of the glass, absentmindedly, between finger and thumb.

'I have several like that in Brook Street, you know, and just as good.'

'What? Bottles of claret?' The frown at the wall deepened.

'No, walls. If it is a wall you want to stare at, old fellow, come and stare at mine. No fear of some fool coming over and asking how you are, or whether you saw so-and-so in

Pall Mall wearing a dashed odd hat.'

Sir Lucius smiled, just a small, lopsided smile. 'Sorry, Am I that obvious?' He sighed. 'I always thought myself a patient man, Giles, but it seems that I am not.'

'Cryptic. Look, walk back to Brook Street with me, and if you feel like telling me what the deuce is up, all well and good, and if you prefer not to, I will promise not to not pry.'

He took his friend by the arm, and led him, unprotesting, up St James's. It was only when sat in a comfortable chair in Lord Godmanchester's book room that Sir Lucius unburdened himself.

'Two days!' he announced at the end. 'What am I to do for two whole days? It was bad enough last night. I am surprised I did not choke myself by tying my tongue in knots as I tossed and turned. Tell me, Giles, was it this hard for you?'

'Sorry, not quite, Lucius. I mean there was always the chance old Sir Marcus might send me to the right about, but the dibs were in tune, and I was never a here-and-thereian, so it was unlikely. I thought Helen was well disposed towards me, but nothing more. Mind you, I was head over heels about her, of course. The worst bit, to be frank, was after we tied the knot. You see, in a way she hardly knew me and there we were, you know, just the two of us. I was so afraid of, well, frightening her. Talk about shy! I do not know which of us was the more so.'

Sir Lucius opened his mouth to speak, but shut it again. Asking 'What happened?' was definitely not the thing.

'In the end I decided honesty was the best policy. I sat

there in the bed, as upright as if receiving castor oil from Matron at school (remember those days?), and told her just what I felt about her, how much I longed to inspire such feelings in her, how all I wanted was to make her happy. And you know what she did?' Giles Godmanchester shook his head, still mystified several years later.

'Er, no.' Half of Sir Lucius's mind was dealing with the thought of being in the same bed as Elizabeth Ashling, and it was exceedingly distracting.

'She burst into tears. Weirdest thing. Panicked me well and truly, it did. Then she said she was crying because what I said was beautiful and she was so happy. Never have quite got the hang of women and crying. And then it was sort of natural to put an arm about her to comfort her, and one thing, you know, led to another. It may seem a terribly hard thing to tackle just this minute, but I tell you what, Lucius, getting married was the best thing I ever did.'

'I have no doubt of that, Giles, nor that it would be so for me, if only I had confidence she would say yes. I just do not know what I will do if she refuses me.'

'But why should she, my dear friend? I can think of no possible reason why she should not be delighted to receive your offer.'

Unfortunately, there were two, and Lady Rendlesham had discovered both of them.

Aurelia Rendlesham was like a spider in the centre of a web; she felt the tremors in distant threads and went to investigate in case there was anything worth wrapping up for later use. She felt, rather than knew, that something had happened when Lord Easby did not appear at functions two nights running where she knew he had been engaged to attend, and then on the third behaved in a slightly peculiar way with Miss Ashling. She knew his body language pretty well, and also that the country dance that he danced with her was one he loathed. There must, therefore, be a reason for his standing up with the lady, and it was most certainly not indicative of victory.

Lady Rendlesham had a suspicious mind, and, thanks to a generous allowance, an open purse. She thought the money she expended on one of her grooms whiling away an evening in an alehouse that Lord Easby's servants were wont to frequent during their leisure hours, well spent, especially when it meant that she found out his lordship had returned from driving Miss Ashling round the park sporting a thick lip, bloody nose and the hint of a black eye. She naturally enough did not assume these injuries were inflicted by the lady herself, but by some gentleman desirous of defending her honour, for some as yet unknown reason. That the man would be Sir Lucius Radstock was not hard to work out. Part of her hoped that he would fail with Elizabeth Ashling, since seeing her on the shelf and dwindling as a spinster made her feel very smug, but at the same time it was hard not to wish to gloat over Lord Easby's failure. He had said he would shrug and move on, but Lady Rendlesham knew how highly he valued himself, and how little he understood failure. This must rankle.

It was two evenings later, on the eve of Sir Lucius's Derby expedition, that she was able to get close to Lord Easby in one of Lady Sumercote's drawing rooms. He did not look, when he thought himself unobserved, a very contented man. Lady Rendlesham could barely contain her delight, and worked her way to his side.

'So, my lord' – she smiled with assumed sweetness – 'I hope you are recovered from your, er, unexpected bloodletting. I do hope it vented any excess passions from your blood.'

He looked sharply at her. 'I fail to un—'

'No, really, my lord, I think you have to admit I know you far too well for silly lies. I wonder what you did that brought about such violence. Oh, do not tell me that you forgot that simpering maidens do not play by the rules that we married ladies comprehend so well. Was the poor little thing overcome by shock?' She tittered. 'You would have been better remaining at my side, Frederick.'

'Hardly, madam,' he snapped. 'Far better the dangers of the chase than deadly boredom.'

Her eyes flashed, and two spots of colour that owed nothing to the rouge pot flew onto her cheeks. 'Indeed, sir. Ennui is so much a part of a woman's relationship with men that we become inured to it.' Her beautifully moulded lip curled. 'For a man who said it mattered not if the lady proved impervious to your self-inflated charms, you look blue as megrim, my lord. You have no chance of her now, of course, and how much more galling it must be to see her falling like a ripe plum into the welcoming hands of Sir Lucius Radstock. You do so like your fruit ripe, as I recall.'

The look he shot her was of loathing, and she almost laughed out loud. This was more entertaining than the most daring dalliance. She was suddenly reminded of an incident as a girl, when a cat had brought a mouse into the schoolroom, and proceeded to play with it before killing it. Her sisters and governess had screamed and hidden their eyes, but she had watched and applauded the cat's ruthlessness in its tormenting.

'I take it Sir Lucius's hands were not so welcoming to you, by the way. How foolish of you, my lord, to take liberties, and one assumes that was what you were doing, in a place where others might intervene.'

'You should be careful of your sharp tongue, ma'am, lest you cut yourself with it.' Easby smiled, but spoke through gritted teeth.

'Do tell. You were teaching her to drive, as I recall. Did she find your hands over-responsive? Or did you meet her out riding upon that grey of Godmanchester's?'

'No more Godmanchester's than mine, my lady. Ah, you do not know everything, you see. That horse was chosen and paid for by Radstock. I only found that truth today.'

Lady Rendlesham caught her breath, and Easby thought briefly that he had at least paid her back for one jibe. A slow smile spread across her face, a smile that was purely private. Then she laughed very softly, and gave the Earl a look that was both disdainful and mocking.

'Oh, my lord, such a fool as you are, but then that is the way of men. You cannot see the weapons before you unless they are those of physical violence, which are, I am sure you will agree, exceedingly clumsy.'

He frowned, not understanding her, which increased her pleasure. The smile lengthened, and the glitter in her hard eyes made him almost recoil at the depth of their calculating malice.

'Poor Frederick. You really ought to withdraw to those encumbered estates of yours, and lick your wounds in private, or are you going to make a last-minute attempt on the Gillingham girl, out of pure desperation? Sorry, impure desperation.'

Her tinkling laugh and the gentle rap of her fan upon his lordship's knuckles led several ladies to assume that Aurelia Rendlesham had taken up again with the dangerous Lord Easby, and to hope, uncharitably, that she might suffer as a result. Only one noticed that his lordship looked most unlike a man engaged in flirtation, and he shortly afterwards withdrew to an evening of gaming.

Lady Rendlesham spent an evening of almost unalloyed pleasure. Only her failure to speak with Miss Ashling, to hint at her knowledge – largely surmised – of the recent incident, and to drip the poison of her most recent acquisition into her ear, kept her from complete happiness. Well, the delights of that encounter could wait, and might even be better for the chance to think first how to get the most from it.

She was not a woman of many virtues, and patience was certainly not one she possessed. Her failure to see Miss Ashling at all the next evening, either at the Castlereaghs' rout, or the three other lesser parties that she deigned to honour with her brief presence, left her irascible. Her shoes, she decided, pinched horribly, and the refreshments at the smaller entertainments were inferior. Both these things she blamed, illogically, upon Elizabeth Ashling.

She returned home with her mind working overtime, and was far more disagreeable than usual with her maid, who frequently had to put up with harsh words and thrown hairbrushes. She submitted to her abigail undressing her but subjected the woman to waspish complaint. The release from corsetry and myriad hairpins did not, as the maid had hoped, improve her temper.

The sound of her husband's slightly unsteady footfall upon the stair made her purse her lips. That was all she needed after a frustrating evening. She hoped that he was foxed enough not to notice the light from under her door, but her hope was in vain.

Lord Rendlesham was not drunk. He would deny he was drunk to anyone who suggested otherwise. He had already informed the friend who walked home with him that he was perfectly sober, also a link boy, two complete strangers, the butler and a chair in the hall.

The thought of his bed was alluring, but at the sight of the narrow shaft of light beneath the door of his wife's bedchamber, an image even more alluring presented itself. He hiccupped softly, and smiled to himself. He was a very fortunate man, possessed as he was of a beautiful young wife. She was expensive, of course, but then keeping her rigged up to the nines was worth it when she drew all eyes to her. She had her odd humours, but then that was what women were like: fragile, delicate things prone to frequent headaches and indispositions.

He knocked tentatively upon the door, and, in a moment of pure revenge, the maid went to open it a fraction, feigning surprise at seeing her employer.

'My lord!' She curtseyed, hiding her smirk as much as possible by lowering her gaze. He did not even spare her a glance, his eyes being only upon the delectable form of his wife, seated at her dressing chest.

She was arrayed in a lace wrapper and her maid had just finished brushing her hair, so it lay in thick dark tresses on the white lace. She looked into the dressing mirror as he entered the room, and groaned inwardly. At least, she thought, she had enough to keep her mind occupied.

'Good evening, my dear,' he enunciated, only a trifle thickly, and nodded dismissal to the maid, which made his wife's smile even more forced. 'I saw your light was on, and . . .'

'Yes, indeed, my lord. I have had much to occupy my thoughts.' Distraction, well, it sometimes worked. 'Did you know that Sir Lucius Radstock looks about to offer himself and all his worldly goods, mostly smelling of horse, to the terribly overrated Miss Ashling?'

'What, not the golden-haired chit? Emily, is it? Chalford's girl.'

'No, my lord, her cousin, Miss Elizabeth Ashling, whose papa drank himself to death and left her so nearly destitute.'

'You don't say! Well, that's a bit rich.'

'Why, sir?' The silk thread trembled again in her arachnoid mind.

'Why, it was he who coined her name, "the Unassailable". Overheard Nuneaton mention it to Foxton in the club yesterday evening, though Nuneaton had broached a third bottle of burgundy and might have been wrong, I suppose. Never saw Radstock as the marrying sort, but, there.

Wonder if it took him unawares, or he's a devilish deep'un and thought to put fellows off the scent.' He paused, and frowned. 'If he did it failed, for I would swear it made more prick up their ears and have a go.'

Lady Rendlesham's eyes widened, and she turned upon the dressing stool to face him directly. 'My lord, are you sure? Did not Nuneaton start the rumour?'

'He advanced it, but said the idea was not his own, and only wished it had been. I wondered if it was a hum because she was largely ignored before that, you know, so it was a dashed foolish thing to say.'

'It was Sir Lucius who invented that title.' She was standing now, holding the back of the chair, eager.

'I tell you that is what Nuneaton said. He is no crony of Radstock's. What reason would he have to make such a thing up, my pretty?'

She hated it when he called her that, but her delight at learning this vital snippet of information helped her ignore it. She even went so far as to step close to her husband, place her hand upon his cheek and gently set her lips to his. His breath was heavy with brandy.

'Thank you.'

Lord Rendlesham was not quite certain for what he was being thanked, but his wife was so rarely approachable he did not bother to enquire more closely, preferring to take advantage of the situation that presented itself. Her ladyship swiftly regretted her impetuosity.

CHAPTER TWENTY-ONE

Lady Rendlesham was in a quandary, being torn between the desire to deal the masterstroke herself and see the effect, knowing that her victim would see the triumph in her eyes, and the acknowledgement that her animosity might render the blow less effective, since it might be disbelieved. She spent a happy morning imagining the look on Elizabeth Ashling's face, the hurt, the crushing disappointment yet again. This time she would not recover. She would go and hide herself in the Sussex downland and not show her face in London again. There was also the added advantage of stripping Sir Lucius Radstock of the contented air he had been exhibiting recently. She had always thought him censorious of her, and, worse still, he had never shown the least interest in her, even when single.

In the end, she decided on a compromise, which would involve her telling one of her friends the juicy and damning details when she knew Elizabeth Ashling was close at hand. Lady Cumnor would be the ideal third party. All it needed was Miss Ashling's presence at the requisite evening party, and that, alas, she knew to be out of her hands. It was, therefore, in eager anticipation mixed with a preparedness for disappointment that Aurelia Rendlesham set out to Lady Sefton's that night. It would be an enormous squeeze, of course, since everyone wished to be seen at the party of one of the Almack's hostesses, and that would mean she needed to ensure Lady Cumnor's close attendance and keep her eyes open to see if the Chalford party were present. Ascertaining Miss Ashling's presence proved surprisingly easy, since she perceived Lady Chalford early in the evening, and overheard her telling another mama how glad she was that 'both the girls' were in such looks this evening.

Lady Rendlesham feared, however, that she was out of luck with her plan of action, because Lady Cumnor was indisposed with a sick headache, as reported by her sister-in-law. Aurelia Rendlesham was not one to give up at the first hurdle, so cast about her for another innocent accomplice. She was almost getting desperate when she caught sight of the ideal lady. Lady Evershott was mild, myopic and deliciously deaf, so almost bound to repeat, loudly, everything she was told in order to confirm she had heard it correctly. She was not a close friend, which meant timing her 'casual conversation' to a nicety, just at the right moment so that Elizabeth Ashling would be close enough to hear Lady Evershott's clear tones. The first opportunity was ruined by Lady Evershott being in conversation with the hostess, and even Aurelia Rendlesham did not think she could interrupt one so influential. She could have stamped with frustration. It was nearly midnight when they were once again in suitable proximity, and she 'pounced', taking Lady Evershott by the elbow, smiling and steering her towards a small sofa as she spoke.

'My dear Lady Evershott! I vow it is a perfect age since I had a chance to speak with you. Is this not a delightful evening. Have you seen Lady Fernilee's rather dashing gown?' Lady Rendlesham left no gap in which Lady Evershott might interject a remark, and nearly pressed her down to the seat. 'What a squeeze this is. Oh, do look at Miss Ashling's pretty gown. She does seem in good spirits, does she not?'

'Indeed, she—'

'And I wonder if Sir Lucius Radstock is in attendance?' She laughed conspiratorially. 'Of course, you will have heard he is likely to make her an offer very soon. Why, did you know' – she dropped her voice very slightly, so as to ensure Lady Evershott would not be quite sure she heard aright – 'he has even bought her a horse, under the guise of merely advising Lord Godmanchester upon a purchase, since he could not make her such a gift within propriety. It must have been a secret to prove his affection to her, for she is terribly keen on horses, and it must sway her decision.'

'A horse? Did you say Sir Lucius has bought her a horse?' Lady Evershott blinked at Lady Rendlesham, who nodded.

Lady Evershott had not been as explicit as Aurelia Rendlesham had hoped, but she was certainly loud enough, and Lady Rendlesham was mightily relieved to see Elizabeth Ashling turn her head slightly, catching the comment, though she could not see who was seated beside Lady Evershott.

'Sir Lucius Radstock, yes.'

'Sir Lucius Radstock, and Miss Ashling? Goodness, and him a confirmed bachelor.'

Lady Rendlesham could have clapped her hands in delight. This was much better. Miss Ashling, who had indeed looked in good spirits this evening, had paled.

'I know. And the strangest thing is that it was he who named her "the Unassailable", which set all the gentlemen in pursuit of her hand, as a challenge, one assumes.'

'Unassailable? Really?'

Lady Rendlesham nodded again, and then made an excuse to withdraw and watch events unfold. Lady Evershott was bound to repeat what she had gleaned, and not sotto voce either. Just as she had hoped, no sooner had she vacated the seat than Lady Evershott beckoned one of her friends to take the seat, and began, in the carrying 'whisper' of the deaf, to tell her friend this juicy gossip. Aurelia Rendlesham watched her victory unfold.

Elizabeth, who had caught enough of Lady Evershott's response to whoever was talking with her to make her stomach turn over and her head spin dizzily, began to feel positively faint as Lady Evershott regaled her new companion with the tale.

This was not history repeating itself; this was worse, far worse. Papa had shunned the grieving child and then Henry had caught a girlish fancy, bruised an immature heart with his shallow desertion, but now . . . Elizabeth thought for a moment that the floor was coming up to meet her, and took a gasping breath, unconsciously reaching out and resting her hand on the arm of Lord Carbrooke, who had approached with the happy notion of describing Miss Amelia's many virtues to one who must surely be in accord with him, and whom, he gathered from that young lady, was sympathetic to their cause. Amelia herself, in the few minutes she had dared engage him in conversation, had been at once ecstatic and fearful, convinced as she was that parental preference for the awful Lord Nuneaton might keep her from the only man with whom, she was now convinced, she might be happy.

He had barely begun when Elizabeth looked quite ill, and then laid her hand on his arm.

'You really do not look quite the thing, ma'am,' he remarked solicitously, secretly rather worried that she might collapse in a heap at his feet. 'Let me get you a glass of lemonade, a chair, your aunt?'

'Aunt.' Elizabeth blinked at him, and took another breath. 'Yes, please take me to my aunt, my lord. I have suddenly the most blinding of headaches.'

'Yes, yes, of course.'

He almost dragged her through the throng, looking about him in some panic until he espied Lady Chalford, whom he approached without any thought of his own concerns.

'My apologies, ma'am, for interrupting you' – he bowed to Lady Chalford and the lady with whom she was chatting – 'but Miss Ashling is unwell, and requested that I bring her straight to you.'

Lady Chalford looked surprised, but one glance at Elizabeth's pale cheeks and blank expression wiped any thought of asking what had happened from her mind.

'My poor dear, you do look wan. Thank you, my lord, I will take her home immediately.' She paused. 'Oh dear, Amelia! What should I . . . ?'

'Perhaps, ma'am, Lady Micheldever might take her "under her wing", so to speak, and later return her home.'

'Yes, yes, an excellent idea.'

'Would you care for me to find her for you, and then Miss Ashling may remain in your care?'

'Yes, that would be best.' Lady Chalford, flustered, defaulted to the mode in which a gentleman might take control simply by asserting a little authority.

Lord Carbrooke bowed and went about his quest, not a little relieved to have put the responsibility of a very sickly-looking lady upon other shoulders. He returned in but a few minutes, followed by Lady Micheldever, to whom Elizabeth's sudden indisposition was explained, and who immediately volunteered to bring Amelia home at the end of the party.

This all meant very little to Elizabeth, who had passed through feeling faint to a state of otherworldly numbness, and with a flame of anger catching the tinder of betrayal. By the time she was handed into the carriage, Lady Chalford was glad to see the pallor had gone, though it was now replaced by a rather dangerous look. Elizabeth sat bolt upright, her hands clasped together tightly. Lady Chalford made soothing noises, which her niece appeared to ignore. Once arrived in Mount Street, Elizabeth stalked into the house in the manner of some potentate of the distant Orient about to order myriad executions, or so it seemed to her aunt. In fact, the only slow and unpleasant fate she was imagining was that of Sir Lucius Radstock, whose deceitful heart she could cheerfully, at that moment, have torn slowly from his traitorous body with her kid-gloved hands. Lady Chalford followed her niece up the stairs, but not quickly enough to reach that damsel's chamber door before it slammed. There came the sound of a cry of frustration, and glass shattering.

'Oh dear,' murmured Lady Chalford to herself. She waited for a minute, then knocked, a little timidly, lest she be met by some missile. There was no answer at all. She opened the door cautiously, and peered round. Elizabeth stood in the centre of the room, bosom heaving, and a small cloud of pink dust on and at the base of the far wall, where also lay the shards of a powder bowl.

'Elizabeth, my dear, try to be calm.'

'Calm? After this?'

'After what?' Lady Chalford enquired, mystified.

In answer, Elizabeth ground her teeth but tried to master the desire to shout, even at her aunt. Her voice, when she spoke, was very low and trembled, but was hardly more than a whisper.

'I am a fool. I knew, oh I knew from the start, but still I let that deceitful toad worm his way into my affections, into my heart even. He seemed so different at last, and he is not as bad . . . He is worse, for the others deserted me through weakness. He has betrayed me intentionally, played me as a fisherman does a trout.'

'I am still at a loss, Elizabeth.'

'Lucius Radstock, Sir Lucius Radstock, Aunt, was the man who gave me the name "the Unassailable". Ah, perhaps you did not know of this. Well, nor did I until rumour finally reached me, about a week ago. It is rife among the gentlemen's clubs, however, and accounts for the number of highly unwelcome suitors who have pursued me, even to the point where . . .' She halted, recalling Sir Lucius's knocking down of Lord Easby. He had seemed so noble, but it was his fault that Easby had ever shown her any attention; it was his fault she had been insulted, hounded, hunted. 'He is to blame for everything. And then, just to add insult to the injury, what must he do but buy Mist for me to ride.'

'Lady Godmanchester's horse?'

'Yes, except it never was her horse. I thought her far too fiery for Helen. He even had my best friend deceive me too. No doubt he made up some romantic tale to persuade her. How he must have laughed at me.'

'But that must, whilst being very naughty, be seen as a sign of the deep affection in which . . .' Lady Chalford tried to find something positive, and failed.

'Affection? No. He just wanted to lull me into being happy so that he could make an offer without fear of refusal.'

'But if you did not know he bought the horse, how could this have influenced you, dear?'

Elizabeth paused. There was a breakdown in her logic, but she was too incensed to worry about it unduly.

'Elizabeth, how is this important if he wants to make you an offer and you have tender feelings for him?'

'Because . . . Because he is dishonest and will hurt me, and . . . I hate him, hate him, hate him.'

Elizabeth burst into tears and flung herself upon her bed. Her aunt was very confused. She would have sworn – both from what had happened over recent days, and even tonight – that Elizabeth was very taken with Sir Lucius, so how his wanting to offer for her was so bad a thing, she had no idea. The name was reprehensible, but must have stemmed from the time before he was attracted to her, and the horse was in many ways a sweet and romantic gesture, especially since his part was concealed. Yet Elizabeth clearly felt positively murderous. Lady Chalford patted her shoulder, sighed, pulled the bell for Ditcham and withdrew to the landing, where she intercepted that reliable tirewoman and explained that her mistress was somewhat overwrought. The maid looked the aunt straight in the eye, with the understanding of one woman to another, and nodded grimly. Nothing more was said. She curtseyed and went into the bedchamber, raising an eyebrow at the pink damage to the wall.

Elizabeth was sobbing into the coverlet. Ditcham sighed, and proceeded, by a mixture of bullying, soothing and sympathy, to get her mistress ready for bed.

The feigned headache was now real. Elizabeth's cheeks stung from salt, her eyes were puffy and red, and sleep seemed an impossibility. There was a terrible emptiness within her. This man had won her trust, despite all her wiser instincts, won it so completely, and yet all the time was deceiving her, making her a mere puppet, whose strings he might cut upon whim. The heart he was breaking whimpered that, if he loved her, nothing else mattered, but the head, thumping as it was, asserted superiority. It had been proved right yet again. Men could not be trusted. He might claim to love, but his actions showed his selfishness, his inability to treat her honestly. There could be no truck with such a man.

No truck, perhaps, but when tiredness overcame her, he was there, lurking in the edges of her dreams, a sombre figure with eyes that pleaded, then grew hard as granite, and no amount of tossing or turning would make him go away.

In blissful ignorance of what had taken place at Lady Sefton's the previous evening, Sir Lucius presented his card in Mount Street the next morning and asked to see Lord Chalford. His lordship was a little surprised to receive this request, his wife's comments upon Elizabeth's budding romance having been heard but not listened to, over recent weeks. However, he instructed that Sir Lucius be provided with refreshment in the library, where he would join him shortly.

When he entered the room he thought his visitor looked a little ill at ease, for he was standing beside the library table, drumming his fingers upon the polished mahogany in some agitation.

'Good morning, Sir Lucius. Er, I am sorry if I have kept you waiting. Have you another engagement that is pressing?'

'No, no,' Sir Lucius replied hurriedly, colouring. 'I . . . It is . . . You see . . .' He faltered, much to Lord Chalford's amazement.

'Do take a seat, and try to calm yourself. You seem agitated. In what way may I be of service to you?'

'Miss Ashling' – Sir Lucius took a deep breath – 'Miss Elizabeth Ashling, that is, your niece. I was . . . am . . . hoping that you will see your way to permitting me to pay my addresses to her.'

There, it was out. He took a gulp of air, and watched Lord Chalford's face register astonishment.

'Good Lord! Elizabeth? You want to marry my niece, Elizabeth?'

'Yes, my lord, I do.'

'Are you sure?' Lady Chalford would have screamed in horror had she heard her lord giving a prospective suitor the opportunity to back down, but Chalford was more than a little stunned.

'Yes, absolutely.'

'Good Lord,' repeated his lordship, blinking. There was a pause, a pause far too long for the state of Sir Lucius's nerves, then Lord Chalford's face broke into a smile and he extended a hand.

'My dear fellow, by all means. Couldn't have wished for a better match for the dear girl.' He shook Sir Lucius's hand energetically. 'To be frank, couldn't imagine any match for her, really. I mean, you are very welcome to pay her your addresses, but she is of age now, and may make her own choice.'

'Of that fact I am aware, my lord, but I have hopes that she might be inclined to favour my suit.'

'Then I will see if she is about. I have not heard of any plans for the ladies to go out this morning. I will send her down to you if you would just wait here. Not a room where you will be interrupted, you see.'

Sir Lucius nodded, feeling already a little tongue-tied, and Lord Chalford withdrew, asking Ribston to tell Miss Elizabeth that Sir Lucius Radstock wished to speak with her in the library, and himself going to knock upon the door of his wife's little writing room, where she often spent the morning at her correspondence, or taking a gentle nap. On this occasion she had pen in hand.

'My dear, I have some news that I think will delight you.'

'Really? Then tell me, for I have been trying this last half hour to compose a most dreary epistle to your Aunt Risborough.'

'Guess who is in the library?'

'I have no idea. Why should I have any idea who is in the library?' Lady Chalford frowned.

'Sir Lucius Radstock,' announced her husband, much in the manner of the master of ceremonies announcing the most important guest at a function, 'and he has just asked my permission to pay his addresses to Elizabeth. There, what do you think to that, my love?'

'Oh dear,' cried Lady Chalford, pressing her hand to her cheek. 'Oh dear me.'

It was not the reaction Lord Chalford had expected.

In the library, Sir Lucius waited, and waited, and waited.

CHAPTER TWENTY-TWO

When the door to the library was eventually opened it was by Ribston at his most impassive, who apologised for Sir Lucius having been kept waiting so long, but said that he had finally ascertained that Miss Ashling was 'indisposed' for the morning. Miss Ashling's presence having been denied him, Sir Lucius withdrew with as good a grace as possible, temporarily disappointed, having worked himself up to a highly nervous state, but in the reasonable expectation that he would be able to put things to the touch in the very near future. It was a pity that she was indisposed this morning. Perhaps the previous evening's exertions meant that she needed to sleep longer. The image of her face, softened with sleep upon some lace-edged pillow, and her hair tousled, crept into his mind and would not be ousted. It stayed with him all the way home, and even as he mounted the steps to his own front door, which was opened to him by a servant who was quite bemused by the look upon his master's face. That it had taken so long to elicit the information concerning this indisposition did not register in the presence of the more overwhelming thought, but slowly a seed of doubt began to germinate. He tried to dismiss it. After all, the last time he had seen her she had been friendly enough. He was pretty near convinced that she felt at the very least some slight *tendre* for him. It was an encouraging thought, and just at this moment, encouragement was an important thing.

He worked upon the assumption that Elizabeth would be present at the Prestwicks', or more likely Lady Jersey's, in the evening, and perhaps, since he already had her uncle's permission to do so, he might find some quiet spot where they would not be disturbed.

He therefore dressed most carefully for the second time that day, but this time purely reliant upon the good cut of his evening dress and the snowy whiteness of his linen. He would have felt the better had he not feared that somehow his demeanour gave away his intent. He went first to Lady Prestwick's and appeared, outwardly, sufficiently composed that his hostess saw nothing unusual about him, excepting a certain buoyancy in his step as he trod up the stairway towards her and bent gracefully over her hand. He said the right things without them sounding trite, and passed on into the crowded rooms, his eyes searching for the dark head. He caught a glimpse, and, heart beating a little faster, threaded his way, at what seemed an interminably slow pace, between nodding acquaintances and good friends alike. Only at the last moment did he realise his error. Lady Rendlesham turned to smile at him, her smile a little brittle as she saw the disappointment in his eyes.

* * *

'Why, Sir Lucius, how fortunate. I so rarely get to speak with you, you elusive man.' She tapped his arm coquettishly with her fan, and her voice implied he was some close friend, rather than a mere acquaintance. 'I was going to ask after your dear mama. I hope Lady Radstock is well?'

'She, er, enjoys good health, excepting the stiffness in her joints, ma'am.' He was frowning, clearly answering automatically, and brought the thought uppermost in his mind to his lips. 'Have you seen Miss Ashling this evening, Lady Rendlesham?'

'Miss Ashling?' Lady Rendlesham repeated, as if trying to put name to face. 'Miss Elizabeth Ashling? Oh, she is not here. I heard Lady Chalford say that she has taken to her bed with a sick headache, poor thing. Such a shame to be so sickly! She has frequently lacked the stamina for the Season, I have noticed. Sometimes ladies suited to the quiet existence of the country, where they appear quite strong, wilt in the Metropolis.'

She noted the deepened frown, but was not so sure that her words were the cause of it. He bowed and turned away, and she watched him, shortly afterwards, make his excuses to his hostess and leave. She permitted herself a small, secret smile. So he was as badly smitten as she was, was he? Well, she had never liked him, and if he chose to make a fool of himself at long last, having seemed so impervious to feminine charms, he deserved no sympathy. No doubt he would now think that the object of his affection was tucked up in her bed, and retire to his own abode to consider the fragility of female health, when she knew for a fact that Elizabeth Ashling, an Elizabeth Ashling putting on a brave face but with hollows under her eyes, was in the next room, and would be going on, as so many were, to Lady Jersey's. Poor Lady Prestwick would soon find her guests sadly depleted in number to those against whom Lady Jersey had taken a dislike. Life was so entertaining.

Sir Lucius was undecided. Without the lure of Miss Ashling's presence he had little inclination to attend even so popular a haunt as Lady Jersey's, but the alternative was in fact remarkably close to Lady Rendlesham's image, and he thought if he pondered much longer he would drive himself mad. Lady Jersey's promised good fare, and good company, since he expected Bensthorpe, the Godmanchesters and Collingbourne to all be present. With a sigh, he turned towards Berkeley Square and the Earl of Jersey's residence. The flambeaux in front of the house illuminated a scene of considerable activity, with carriages setting down their noble occupants, and noisy link boys arguing over who was next in line to offer to light the way for any – and there were very few – who chose to leave.

He trod up the steps amidst the bustle, acknowledging a lady, his mind only half on the occasion. He looked a little *distrait* to Sally Jersey, but he managed to make her smile, nonetheless. It was not long before he came across Lord Bensthorpe, in deep discussion with Mr Southram.

'Lucius, my dear fellow! Just the man we need. Southram here says that Monty Westrupp is selling his black hunter. I think it must be a hum, but surely you will know the truth of it.'

Sir Lucius shook his head, though he smiled. 'I am sorry

to disappoint you, Bensthorpe, but I have to confess it is news to me too. Not up to your weight, though, I should say.' He surveyed Lord Bensthorpe's slightly rotund figure, and then looked at the younger man. 'Would do for you, Southram.'

'Ah yes, Sir Lucius, but it does depend very much on what he wants for the gelding. Paternal generosity is not unbounded, and, er, the old man did have to bail me out a trifle last quarter day.'

'But it is a fine animal. Your father appreciates a good horse.'

'He does, my lord, but he also appreciates a dutiful son. I am sure he would think buying the horse would be rewarding my folly.' Mr Southram pulled a wry face, and sighed. 'Nothing for it but to win a fortune at hazard, I suppose.' Since Mr Southram was not noted for playing for high stakes, and his only debts were for tailoring and on the Turf, this was accepted as the jest that it was. 'Any idea how you play it?'

Lord Bensthorpe patted the youngster on the back. 'Not going to get you into bad habits, Southram.'

'Now there's a thing. Sir Lucius, name your next colt Bad Habits and I volunteer to back him throughout his career.'

Sir Lucius smiled more broadly, and left them to their bantering. He caught sight of Giles Godmanchester conversing with his host in one corner of the room and threaded his way towards them. He was within a few feet when Lord Jersey stepped back to move on. There, right before him, a glass of champagne in her hand, was Elizabeth Ashling. She froze, the glass partway to her lips.

They stared at each other for a moment. Both were tongue-tied, but for wildly different reasons. He had been so certain that he would not see her that it was as if she had appeared from his imagination, his thought made tangible.

'Miss Ashling.' He began to smile, but it died on his lips.

'You.' Her voice throbbed with emotion, and it was not adoration.

He frowned. The one word was so heavily loaded with loathing that it made him reel. 'What on earth . . .'

'How you can have the effrontery to stand before me, I do not know.' She spoke in a low, impassioned voice, barely above a whisper.

He looked genuinely puzzled, and not a little hurt, but rather than lessening her wrath, it seemed to fire her further.

'Very good, Sir Lucius,' she sneered. 'Had you considered a career on the stage, in tragedy? I am sure you would do very well. Or do you see yourself as the romantic hero?'

'Miss Ashling, I have absolutely no idea what I have done to—'

'Not here. Not now. Whatever it is . . .' Lord Godmanchester looked at his friend and then Elizabeth, his voice an urgent undertone. That his pleas registered in some way was shown by the lowering of their voices, but otherwise he might have saved his breath.

'No idea? That is rich. You make me the talk of St James's, my name bandied about in gentlemen's clubs, the object of vulgar wagers, no doubt, and offensive hounding, and do not think it might upset me? You even have the gall to pretend to be my knight in shining armour, defending me from the "wicked" Lord Easby, when without your instigation he would never have given me a second glance. Did you watch that morning, biding your time to appear at most advantage? And then you deceive me, using my own friends, into riding your horse. Mistral, hah! The Trojan Horse must have been her real name. Was that some game, a secret jest?'

He looked at her with dawning horror and understanding. It was all so very wrong, and yet true. In his anticipation he had now nearly forgotten his part in her being so popular, and most certainly regretted it. He had no idea whence she had come by the information, but it had clearly left her incandescent with rage.

'Miss Ashling, I assure you that—'

'You could assure me that the sun will rise in the morning and I would not believe it, sir.'

'Let me at least finish what I have to say?'

'Why? I cannot believe a single word of it. You have lied to me, deceived me into thinking . . .' She halted, unable to go on for the lump in her throat, the tears that threatened to betray her.

'If you would but let me explain.'

'Explain? What?' Her whisper was fierce, and she almost spat her response. 'How much entertainment you got from watching me trying to fend off unwanted suitors?' Her eyes accused.

'No. I never intended . . . I did not know . . .' Even as the words came tumbling urgently from his lips he knew that that had been the thought in the fateful moment when he had begun to give Collingbourne the name. It had been so brief in its duration that he had almost persuaded himself it had never existed. He coloured, and halted, and his silence, taken as admission of guilt, fuelled her rage the more.

'First you think it amusing to persuade your friend to pass off a horse as his so that I ride an animal that belongs to you. I scarcely dare imagine what perverse delight that was meant to give.' Her lip curled. 'Then I find you are the originator of the vulgar soubriquet that means I am positively hunted by men who wish to say they conquered the Unassailable. Thank you, Sir Lucius. Thank you so very, very much.'

'That came first, and I had no idea—'

'First? Was there then a long list of things? Tell me, Sir Lucius, what other ideas did you have for me?' Her eyes flashed.

He was goaded into reply, goaded into saying what was the last thing he should have mentioned at that moment. 'I was going to ask you to become my wife.'

The words sounded hollow, even to him. Lord Godmanchester winced. As a declaration, it was one doomed at birth. Elizabeth stared at him, her lips parted, as if he had just announced he was a cannibal. Her long fingers gripped the stem of her glass so tightly that a crack broke the silence between them. She stood, looking at him still, as blood began to drip steadily from her hand where the broken stem dug into her palm. There was no pain, for it was lost in the pain of hearing what she had thought she dreamt of hearing and now knew to be a cruel twisting of the knife in her heart. He had lied to her, made her the object of gossip, and now thought he could simply ask for her hand? If he had any feelings for her, such a thing would have been impossible.

'Miss Ashling, you are hurt.' Lord Godmanchester stepped closer, but also shielding her from other eyes.

'I fear the glass has broken,' she announced, in a slightly surprised but disembodied voice. 'Oh dear!'

The room began to spin, and she felt as if she were being sucked into some black whirlpool from which she had no inclination to even attempt escape. She heard a voice, focused hard to catch the words.

'Let me . . .' Sir Lucius grabbed a napkin and made to take her hand.

'Do not touch me.' Her own voice sounded far away, disjointed. 'I would rather . . . bleed to death.'

With which she crumpled, descending into blackness. Whatever her wishes, Sir Lucius caught her before she reached the ground, pressed the linen over the wound and lifted her inanimate form to carry into an antechamber, away from prying eyes.

'Find Lady Chalford, Giles, and Lady Jersey.'

'Yes, of course.'

Several young ladies were showing alarming tendencies to swoon at the sight of the blood upon the floor and upon Miss Ashling's person, and there were the makings of 'a scene'.

'Make way, please; there has been a slight accident. Nothing to cause concern.' Lord Godmanchester sounded calm and in control, and went before Sir Lucius as far as the nearest door, where a footman, who had been contemplating what viands might be left over to form his own late supper, sprang to alertness, opened it and led Sir Lucius into the wide passage and then opened the door into a small chamber, where Sir Lucius laid his light burden upon a sofa, kneeling beside her. He dismissed the footman to stand at the door and direct Lady Chalford and his mistress to the room, but his eyes were upon Elizabeth.

She had lost all colour, the whiteness of her skin in sharp contrast to the dark hair, one strand of which lay upon the column of her neck. He knew a desire to move it back into place with a finger, but that seemed strangely indelicate, too intimate a gesture. He concentrated upon the wound. The palm of her left hand bore a deep gash. He pressed the napkin into a tight pad over it, and bound her hand, fingers clenched over the palm, with his own handkerchief. For one or two brief minutes they were totally alone. He looked down at her, and felt that just for this moment she was his, and the need to kiss the injured hand was too much. He lifted it, and his lips just touched the fingertips that tasted slightly of the salty, ferrous taste of blood. Then the door opened, and the private moment was gone. Lady Jersey entered, all concern for one of her guests. Sir Lucius looked up, his face impassive, his voice calm.

'Lord Godmanchester has told me . . . oh!' Lady Jersey saw the red staining on the white linen.

'The glass broke in Miss Ashling's hand, ma'am. There is nothing in the wound, but it is deep and bleeds heavily. She should be conveyed home immediately and a surgeon called. I think he is likely to stitch the palm.'

'Oh dear me!' Lady Jersey bit her lip. 'How could such a thing happen?'

'Perhaps there was some weakness in the stem, ma'am. I fear I told Miss Ashling something that was a surprise to her, and she must have gripped it more tightly very suddenly. The broken stem cut into her palm.' Sir Lucius was thinking quickly. Nothing that he said was untrue, and it was important that Miss Ashling did not once again become the subject of wild rumour. He hoped against hope that nobody had overheard what had passed between himself and Miss Ashling, other than Giles Godmanchester, and that the peer's broad back had shielded the actual incident from onlookers. 'It could not have been foreseen and . . . it was a genuine accident, for I was talking with her at the time.'

'Oh, my poor Elizabeth!' At this moment Lady Chalford entered the room and her hands went to her cheeks. She swayed for a moment, and Lady Jersey feared she too might faint.

'Dear Lady Chalford, do be seated. It is most, most unfortunate, but . . . I will seek out your daughter and bring her to you.' Lady Jersey was hoping the incident would not mean her party was remembered for the drama rather than being one of the highlights of the Season, and felt her place was among her guests, reassuring and downplaying the whole horrible thing. She gave Lady Chalford a weak smile and flitted away.

'And I shall go and summon your carriage immediately, Lady Chalford.' Sir Lucius spoke with authority and calm, which cut through Lady Chalford's mist of panic. 'The wound is bound for now, so you may travel to Mount Street without alarm, but please do so straight away, and summon a surgeon. She will revive very quickly, I assure you.' His words were reassuring, but his expression very serious.

'You are sure, Sir Lucius?'

'Yes, I am sure.' With which he rose, gave the briefest of bows and left the room, returning a couple of minutes later to find Lady Chalford fanning her niece's face, Miss Amelia Ashling holding a glass of water and Elizabeth propped up against a velvet cushion, groaning and muzzy. He gave Lady Chalford the information that her carriage awaited below, and since Elizabeth had not revived enough to remonstrate, or indeed be aware of who was present, he brushed aside the footman who was awaiting instructions, and lifted her into his arms once more. He carried her downstairs and placed her tenderly in the waiting vehicle. Only as it drew away did Sir Lucius permit himself the luxury of a deep breath of summer night air. He closed his eyes for a moment, and then turned on his heel to walk home, frowning.

CHAPTER TWENTY-THREE

Sir Lucius returned to his house with his mind a whirl of concern, crushing disappointment and anger at himself. What had risked becoming a very public quarrel had been overshadowed by Miss Ashling's accident, and though some might wonder how she had come to break the stem of the glass, most had focused solely upon the effusion of blood and the near-hysterical reaction of several young ladies present. The sight of blood did not, of course, discommode him, but the look in Elizabeth Ashling's eyes haunted his dreams. The pain might in part have been caused by the gash to her hand, but the desolation was entirely his fault. He told himself that if she did not care for him at all, there would only have been disdain, but it did not make him feel any the better. If he could not get her to listen to him, hear him out, what chance was there that he could persuade her of his genuine feelings for her? It was an unusually terse Sir Lucius who snapped at his valet both as he made ready for bed and upon rising in the morning.

He rode, hoping the exercise would calm him, but all he thought of was how she had looked, totally happy and at ease upon the grey mare, how she had dropped her guard upon horseback, and forgotten, be it ever so briefly, how she despised the male sex. She would not ride the mare again, not just because of her injury, but because of his deception. If only she would believe he had bought the animal not from some devious motive, but because she had deserved it. It was only after that he had discovered feelings for her, though he doubted she would believe they were honourable either. He had sneered at Henry Freshford, but had he not done worse, in her eyes? Freshford had been weak; he had been deceitful. She clearly thought he was out to make her fall in love with him upon a callous whim, like some puppet to be manipulated and cast into a corner when the play was ended.

It hurt his honour almost as much as it hurt his heart, and he returned to his house, grim-faced.

Ribston betrayed no sign of emotion when he opened the door of the Mount Street house to a rather haggard Sir Lucius Radstock, but was quite capable of adding two and two together, especially given the additional advantage of below-stairs gossip, to which he paid, of course, no attention. He took Sir Lucius's card, but with the dampening comment that he rather thought Miss Ashling was keeping to her room, seeing as how she was unwell. He gave the card into Ditcham's hand at the bedchamber door, but did not need to step over the threshold to learn how badly it was received. He wondered if the angry outburst might even reach down to the morning room itself.

Shortly afterwards, he returned to where Sir Lucius was pacing like a caged beast, with the half-truth that Miss Ashling was in no fit state to entertain visitors today, and indeed, it might be some time before she was well enough to do so. Sir Lucius's face was instantly one of concern. Had she been attended by a doctor; was she feverish? The questions bordered on the personal, but Ribston, seeing a man in desperate straits, tried to ease the poor man's mind of such fears that must have beset him, though in truth, he saw no likelihood of Miss Ashling being 'at home' were he to call every day for a month. So Sir Lucius withdrew in as good an order as possible, frustrated, worried, disappointed and angry with the world, and, as any gentleman would do, sought refuge in his club.

Lady Godmanchester, who arrived some time later, was not turned away, though Lady Chalford received her first, and in some agitation.

'My dear Lady Godmanchester, I am quite overset. Elizabeth is determined, yes, determined, to return to Sussex. I have told her that it will make things worse, though how much worse they could be I am not sure. For all that we try to pass last night off as a mere unfortunate accident . . . oh dear . . . and I was hopeful . . . and my Amelia, my poor Amelia! What of her chances now? Oh, it will be the same all over again; I should not have made her come. Now where did I set down my *sal volatile*?'

She continued in a similar vein for some time, and Lady Godmanchester was required to use all her gentle good sense and even a few white lies to return the agitated lady to any semblance of calm. She told Lady Chalford that if Elizabeth retired to the country it could easily be explained by her not wishing to linger in the stuffy capital, unwilling to go about with a bandaged hand, which would make so many simple things awkward, and with only the last few weeks of the Season remaining. Then a thought struck her.

'Lady Chalford, how would it be if I persuaded Elizabeth to return to Thornby Park with me? Godmanchester is keen that I do so, and in truth, I am finding the exigencies of London too much. I tire too easily and feel the heat. It is but lack of company that gives me pause. If Elizabeth would come with me, I would be eternally grateful, and you could say, quite truthfully, that she was doing so for my benefit.'

'Oh, if she would . . . Dear Lady Godmanchester, it would be the best solution to this most terrible situation. And if Elizabeth is not here, and the gossip subsides, though it sounds dreadful, I am sure that by the end of the Season, Carbrooke will have made Amelia an offer.'

'Amelia is a very pleasant girl, and I am sure Lord Carbrooke would not be put off by tittle-tattle over nothing. After all, what fault of Amelia's could it be if her cousin has an unfortunate accident? Now, may I go up to her, dear ma'am?'

Lady Chalford sighed, and nodded.

Elizabeth had spent a very uncomfortable night. Her hand throbbed, and the surgeon putting several stitches into her palm had tried her already strained nerves to the utmost. He had given her laudanum to dull the pain, though she disliked it, but it had brought her sleep. That it was sleep tormented by unhappy dreams meant that she awoke unrested, and filled with the misery that the previous evening's events had prevented her from expressing, even in the privacy of her chamber. She had not partaken of breakfast, and it had taken all Ditcham's cajoling and indeed bullying to get her to leave her bed and dress. She had viewed her mistress's pale face and the blank look in her eyes, and shaken her head. She had seen this before, and it was not a good sign.

The announcement that Sir Lucius Radstock was below, and sought an interview, had produced signs of emotion, in the form of a furious tirade, the gist of which was that Elizabeth did not want to see the man, nor hear his name again, as long as she lived, and it had given the faithful tirewoman much food for thought. The anger had been followed by tears, and it was a very pale lady with red-rimmed eyes who received her best friend.

Lady Godmanchester came forward, her hand held out to take Elizabeth's uninjured one. 'My poor Elizabeth. Are you in much pain? Has the doctor seen you this morning? How did you sleep?'

Elizabeth smiled wanly. 'Yes, no and not well are the truthful answers, but there.'

'Your aunt said that the surgeon had to stitch the wound. You must be very brave, my dear. I am sure I would have fainted clean away.'

'I . . . It was not pleasant, but such things heal quickly enough, and I had other . . . things to distract me. Helen, I am going back to Sussex. After last night, I cannot face the looks, the whispers. Not again. You understand?'

'Of course, though, I assure you, you are making too

much of the incident. The accident will be talked of for a day, and might have happened to anyone.'

'Please, Helen, don't. You know as well as I that it is also more than that. I could not face him, I simply couldn't.'

'Elizabeth, at the moment I see that, though in the long term you are bound to—'

'I have no inclination to remain in London, Helen. I will be safe at home.'

'Well, I think that a shame. And I also have an idea that will prevent any gossip attending your departure before the Season's end.'

'There can be none.'

'Yes there can. Godmanchester is pestering me to return to Thornby Park, and indeed in many ways I would like to do so. London is becoming very stuffy, and I get tired easily. But I will have months and months ahead of me in seclusion at Thornby, and I am going to be so bored, I just know it. Come with me, to keep a poor, sickly woman company. It would be so much nicer. Do say yes, please. There will be nothing to do but walk with me about the grounds, play with baby George and enjoy hours of doubtlessly meaningless chatter, but it would be better than solitude for us both.'

Elizabeth bit her lip. Hopefully, there would be no recriminations from her aunt, who was caught between the need to remain in London to finish the Season with Amelia, and the fear that letting Elizabeth return to the country alone might seem unfeeling, if her injury was the excuse. If anyone would understand, it was Helen. She did foresee one large obstacle, however, and this she voiced.

'But Lord Godmanchester and Sir Lucius are the closest of friends. What if he were to invite him to stay? Indeed, what would be more natural than for him to invite him?'

The thought had struck Lady Godmanchester also, but she clasped her hands together resolutely and said, 'I would beg him to spare me the embarrassment, and' – she blushed – 'if he truly thought it would upset me, he would not bring Lucius to the house while you were there. After all, I would not be asking him to sever the connection, that would be unfair, just to refrain from inviting him while you visited. I can be very persuasive.'

So, thought Elizabeth, could the duplicitous Sir Lucius Radstock, since he had managed to get the honest Godmanchesters to be party to his fraud concerning Mist, whom she now only called 'the Trojan Horse'. This, however, she kept to herself.

'Would my aunt agree, I wonder?'

'Oh, I should think she would,' replied Lady Godmanchester, feigning innocence.

There was a pause. Elizabeth gazed into space, thinking, and then smiled wearily at Lady Godmanchester. 'Forgive me. I must seem churlish to even hesitate at such an offer. Please, blame it upon a poor night's repose and my own "indisposition".'

'Of course.' Lady Godmanchester patted Elizabeth's uninjured hand.

'I will come, if my aunt permits, and do so with gratitude, my dearest of friends.'

'Oh Elizabeth, I am quite excited about the thought of showing you Thornby, and most importantly, you can meet baby George. It is very unfashionable to say so, but I do so miss him.' She sighed. 'London would not be good for him, with all the noise and so many diseases in the air. Country air is so much sweeter. He is such a darling baby, too. I am sure you will fall in love with him, and he says the drollest little words. Let us go and speak to Lady Chalford. We might even be able to set out the day after tomorrow.'

'She's doing what?' Sir Lucius exclaimed, frowning at Lord Godmanchester.

'Helen invited her to Thornby Park. It seems Miss Ashling was all for bolting back to Sussex, which was causing great fluttering in the Chalford dovecote, and since I had been trying to get Helen out of London anyway, Helen thought it a tidy solution – which in many ways it is. Less gossip all round, and a feasible reason, just about, for Miss Ashling's withdrawal.'

'I see.' The frown did not lift. 'She wouldn't see me this morning, when I went to try and explain, to apologise. At least at Thornby she won't be able to avoid—'

'Lucius, I am sorry, but you can't come to Thornby.'

'But surely—'

'You are my closest friend, Lucius, and I would do anything for you, except upset my wife, especially while she is in a delicate condition.'

'But I have no intention of upsetting her.'

'If you come to Thornby Park, can you imagine what it will be like if Miss Ashling will not leave her room lest she meet you, takes her meals apart also? As a hostess, as a friend, Helen will be in a hellish predicament and will be distressed. If I have to choose between my wife and my friend, then . . . There is no choice, can be no choice. I am truly sorry.' Godmanchester ran a hand through his hair.

Sir Lucius gave a twisted smile and laid a hand on his friend's shoulder. 'You are the best of fellows, Giles, and honourable in the extreme. It has always been one of the things I most admired in you. I may not like your decision, in fact I am damned put out by it, but I do not hold it against you, nor think it damages our friendship. It does, however, put me in a tight spot. If Miss Ashling were returning to Sussex, then I should seek her there, but as it is I am prevented from doing the one thing I want – in fact, need – to do. She may not forgive me, but, by Heaven, she must be brought to realise that I never intended her hurt, even before I . . .'

'Fell in love with her. I know, my dear Lucius.'

Sir Lucius sighed. 'I never thought it would happen, Giles. It crept up upon me.'

'It does that, my friend.' Godmanchester smiled.

'But you were fortunate. Your Helen returned your affection, or at least was prepared to do so. Elizabeth Ashling views all men as perfidious and none more so than me.'

'Write to her. Just not quite yet, though.'

'It isn't the same, and what hope have I that she will not tear whatever I scribe to her into pieces without ever reading a word?'

'I know Helen would try and persuade her to read it, and then, perhaps, she could be brought round to seeing you.'

'But you know as well as I do, it is not just seeing me

that I want, not really. What do you give for my chances, Giles?'

'Oh, never say die, Lucius. You can be a jolly persuasive chap when you want. She may yet come round, and I know Helen was convinced that she was not impervious to you before she found out about the horse and then the source of her appellation.'

'I'd give a monkey to find out who told her about the horse, indeed who knew, other than us.'

'Well, they never heard it from me.' Godmanchester sounded aggrieved.

'Of course they didn't, so don't fly up in the boughs about it.'

'Well, if you ask me, the likeliest person to tell Miss Ashling anything unpleasant is the Rendlesham woman. Seems they were at daggers drawn through their first Season. Or rather,' Godmanchester revised his statement, justly, 'she cordially disliked Miss Ashling, until such time as she snapped up her marquis. Just shows that Rendlesham was even more of a fool than we thought him.'

'Is that possible?'

'In view of his remarriage, yes.' Godmanchester grinned. 'If she found out anything, she would be certain to make trouble with it. Now, as for you, stay up in Town, act as if nothing has happened, so that the gossips will find it harder to concoct a farradiddle just too close to the truth for comfort, then write that letter, and let time and Helen do the rest. Oh, and I am going to tell another lie.'

'Indeed.'

'Yes. I am telling Miss Ashling I have now purchased the

grey mare and so it need not remain eating its head off in my stables here. I am taking it back to Thornby with us.'

'Do you want it for your wife after all?'

'No. Too spirited for her. But I have hopes that you might yet, er, "buy it back from me". If you are successful and in a good mood, I might even sell it at a profit.' He smiled, though it was a little forced. 'Now, let's have a game of billiards, and put all things female out of mind for an hour or so.'

CHAPTER TWENTY-FOUR

Sir Lucius realised the good sense of his friend's words, and also knew that if he returned to Paley and his horses, he would be no better off, since they would be the last thing to take Elizabeth Ashling from his thoughts, and his mama would see through any pretext and shake her head over his handling of everything, with good cause. He told himself that going about Town as if unconcerned and with no strong connection to Miss Ashling would be doing her a service in quashing any rumours, and, alas, be just the relationship she desired. All he could do, as he saw it, was to protect her in whatever way he could, though she would never know of it. He had an invitation to Lady Etchingham's rout party, which should be well enough attended for him to be able to be seen acting entirely normally, and by a good number of those who thrived upon gossip, including Selina Etchingham herself. He sent round to Lord Godmanchester, asking if he too might put in an appearance, but received a reply that his friend was escorting his wife to the opera for her last evening in London, and was therefore unable to oblige.

Lady Etchingham, standing at the top of the elegant stairway, receiving her guests, watched Sir Lucius Radstock's approach with interest. Rumour had it that he had aspirations when it came to Miss Ashling and had been talking with her when she had suffered 'the accident'. He did not look, she admitted to herself, a man torn by worry this evening, but then perhaps he had received positive news about the lady's recovery. He drew close, and bowed over her hand.

'Good evening, Sir Lucius. I am so glad to see you this evening. I had wondered . . .' Lady Etchingham left the sentence unfinished, but arched an eyebrow questioningly.

'Oh, I assure you, ma'am, there is nowhere I would rather be, and I am sure that is true for all your many guests.' His answer was smooth, but he knew for certain he would be fending off prying questions for the entire evening. These would come from the ladies rather than the gentlemen, and it would be far easier to seek 'cover' within their ranks, but that would be cowardly, and doing Miss Ashling a disservice. He therefore made several circuits of the public rooms, engaging in conversations and presenting the face of a man without care. He felt that he was doing very well, quietly reiterating, when asked about 'what happened at Lady Jersey's', that it had been a most unfortunate accident, that there must have been a weakness in the stem of the glass, and that he had heard from Lady Godmanchester, who had visited Miss Ashling, that a full recovery was expected, given a little time. It was at the point before guests began to drift away to their beds or other parties that he overheard a woman's voice, raised in a stage whisper.

'Well, we all know what made Lady Caroline Lamb slash at her wrists, poor thing. Perhaps Miss Ashling was also openly rejected, yet again, and could not face the repetition. She was never "strong", you know. I suppose Lady Chalford might even send her back to the country and somewhere where she can be, ahem, "cared for" quietly. Such a shame.'

For a moment he froze. To compare what had happened with the very histrionic scene that Lady Caroline had made, some years earlier, when confronted and rejected by her former lover, Lord Byron, was worse than he had even imagined. Lady Caroline had always been – erratic, indeed wayward, and so distant in character from Miss Ashling that it would have been laughable, had it not been so damaging at this moment.

He addressed the lady's back, in a cold, clear voice. 'Your supposition is wrong, Lady Rendlesham, and so far-fetched as to be ridiculous.'

Lady Rendlesham turned to face him, caught between triumph and just a little fear. She was not a woman who gave in easily, and certainly not gracefully, and she had one singular advantage – she was a lady and in a public place.

'Sir Lucius. Really, sir. A lady is never wrong.' She looked almost coy, but her eyes glittered with anger.

'Indeed. But I say again, you are wrong.' The implication was calculated.

'How dare you!'

'And how dare you make insinuations, without any

basis, ma'am. I did not "reject" Miss Ashling, and the accident was just that, a most unfortunate accident that cut the palm of her hand. The palm.'

'Well, you would say that, sir, if you felt some self-blame, so your words do not really count, do th—'

'I rather think that my word counts.' Lady Jersey's voice, not raised, but very clear, interrupted. 'I myself attended Miss Ashling, and the injury was to her palm.' That she had only seen a blood-stained cloth pressed to the hand was close enough to full proof for Lady Jersey, who also disliked Aurelia Rendlesham.

'And I heard Miss Ashling say, "I fear the glass has broken."' A young lady, emboldened by being on the same side as the Patroness of Almack's, spoke up in a soft voice. 'I am sure nobody intending to harm themselves would say that.' The young lady then reddened as eyes turned upon her. 'Would they?' She faltered slightly.

'No, my dear, they would not.' Lady Jersey's voice was gracious, and also grateful.

The young lady's mama, who had, for a moment, seen her daughter's chances of a successful Season crumble to dust from her temerity, now beamed at her progeny. The gratitude of Lady Jersey, however brief, would mean her dear Jane being presented with more eligible gentlemen as dance partners, perhaps even an invitation to one of the lady's more select dinners. Jane's chances of finding a good husband were increased.

'And I am in agreement with Sir Lucius, Lady Rendlesham. You are wrong.' The voice lost all graciousness and became icy.

Lady Rendlesham reddened as if she had been slapped. Lady Jersey was not an enemy it was wise to have. Several of those who had been listening to Lady Rendlesham moved very slightly back from her, distancing themselves and isolating her. Sir Lucius, whilst still seething, realised that Sally Jersey could do what he could not, and crush this poisonous snake of a woman.

'I – may have made an error,' faltered Lady Rendlesham, 'though it was an easy one to—' The last attempt to fight back was an even bigger error.

'The doors of Almack's are closed to you, Lady Rendlesham. Please do not cause yourself further embarrassment by attempting to gain admission.' It was Lady Jersey's *coup de grâce*, a sanction used sparingly but always to great effect. There was an audible gasp from some ladies present, and Aurelia Rendlesham could do no more than curtsey her acceptance of defeat and withdraw. Lady Jersey cast Sir Lucius a swift glance that showed both triumph and understanding, nodded graciously and then declared that she, for one, was in need of one of the delightful ices that Lady Etchingham had so thoughtfully provided on this sultry evening. Sir Lucius withdrew quietly, but before he left the party, sought out Lady Jersey.

'Thank you,' he said, simply.

'Not at all, Sir Lucius. *On dits* are delicious, and gossip interesting, but lies out of spite are intolerable. Aurelia Rendlesham is a poisonous woman and – well, it was a pleasure. And just.' She paused. 'She failed to realise that it is *this* lady who is never wrong.' And then, with her tinkling laugh, she offered him her hand. He bent over it, and if, when he wrote later to Lord Godmanchester, he admitted that he felt he had done very little, he did say he had played a part in the fall of 'the Rendlesham woman'.

Elizabeth left Mount Street the next day, thankfully in ignorance of what had taken place the previous evening, and with a hug from Amelia, who was too caught up in her own blossoming romance to be cast down for long by her cousin's indisposition and departure, and a watery embrace from her aunt, who secretly felt guilty at the relief that departure would bring. Lord Carbrooke had arranged to call upon his return from a brief visit to his parents, and with the express purpose of an interview with Lord Chalford. Her ladyship was thus torn between triumph and the vague fear that Elizabeth's matrimonially cursed presence might make history repeat itself in some horrible way. To be sure, Carbrooke was not the great matrimonial prize that Lord Nuneaton would have been, but rank and wealth were not quite everything. She had come to terms with events, and her maternal desire to see her daughter happily, as well as suitably, wed was uppermost. Carbrooke was perhaps a little young, but in the eyes of a seventeen-year-old, far more appealing than a confirmed bachelor of nearly forty; he was personable, affectionate and wealthy enough that his wife would never have to penny-pinch. Amelia's mama might have been flattered by Nuneaton's attentions, but not once had the mention of his name brought the glow to Amelia's cheek that the Viscount Carbrooke's did, nor had she ever waxed lyrical as she did over the small services that her younger beau performed for her, whether it be picking up a dropped glove, or taking her up in the park, with her maid of course, in his phaeton, and driving her home when an unexpected downpour threatened.

Lord Godmanchester had no intention of taking his lady home at more than a gentle pace, as befitted her condition. He had expected to be confined in a carriage with two ladies who would chatter, but in fact both, for their own reasons, were more inclined to sit in companionable silence. He had bespoken rooms at The Swan, in Bedford, where they would stay the night before finishing the journey the following day. Elizabeth leant back against the squabs and closed her eyes.

'Is it wrong of me to think "thank goodness", Helen?' She broke the silence.

'No, my dear friend, it is not. After all, you have departed upon the most cordial of terms, and what you are thankful for is the prospect of not being in this stifling metropolis, not parting from your relations.'

'If that were but entirely true. I am conscious, when in that house, of being a failure, a disappointment.' Elizabeth sighed. 'Nothing is said, I grant you, but I feel it nonetheless. At least my aunt can forget that once Amelia is settled.'

'Your cousin looks likely to make a very happy match.'

'Oh yes. Carbrooke is a pleasant young man, neither slow-witted nor so intellectual that he will notice that Amelia is . . . not bookish. They will deal extremely well together, and after a few Seasons in London I have little doubt he will spend most of his time on his estates, and Amelia will settle very contentedly into the role of country lady. She confessed to me that though she was having "a very nice time" in London, she found it very fatiguing, and would in some ways prefer to be back in Sussex. It wasn't something she dared admit to her mama, of course.'

'Oh no. I sometimes think the mamas put so much time and energy into a come-out that they forget that there is anything except the Season.' Lady Godmanchester giggled, and placed her hand upon the just burgeoning roundness at her waist. 'If this babe is a girl, remind me of this conversation eighteen years hence.'

Lady Godmanchester, despite the tiring nature of the journey, became quite animated as they neared Thornby Park, in eager anticipation of seeing her son, wondering how much he had grown, and with all her natural maternal instincts to the fore. It was easy for Elizabeth to let her rattle on, and to contemplate a few weeks of rest, before addressing how she should set about setting up her own establishment.

Unfortunately for Elizabeth, she found that whilst her host and hostess made every disposition for her comfort, rest of the body was not mirrored by rest of the mind. She told herself that this was because the only person she could think of as a companion at Dowlands was an elderly cousin of her mama's, and one with whom she had nothing in common, for Cousin Jane's 'nerves' made her a permanent semi-invalid and she considered even going out to church an expedition. The alternative, and it was unpalatable, was returning to live several more years at Marden, and, with Amelia married, the far younger company of her cousin Anne. Like it or not, she knew her aunt felt her spinsterhood as a blemish, and for all her kind affection, would never cease to bemoan it. She had gone to London reluctantly, thinking that life at Marden would suffice her until she was able to live alone, forgetting how it would be without Amelia's companionship, and London had ruined everything.

The truth was that even the anticipation of life at Dowlands now seemed a pale limbo. She had thought herself safe, but then one man had breached her security, robbed her of her equilibrium. She never wanted to see him again, for if she gave in, he would break her heart. That her heart whimpered that it was broken already just showed how weak a heart could be.

She wandered Thornby Park like some unsettled ghost, and though her hand began to heal and the pain died away, she had little appetite for either food or activity. Riding was not feasible until such time as her hand could bear the pull of a rein upon it, and Lady Godmanchester's walks were, given her natural tiredness, mere ambles within the grounds. Elizabeth even found the Godmanchesters' connubial contentment hard to bear. The sight of them exchanging looks where the other need not speak brought home her isolation to her. She told herself that Helen had achieved a miracle, and found a true and honest man. Lucius Radstock was not as worthy, since he had already shown his false colours. For every moment that the thought of him crept into her mind, and the dream of what it would be like to share her life with him, there was the counter, the numbing reality of that moment when the world fell apart, and there was nothing but the abyss. She had faced it twice, the more fool she, and she was not to be duped again. Her heart had told her to trust, and where had that got her? If her heart yearned now for the tall figure with the beguiling eyes, her head told her that from a third betrayal there was no returning.

For the first week, Lord Godmanchester studiously avoided any mention of his friend in conversation when Elizabeth was present. It was remarkably difficult, since he and Sir Lucius were planning on going to Newmarket for the races in a few weeks' time, and besides, so many things involved him.

'I nearly ruined everything over dinner,' he bemoaned, as he sat in his wife's bedchamber, while her maid laid the final touches to her bedtime toilette. With a word of thanks the servant was dismissed, and he came to lean over her, smiling into the mirror and massaging the muscles of her elegant neck.

'Mmm, don't stop, Giles.'

'How long must it go on?'

'Until the muscles relax, my love.' Lady Godmanchester almost purred.

'Not this, madam. Pretending Lucius doesn't exist.'

'You know, she is not happy.'

'Even a mere man can see that.'

'I would never describe you as a "mere man", my lord.'

'Ah, not while I can provide this service.'

She reached up a hand to stroke his cheek. 'You provide everything I need, always.'

He turned his head to press a kiss into her palm.

'Would you stay tonight, Giles?'

'I thought, in view of your condition . . .'

'I am not sure of, well, that, but I would like you to hold me. I want to fall asleep in your arms.'

He responded huskily, and for a while Lucius and Elizabeth were forgotten, but before she fell asleep, Helen remembered the abandoned conversation.

'I think poor Elizabeth is torn.'

'Mmm? Sorry, you are mumbling into my chest, dearest. Say that again.'

'I said' – she raised her head onto his shoulder and blew into his ear – 'that poor Elizabeth is torn. I am convinced she has feelings for him, strong feelings, but she does not trust them. It makes me wretched to think of her so miserable.'

'Then do not think. I do not want you wretched, and in this, she has to work things through for herself.'

'But, perhaps, I might manage the odd nudge?'

'Helen?'

'The ban on mentioning Lucius's name is lifted, as long as you do not lace your conversation with it, and I think you might write and tell him that if he wishes to write here, in another week he may do so.'

'Yes, my lady. Any further commands?'

She whispered in his ear.

It was generally agreed that Lucius Radstock was an even-tempered fellow, but his close friends found him abstracted, and even a little curt, following Miss Ashling's sudden withdrawal into Northamptonshire. Lord Collingbourne, who had come upon him in Piccadilly and fallen into step beside him, assuming he was heading for his club, regarded him in deep concern, having asked a question three times without receiving an answer.

'Oil of cloves,' he declared, as loudly as he thought seemly in a public thoroughfare.

'I beg your pardon?' Sir Lucius looked at him in sudden surprise.

'No. That is for toothache. Oil of something else, then, to soften wax in the ears.'

'What on earth are you talking about, Collingbourne? And why yell at me?'

'Sorry, my dear fellow, but I thought you must be suffering from deafness. I enquired three times whether you thought Sink or Swim had a chance up against Twinkletoes at Epsom next week, and not a word did I get in reply.'

'Forgive me, I was lost in thought.'

'What is your opinion?'

'On what?'

'Sink or Swim, or Twinkletoes.'

'I really have no idea. It is scarcely important.'

'It is when you have laid a pony on Sink or Swim,' Lord Collingbourne replied, with some acerbity. 'You'll be telling me next you are not attending the meeting.'

'How percipient. I am not.'

'What? Now, stop roasting me, there's a good chap. It is not yet noon, and I had a very convivial evening with Hemsworth last night, so the old head is not up to coping with your dry wit.'

'I am not going.'

'But . . . But you always go.'

'I am sorry to disappoint you, but not this time.'

Stunned by this unwelcome news, Lord Collingbourne turned instinctively to the left to head down St James's, and almost fell over his friend, who had not deviated from his straight course.

'I say, sorry, Lucius, but I assumed we were going to White's.'

'You may be, but I am not.'

'Tattersall's?'

'No. I am going home.'

Lord Collingbourne's wits might not be sharp, but he was perfectly able to grasp the fact that his friend was in no mood for company. He bade him a kind farewell, adding that he hoped he felt better soon, and went to restore his spirits within the comforting familiarity of his club, where he came across Lord Bensthorpe, reading *The Gazette*. Bensthorpe looked up.

'Why the long face, Collingbourne?'

'Morning, Bensthorpe. I've just come along Piccadilly with Lucius Radstock, and the poor fellow is not himself at all. I thought at first it was his ears.'

'His ears? How can his ears make him look different?'

'Look different?' Lord Collingbourne frowned. 'Looks just the same as normal, if rather more serious. No, he's not well, I tell you. I thought it was his ears, because he did not hear me ask a question, several times, but it is not that. Blocked ears would not stop him going to Epsom next week.'

'But he has a colt running on the Thursday.'

'That's as may be, but he told me he was not attending. And,' Lord Collingbourne added, as a clincher, 'he said that whether Sink or Swim can beat Twinkletoes was unimportant.'

'Lucius Radstock said that?' Lord Bensthorpe sounded suitably shocked.

'He did. You know, he was so preoccupied, I wonder if he has had bad news. Notice to quit. I mean, if he had something infectious he would be covered in spots and not walking down Piccadilly.'

'Dash it, Collingbourne, he looked fit as a fiddle only last week.'

'Ah, but remember Launceston. He was the life and soul of the party one night, and cold as a leg of mutton next day.'

'But that was an apoplexy.'

'Before you all start buying black ribands for Radstock, perhaps I might suggest another reason for his, er, "malaise"?' drawled a voice behind them.

They had not noticed the approach of Lord Easby. They eyed him with interest, if little pleasure.

'And what would that be?' enquired Lord Bensthorpe, with a trace of suspicion.

'The departure of the oh-so-disdainful Miss Ashling from our midst.'

'Good grief. I had not thought of that. Of course!'

'I only put it forward as a theory, of course, not being, shall we say, one of his intimates, but it has more validity than Collingbourne's assumption of some sudden deadly ailment.' With which, having dropped this stone into the pool of conjecture, Easby bowed and moved away, leaving the two friends staring at each other.

* * *

Sir Lucius did not return home to the solitude he craved. He was surprised to find his front door open, and a large number of trunks and valises being carried within. Sansom was overseeing this procedure, and beamed at his master.

'Her ladyship has just arrived, sir. Her room is being prepared and you will find her in the Green Saloon.'

'My mother? She gave no warning of descending upon me. I will go to her, of course. Has she partaken of luncheon? I know how little she eats before embarking upon a journey.'

'She desired me to delay any repast until you arrived home, sir. I took it upon myself to say that you were expected back quite soon.'

Sir Lucius handed his hat and gloves to the footman, and took the stairs two at a time up to the Green Saloon, where he found Clarissa, Lady Radstock, seated near the window and surveying the street. He approached and bent to kiss her hand and then her cheek.

'You should have warned me, Mama. I would have been here to receive you. Have you come to consult the doctor about your arthritis, or merely to condemn the latest fashions and then buy several charming new hats?'

He smiled at her, but she noticed that it was perfunctory. So the gossip was true. She had hoped that her friend Lady Ellesmere was making much of a mere lovers' tiff, but she had not seen her son look so serious since his father's death. Sir John's demise had been totally unexpected, and had rendered her quite unable to deal with the legal and practical consequences. Lucius had returned to the ancestral home immediately, and taken everything into his very capable hands, but there had been inquests and coroners and an awful lot of paperwork that he had had to go through with the family lawyer, whilst dealing with his own natural grief and concerns about her health, which had not been good. And yet this was not the serious look that came from burdens and care. This was different, and unsettling. He looked lost.

'My arthritis is actually much better, I am glad to say. I hate being so "invalidish", and walking with that stick as if I were seventy. No, I was merely in need of a little entertainment, and the last few weeks of the Season seemed likely to provide it. I hear that Monkwell is making a fool of himself over some schoolroom miss half his age, with no fortune and a harpy for a mother, and that Lady Kesteven is likely to present Kesteven with Montagu Westmore's brat. It is a good job both he and Kesteven are fair and blue-eyed, but if the child has Westmore's hook of a nose . . .'

'You seem to know every *on dit* already, Mama.' He paused. 'So, have you come to find out if the gossip about me is true?' There was a slight edge to his voice, and the eyes had hardened. He was deeply attached to his mother, but he had no wish to see her involve herself in this most private of problems, and one which, if soluble at all, was dependent upon only himself and Elizabeth Ashling.

'Yes. I am your mother, so it is natural that I should wish to do so. However, if you think I am going to burden you with advice, you may rest easy, for I am not. If you are in a coil, it is of your own making, and you are the best placed to extricate yourself, one way or another.' She eyed him shrewdly. 'My ideas are a generation outmoded. I do not understand the flouncy ways of the misses of today.'

'Flouncy? Oh no, Mama, whatever else, Elizabeth is not "flouncy", if you mean she is blowing hot and cold, and testing my mettle. She is perfectly sincere in her beliefs. What I cannot fathom as yet is whether her professed loathing of me is based purely upon my own errors, or is still grounded in past events over which I can have no control. As I told you, I had thought we were in a fair way to an understanding, but then . . .' He sighed. 'I am perforce reduced to kicking my heels and waiting before I can do anything, and the waiting is intolerable. I fear you will find me poor company, Mama.'

'I did not come so that you might dance attendance on me, Lucius. I shall do very well visiting my friends who are in Town, and perhaps organising a card party or two here, if I may. Should you wish for my advice, and I doubt that you will, I am here.'

'You are the best of mothers.' The smile was genuine this time.

CHAPTER TWENTY-FIVE

Actually composing a letter to his best friend proved quite difficult, and Lord Godmanchester remained closeted in his study for the best part of the following morning before he managed an epistle that he considered neither too depressing nor giving false hope. In addition, he was at a loss as to how to gauge Elizabeth's state of mind. Helen had made her views clear to him, but he wondered how much his dear wife was inclined to the romantic, and merely wishing that a happy outcome could be achieved. She believed what she said, but was it self-delusion? Elizabeth's misery was plain, but he had no solid reason to assume that a letter from Lucius would make things better even to the degree that she would face him, let alone cast herself into his arms, accept his offer and start ordering bride clothes.

In the end, he began by discussing the proposed visit to the Newmarket meeting, and then worked his way around to the current state of affairs at Thornby Park.

Helen is blooming, and I am so glad that she agreed to return to the country. Elizabeth also is better, in that her hand now gives her only slight discomfort, though it precludes her from riding as yet. The local doctor, a sound man, is removing the stitches tomorrow. However, she is clearly in very low spirits, and shows a very poor appetite. Your name has not been mentioned in her presence, but my darling wife now thinks that this moratorium may come to an end, and has suggested that you might care to write to explain yourself at the week's end.

In all truth, Lucius, I do not know how your missive will be received. The workings of the female mind are a mystery unto me as to every other man, married or not. Helen assures me that she thinks your situation far from hopeless, but whether that is feminine intuition or wishful thinking I do not know. I can only say 'nothing ventured, nothing gained' and wish you the very best of good fortune. I know that Helen will make every effort both to get Elizabeth to read it and to accede to seeing you here.

He then concluded by hoping that his friend had not been driven into Bedlam by the frustrations of having to bide his time in inactivity, and remained etc etc.

It was not, it had to be said, a long letter for so many hours' work, but at least it had not been cast into the fireplace as its predecessors had been, and Lord Godmanchester sealed and franked it in a positive frame of mind.

* * *

Sir Lucius Radstock was doing a fair impression of the caged beasts at the Royal Exchange, pacing up and down the drawing room until his mother took him to task.

'For Heaven's sake, do stand still or sit down, Lucius. You are giving me the headache.'

'I am sorry, Mama. I was thinking.'

'Surely you can think standing still?'

He sat upon the edge of a chair and leant forward, hands clasped together, resting his chin upon them. 'I had a letter from Thornby.'

'And?'

'Giles suggests I wait until the end of the week before even writing to her.'

'Is the young woman in some form of quarantine, then?'

'From me, yes, it seems.'

'Forgive me, but why should you still wish to press your suit upon a girl who seems to be doing her best to forget you walk the same earth?'

'Because I happen to think we would be very happy together; because I do not know whether she wants to forget me or just thinks that she ought because I am a man, and, ergo, untrustworthy, and for which I fear I have inadvertently given her cause; and because I love her.'

'You are sure, my son?'

'As certain as I am of anything in this world. I never felt this way before, I admit. The "passions" of my youth were short, sharp and shallow. I do not just want her, Mama; I want to guard her from the world, make her happy, see her eyes light up with joy, dry her tears. Oh, everything.'

'It does seem a very comprehensive list.' Lady Radstock paused. 'And what if she will not have you, Lucius?'

'I do not know, Mama, I truly do not know.'

Setting pen to paper actually proved one of the most difficult things Lucius Radstock had ever done. There was so much that he wanted to say, needed to say, and yet it crowded his mind so much that making sense of it all, let alone conveying it in a way that would lead to Elizabeth Ashling agreeing to meet him face to face, seemed impossible. Sheets of screwed-up paper littered his desk and tumbled on the floor like so many snowballs. Several times the ink dried upon the nib as it was poised but not put to scribe the next phrase. Even the salutation proved a trial. 'Dear Miss Ashling' might be correct, but to his mind he could as well have been requesting the settlement of a bill. 'My dear Miss Ashling' sounded better, but would she consider it presumptuous or patronising? It did have the advantage of being true, for she was very dear to him. He only wished he might scribe 'My darling Elizabeth', but this made him gloomier than ever, for surely he would never now have that right. He sighed, putting down the pen and running his hand through his ordered locks. If he made a mull of this, everything was at an end, and it was so very difficult.

He took a deep breath, and picked up the pen once more.

My dear Miss Ashling,

I entreat you to read this, and not simply discard it in your understandable wrath. I am left unable to give you the truth by any other means, and a true explanation is both what you deserve and what I cannot bear that you do not possess. You have become aware of certain facts in a manner that has left you believing them to be a total betrayal of your trust, your friendship, and even malicious in intent. I swear to you that . . .

He stopped. How could he swear he had never intended any such thing, when he recalled what he had felt at that moment of stupid peevishness? How bitterly he regretted that transient thought. He took a fresh sheet and began again.

. . . I value your trust and friendship. Indeed, I can only assure you that your happiness has become paramount with me, and I would not do anything to jeopardise it.

The bare facts that you threw at me are true. I cannot deny either, and in the matter of the mare see no reason why I should wish to do so, since I did not conceal my purchase to deceive you, but so that you would not feel in any way obliged to me. However, I was indeed the man who gave you the name 'the Unassailable', but unintentionally so, though you may not believe it. It was half-uttered and retracted in a moment of annoyance, and I did not think it was overheard. You cannot know how bitterly I have regretted it. You had just danced with me, that evening when I thought I had assisted you by sending off young Escott. I had, in my masculine arrogance, expected some small degree of thanks, and your response was frosty. I recalled the first words I had ever heard you utter, that you would 'grant men nothing', and it was fatally easy to see you as one of those women with a natural antipathy to the male sex. I did not think to consider that there might be a good reason for such an attitude. In that one foolish, and, I fear, unforgivable, moment I did, yes, think it would serve you aright if you had to hold more gentlemen at arm's length. I am ashamed to admit it, but I have said you deserve the truth. I knew my error about you so very soon afterwards, from the first time I saw you in the park, mounted upon that awful hired hack. You were a different person, a real person, not just a wooden 'doll'. It was too late, even then, to quash the title 'the Unassailable', but I made every effort to prevent your name being bandied about. That it led to men of the stamp of Easby 'pursuing' you is something that I accept may be beyond your forgiveness, since I cannot forgive myself. My actions, when I came upon the extent of his impertinence towards you, were entirely spontaneous, and those of a gentleman, though the murderous anger would have been less had you not been so precious to me.

The other accusation is that I used subterfuge to provide you with a mount. Of this I am not, and will not, be ashamed. You have viewed it as an attempt to deceive you, use you in some way, but you are completely mistaken. I bought the grey mare because I was so appalled at a true horsewoman being forced to ride such an animal as had been provided for you, and then also because I knew I had done you a great disservice, and providing you with a horse that might give you pleasure might, though anonymous, atone in some way for my 'sin'. The world at large would not accept such a gift as permissible so subterfuge was my sole recourse. Since you were not to know of my action, it was clearly not intended to make you think the better of me.

Lady Jersey's party haunts me. I had such hopes, such honourable hopes, and they were dashed in an instant by your disgust and anger. I was not thinking, and compounded my folly by letting my feelings dictate my words, making you an offer that was so abhorrent that it led to your injury.

His mind was suddenly flooded with the remembrance of her in his arms. At the time it had been a practical act, but now he recalled the lightness of her weight, the touch of her hair brushing his cheek as her head lay against his shoulder. His throat tightened.

My cause is surely lost. Even aspiring to your mildest regard is ambitious. Yet I have to tell you that I have never felt for any woman what I feel for you, and that the life that seemed perfectly contented is now revealed as empty because I know you cannot bring yourself to be part of it, Elizabeth. Forgive the intemperate words; you have to know the truth of me.

If you can bear it, I would beseech you to permit me a few minutes of your time to make this clumsy explanation in person, for words upon paper are so inadequate, and that you might find it in your heart to dismiss me with forgiveness. Giles Godmanchester would, I know, convey any message.

I remain,
Your eternally devoted servant,
Lucius Radstock

His hand trembled at the signature. He looked at it, as if surprised, and then clasped his hands together before him on the desk to steady them. He read the letter through, and sealed it, aware that his future lay in its reception.

The post was brought as the ladies finished breakfast, for Helen Godmanchester was thankfully past the weeks of sickness and some mornings felt well enough to enjoy tea and toast with her friend. The butler brought in a tray with several missives upon it, and presented one to Elizabeth, who thanked him, expecting it to be from Amelia or her aunt. The hand was unknown to her, and she frowned. Lady Godmanchester, who did recognise the writing, smiled innocently.

'I hope the letter is good news, Elizabeth?'

'Good? I . . . Helen, do you know this writing?' She held the letter, unopened.

'Why yes. It is Lucius's writing. I am very pleased. It is about time he screwed up his courage and wrote you an apology.' Her ladyship sounded very calm and matter-of-fact.

'Screwed up his . . . I won't read it.' Elizabeth flushed, wishing her pulse had not increased with the thought that he might be afraid to write to her, and trying to be resolute.

'Is that fair, to either of you, my dear? Whatever lies between you, is it not right that you let him at least apologise, explain—'

'Explain? There can be no explanation, nor excuse.' She closed her eyes. 'Oh, Helen, he has made me so miserable.'

Her friend leant over and took her hand. 'Are you not also making yourself miserable, Elizabeth? At least read what he has to say. It might make things easier.'

Elizabeth wavered. Then, with fingers trembling as much as those that had sealed it, she opened the letter. She read in silence, and only by the ebb and flow of colour and the biting of her lip could Helen Godmanchester assess her emotional turmoil. Mastering her curiosity, that lady kept silent. After a few minutes, Elizabeth laid the letter upon the table. She said nothing, but her bosom rose and fell swiftly in her agitation.

'I can't. I must not. If I do . . .' she murmured, more to herself than her hostess.

'Not do what, Elizabeth?'

'Not meet him. If I do, I will be weak.' She saw her friend's perplexed frown. 'I will let him persuade me with soft looks and kind words, and he will break my heart.'

'Forgive me, my dear friend, but is your heart not broken now, here? Could he not mend it? If he loves you?'

'Men do not love.'

'You are wrong.' Lady Godmanchester shook her head, confident in her knowledge. 'Men do love, and their love is worth a great price if won. If Lucius Radstock has written you a letter that makes you even think of meeting him, then it is he who is opening himself up to be hurt. Can you not see that?' Her voice was very gentle. 'Do you not love him, Elizabeth? Is that not why you have been so low?'

Elizabeth turned to her friend, laid her head upon her shoulder and wept.

It was not to be expected that their meeting would be easy. Sir Lucius arrived at Thornby Park, grim-faced, and his friend thought him rather haggard. Elizabeth was, thankfully, out in the grounds with Lady Godmanchester when he shook his host's hand and was invited into the house.

'How is she?'

It was the question that had burnt within Lucius Radstock every mile of the journey, and took precedence over polite platitudes. Lord Godmanchester did not, for a moment, think his friend was asking after his wife's health.

'Quiet. Not at ease, I can tell you that much, even less so since your letter. Helen will not reveal all that they speak of, for there are things between women that are not for even a husband's ears.' He paused. 'I can only say that if she has been this miserable over a breach between you, surely it must indicate that she has deep feelings for you. Anyway, come along in and clean the travel stains from yourself. Helen and Elizabeth are promenading slowly about the rose garden, I believe, and will be back shortly.'

Sir Lucius did as he was bid, presenting himself in the morning room some twenty minutes later. Lady

Godmanchester looked to be blooming. He smiled, and complimented her upon it, and then turned to Elizabeth. The contrast was almost shocking. She was pale, and there were dark shadows beneath her eyes. He had never seen her look less beautiful, and never wanted so much to look after her, drive away her miseries. The formalities meant nothing; he spoke, she answered. Lady Godmanchester smiled upon them and, with a complete disregard for social niceties, declared that since they had things to say to each other, she would go and see if little George had run Nurse ragged, as he had been threatening to do after breakfast.

The door closed, and they were left facing each other. Elizabeth was white-faced; he thought she looked haunted. She indicated a chair and invited him to sit, coldly, politely, as if they were mere acquaintances.

'No, I thank you. I . . . How is your hand?' He sounded calm, though his heart was racing.

Elizabeth remained standing also, as if to be seated put her at a disadvantage. 'Healing, thank you.'

There was an awkward pause.

'You read my letter.' It was a fatuous statement, since if she had not read it he would not be standing before her now. 'Did you, do you, believe what I wrote in it?'

She averted her eyes. 'I do not see that it is very important, whether I do so or not, Sir Lucius.' Her voice was flat.

He took two strides towards her, and she stiffened as he held out his hand. He let it fall.

'It is, of all things, the most important to me. Whatever you feel, you must know the truth, know that whatever hurt I did you was not intended. I regretted it even as I said it, made efforts to disguise it, retract it. I was stupid, thoughtless, chagrined, call it what you will, but . . .'

'It is best forgotten, sir, so we will not mention it again. Indeed, there should be no reason for us to meet, since I do not intend to visit London in the future. You have confirmed to yourself that I have accepted your apology, though travelling all this way seems rather a waste of your time—' She heard her own voice as if it were another's.

'You know that was not the main reason.'

'—and effort.' She ignored his interjection. 'Let us shake hands, and part without bad feeling between us.'

She held out her hand and he took it, not to shake it, but rather to turn it, palm uppermost, so he could see the short, still livid scar. Before she could close her fingers or snatch the hand away, he bent and kissed it, very softly, and then straightened to look her in the eyes.

'Elizabeth. At Lady Jersey's . . . it was the wrong time, the wrong place, the wrong words, even. I took you by surprise. That your anger, your revulsion even, led to you being hurt . . . I blame myself, and it weighs heavily upon me. You know why I had to come and see you today. What I said that night I meant, though it came out so badly. Before I was traduced to you, I thought perhaps you were not without some feeling towards me, that my offer might not be, despite your demeanour to almost every man in London, unwelcome to you. I do not make it upon a whim, or out of guilt, but because I love you. I love you and cannot imagine ever being happy again without you.' His grip tightened; his voice dropped.

'I am not a man who has simply decided it was time I settled down and set up my nursery, and picked the likeliest filly up to my weight, among those trotted out for inspection. Yes, you may look shocked, but that it how it has always seemed to me. Every Season the matchmaking mamas bring out their young stock, and parade them as if it were Tattersall's ring. Well, I am happy to pick horseflesh that way, but not a wife. I knew there would have to be more, but had never found it, until you, until I saw you out riding. When we were introduced, when we danced together, you were just a beautiful woman with some unexplained dislike of my sex, but in the fresh air, especially upon a horse worthy of you, you were a different person. You were open and vibrant, unafraid, admirable, and that admiration became adoration, became love. You built a wall about you, to protect yourself, and if I cannot break it down, then I am willing to scale its heights and live within it with you. I would be your protection. I am asking you to marry me, Elizabeth, because you mean more to me than anything in this world.'

She stared him, not angry this time, not revolted, but confused. She tried to pull her hand away, but half-heartedly, and he did not free it.

'No, please, it isn't fair.' Her voice was barely above a whisper, and there was a catch in it. 'You don't mean it. They never do.'

'They?' he queried, but she ignored him, talking half to herself.

'You let down your guard, you trust, you offer your heart, and ultimately a man will drop it into the dust and walk away, sooner or later. Please, not again.' She blinked at him, her eyes misting, and frowned as if she had forgotten he was there for a moment. 'I could not bear it again.'

'I will not let you down. I love you.'

'Ah, no. That is the lie. I shall not be deceived, must not let myself be deceived, a third time.'

'A third time, Elizabeth?' If she was recalling Freshford, he understood, but he had no knowledge of any suitor since.

'With Henry, I thought it was different. It seemed so natural, so easy. He said he cared. He said the same old lies, but they sounded so sincere, right up to the point when he abandoned me. When . . . when my father died, he came to me, all consolation, and I felt so safe. Yet after that day I did not see him again, nor did he even write to explain. He just dropped me like a stone into a pool, to sink. One word from his family and I was not even worth an explanation.' She spoke without anger, but with immense disappointment.

'Freshford was a weak fool. A man who loved you would not have abandoned you.'

'But my father did.'

It was such a simple statement, and explained so much. He had wondered why the disappointment at eighteen had been so profound, and had come to the conclusion that it was as much to do with embarrassment at the humiliation as any broken heart, for adolescence saw hearts break and mend easily enough. Now, he saw that Freshford had been the final confirmation of perfidy, just when a vulnerable girl had thought, hoped, that the giddy spiral of 'falling in love' meant that it would prove stronger than the bond of paternal affection.

'We were happy, a happy family, a loving family. I loved Papa, as I loved Mama, and Charles, my little brother. I had a perfect existence, until I was ten. And then suddenly, they were gone, Mama and Charles, and there was just the two of us, and Papa turned his back on me, avoided me. He rarely spoke to me, hid himself away, and when my aunt offered to take me to Marden when I was thirteen, he was glad to be rid of me. What love was there then? None.'

Sir Lucius paused, and then said gently, 'Forgive me, but your uncle is fair, and I dimly recall that it was so with all the Ashling brothers. I take it you are more like your mother.'

'Very like, according to my aunt. I sometimes catch a glimpse of myself in the mirror, and it reminds me, but perhaps that is just fanciful, and because of us both being dark.'

'Then is it not entirely possible that your father, bereft of an adored wife, could not bear to see the daughter so like her, and yet not her? Grief takes people in different ways.'

'But I too grieved. I was so alone. I needed him, needed to be loved still.' It was a cry, the cry of a lonely and confused child.

She stood with tears on her cheeks now, and took a great shuddering breath. He had been unconsciously stroking the back of the hand he held with his thumb, but now drew her to him, unresisting, and put his arms about her, kissed her hair.

'You are loved. I love you. I will not abandon you, Elizabeth, and I do not think your father ceased to love you. Think, my darling. What need had he to invest in schemes, a man who lived quietly, reclusively? Perhaps all that he thought he could do for you was provide more for you, not to have men court you for your wealth but so that none would be dissuaded by what he thought a mere competence, hoping that you would find someone who could give you the love he could no longer make plain. Look at me, Elizabeth.'

She shuddered as a sob caught in her throat, but obeyed, and saw his face very serious, yet with tenderness in his eyes.

'My love for you will not waver, but I need to know. Do you hold off from me because I mean nothing to you, or because you are afraid to listen to your heart? I cannot command you to be my wife, only beseech you, beg you, and I am not too proud to beg. If I mean nothing, be assured always of my . . . friendship; know that you can call upon me in any trouble; know—'

'Lucius.'

It was but his name, whispered tremulously, but it gave him his answer, and he felt her relax against him. His hold tightened, possessively, and he bent his head, his mouth seeking hers. If the first kiss lingered tentatively, the second, as he felt her respond, was hungry. She pulled back, but only to fling an arm about his neck, and match that hunger with her own.

Whether it was as the consequence of the flood of emotions, or just the sheer overwhelming sensation of his embrace, her knees seemed to give way, and she could not thereafter say whether he led, or half carried her, to the sofa, where they were disturbed some time later by Lady Godmanchester, who, she said mendaciously, sought her embroidery, which she had set down somewhere and mislaid. She pretended not to notice how closely together they were sitting, nor the touching fingers, nor Elizabeth's heightened colour, but went away to tell her lord that all was well.

'Do you think she guessed?' murmured Elizabeth, leaning comfortably against Sir Lucius's shoulder once more, as his arm slipped back around her waist.

'Oh, she did not guess, my love. She knew.'

Elizabeth giggled, a sound he had not heard from her before, and he grinned down at her.

'Am I to have a giddy wife?'

'Not giddy, sir. I am no feather-head, I assure you. It is just, at this moment, as if I had taken too much champagne. I did so once, when I was young, and after the giggles I had the hiccups.'

'I sincerely hope you are not going to progress to the hiccups now. Kissing you would become extremely awkward, and I do so like kissing you.'

She offered him her lips to prove this would not be the case.

'And,' he remarked, a few minutes later, 'what do you mean by "when I was young"? If you are old, my child, at twenty-one, what does that make me, since I am nearer thirty than twenty-five?'

'Positively ancient,' she purred, and snuggled even closer. 'I shall buy you an ear trumpet and a gout stool as wedding gifts.'

'I can scarcely wait.' He grew more serious again. 'I will leave you tomorrow, and go back to London, but return within a couple of days. I must see Lord Chalford and tell him the news, and have the notice put in the papers, though I hope to be spared your aunt falling upon my neck in relief.'

'Relief?' Elizabeth raised an eyebrow.

'Indeed, at getting you off her hands before the child Amelia, my sweet. I refuse to let Carbrooke beat us to it. I would like the preparations well advanced for when we return, and I know Lady Chalford will want to send you off in style. It will be "St George's, Hanover Square, and all the trimmings", my love, without a doubt.'

She pouted, but her eyes danced. 'I see. Then she will be delighted, even though it is you, Sir Lucius.'

'Touché. You know, I was right. You and the Trojan Horse are very similar.'

'We are?' She eyed him suspiciously, for his eyes danced even more, and his lips twitched.

'Yes. You told me once she was "quite a handful, but with a lovely soft mouth".'

'Ooh, Lucius!'

SOPHIA HOLLOWAY read Modern History at Oxford and also writes the Bradecote and Catchpoll medieval mysteries as Sarah Hawkswood.

@RegencySophia
sophiaholloway.co.uk